THE SWEET LIFE CAFÉ

HELEN ROLFE

First published in Great Britain in 2026 by Boldwood Books Ltd.

Cover Design by Alexandra Allden

Cover Images: Shutterstock

A CIP catalogue record for this book is available from the British Library.

Paperback ISBN 978-1-83561-131-9

Large Print ISBN 978-1-83561-130-2

Hardback ISBN 978-1-83561-129-6

Trade Paperback ISBN 978-1-80656-177-3

Ebook ISBN 978-1-83561-132-6

Kindle ISBN 978-1-83561-133-3

Audio CD ISBN 978-1-83561-134-0

MP3 CD ISBN 978-1-83561-135-7

Digital audio download ISBN 978-1-83561-128-9

This book is printed on certified sustainable paper. Boldwood Books is dedicated to putting sustainability at the heart of our business. For more information please visit https://www.boldwoodbooks.com/about-us/sustainability/

Boldwood Books Ltd, 23 Bowerdean Street, London, SW6 3TN

www.boldwoodbooks.com

For my mum and dad who have gone to the stars... miss you every single day

Love, me xxx

PROLOGUE

Celebrating the life of Gayle Rafferty.

Please join friends and family as we honour Gayle Rafferty during this funeral to be held on 26 September of this year.

Dress code: informal, bright colours – absolutely no black allowed (unless it's your shoes)

Location: The Sweet Life Café, Bay Street, Anchor Island

Time: 4 p.m.

Arrive hungry with plenty of room for pudding...

No need to RSVP. The more the merrier

1

ADDIE

Addie Rafferty was running late. Again. She picked up the pile of post from the doormat and dumped it, along with a collection of junk mail, on the table. The blue envelope on top caught her eye with its Anchor Island postmark, but she didn't have time to deal with whatever it was right now. She had to get to work. She'd already been late several times recently and she didn't need another black mark against her name. This job was the only way she could afford this flat which wasn't homely by any stretch of the imagination but was at least a roof over her head. And with her seven-year-old son, Isaac, to think about too, she had to keep making ends meet the best she could, and perhaps accept that this was just the way it was.

Having skipped breakfast in a rush to get Isaac organised for staying at his grandparents for the weekend, so she could put in more hours for work, she reached for the last remaining teacake from the batch she'd baked with him on Sunday, grabbed her bag and left to walk the short distance from her flat in Harrow to the Tube station.

The blue envelope was still on her mind as she boarded the

Tube and began the relatively short commute into London. It hadn't looked like Aunt Gayle's writing on the front, but who else would be sending her a letter from Anchor Island? Addie and her sister, Susanna, rarely heard from Aunt Gayle, and vice versa. The last time Gayle had been in touch it was a few months ago with a birthday card for Addie, and before that a short letter to remind them that their father's things were still in her attic. They'd been there for thirty years, ever since he died and the girls went to live with her. Addie had taken charge of replying to say that she and Susanna would come and sort through things soon, although both she and Susanna had known it would be a big leap when they eventually did it given neither of them had been back to the island in almost twenty years. Even Isaac's relentless questions about her years growing up on an island in the English Channel hadn't instigated a visit.

As the Tube continued to head into the heart of the city and the office where she worked as a senior digital designer for a web agency, Addie pushed away her concerns about Anchor Island and Aunt Gayle and thought about the day ahead instead. She had a big presentation to deliver and although she liked to think she wasn't bad at what she did for work, the fact was, it wasn't her dream job, never had been, and on some days that made it so much harder to give it her all.

On the train she was surrounded by a mishmash of people – some dressed in jeans, others in smarter dress like the woman in a sharp suit with pointed stilettos. Did she do her whole commute in those? Addie had long since given up on heels, favouring trainers until she reached the office. Another man leaned against the metal safety pole frantically scrolling on his phone. On the seat closest to him a woman was tapping away on a laptop, seemingly desperate to get finished whatever it was she was in the middle of.

Addie wondered how many of these people were working in their dream job. How many people truly got to do what they loved when there was the pressure of bills to pay and hungry mouths to feed? Sometimes you had to do what was necessary. And that's exactly what Addie had done. She'd wedged herself into a life that did what she needed it to do – it provided. She earned good money, the rented flat she'd lived in for the last five years was close to a half-decent school for Isaac, and while she wasn't on the property ladder, she still had some savings put by in the vague hope that she would be one day.

As the Tube shunted her closer and closer to her destination she thought about the upcoming weekend. Except it wasn't a weekend, not for her – she'd be catching up with work, albeit from home. To at least make it bearable she planned to stay in her pyjamas all day and the second she was finished she'd bake a lovely pudding to enjoy after her dinner. Chocolate soufflé would be perfect and already she was thinking about enjoying it with a glass of wine. She'd picked up a bargain bottle of Pinot Grigio on a special deal from the corner shop the other day, when she'd raced in to buy bread so Isaac would at least get a sandwich in his packed lunch. She couldn't really afford it and didn't buy wine often, but sometimes she needed a little something for herself to take the edge off the grind of day-to-day life.

She thought about Isaac, with his crazy blond curls and dazzling smile, who loved chocolate soufflé just as much as she did. Her little boy was the love of her life, and it pained her that she couldn't give him more. Instead of a grotty flat with no outside space of their own, she longed to give him a garden, fresh air rather than a sea of smoke from the crowd of teenagers who hovered outside their building. She wanted to give him a bigger bedroom to build his Lego, she wanted to spend every weekend baking with him rather than working, she wanted to bask in the sound of his gentle giggles and make the most of the time they had before it was too late and he was all grown up.

At least Isaac had Maurie and Jarrett, his paternal grandparents. They filled some of the void Isaac's disinterested father, Jonty, had left when he'd taken off for South America and never came back. Maurie and Jarrett's house in Ruislip was a real home too, a place where Isaac had his own bedroom and a great long garden to run around in and play outside whenever he felt like it.

It should've been a quick walk from the Tube to the office but the gods of whatever it was that controlled being on time were conspiring against Addie today. First there was a problem at the ticket barrier, with queues backed up. Then she was lost in a swarm of people trying to get up to street level, and after being jostled about, when she finally emerged there was a street cordoned off due to a police incident, and she was forced to take a longer route to the office. To top it all off, she was about to enter the building but collided with someone and ended up with coffee down the front of her shirt.

She'd planned to go straight to the bathroom after dumping her bag to deal with the coffee spill before it really set in to the material of her shirt. But she didn't get a chance. She'd only just put her bag down when her boss passed by her desk and said, 'A word, please.' He didn't need to add the instruction to follow him into his office.

She exchanged a look with her colleague, Sally, who was sitting opposite. 'Probably about my meeting later, I'm a bit nervous.'

'You've got this,' said Sally. 'They'll love you.'

She looked at her shirt and pulled a face that suggested they wouldn't, not if her personal appearance was any indicator of her competence.

Presenting to potential clients still had the power to make

Addie anxious no matter how many times she'd done it before, and today's client, if they chose this web agency, would be a big coup for the team. She needed to review the presentation she'd put together, the presentation that would show the client how she'd translated their concept into engaging online content, which would generate sales and boost their business.

The goldfish bowl office with a glass partition had no door, so she went inside and took a seat when her boss, Raymond, looked up and gestured for her to do so. She hoped he wasn't about to throw another project her way given she already had a ton of work to catch up on this weekend.

Raymond eventually finished whatever he was typing on his keyboard and looked over the top of his thick-rimmed glasses. 'Is everything all right, Adeleine?'

'Of course.' She forced a brightness into her voice. 'I know I was late again today.' She looked down at the front of her shirt. 'Problem at the Tube station, a road closure, and someone with a full coffee cup knocked into me.'

'Right.' He chose his words carefully, or at least that's how it seemed. 'Is there anything I need to know?'

Well, let me see... she thought. *My job doesn't interest me, I'm just doing it for the money, and to be honest I'd rather be at home with my son this weekend or baking all day rather than working. Oh, and you keep calling me Adeleine which nobody else does. So please, stop it!*

Raymond had always used her full name. She'd given up trying to correct him. And, she supposed, in a heavily male-dominated team, Adeleine did sound a bit more serious than Addie. It was just that nobody called her Adeleine any more – it was what her dad had called her and since he'd died she'd found it painful to hear, so she'd switched to the name her friends at school used.

'I'm fine, honestly,' she said, instead of sharing what she was thinking. 'Everything is under control.'

'Are you sure?'

'Totally.'

He nodded, accepting she wasn't going to divulge anything further. 'You're meeting with a client today, Adeleine.' He steepled his fingers beneath his chin, elbows on the table. 'It's an *important* client. This could mean big business for us.'

'I'm fully prepared. I promise. I plan to do a quick review of my presentation and then I'm set to go.'

'First impressions really count.'

So he'd seen the stain. Not hard, really – it stood out a mile.

'I can pop out, grab another shirt from somewhere nearby,' she said. Not that she had the time, nor the funds to splash around, but what choice did she have?

'See that you do. And Adeleine,' he added before she could scoot back to her desk. 'Perhaps keep a spare set of clothes here just in case and maybe get an earlier train.'

He'd delivered his instructions as if they were easy. An earlier train was impossible given the time before school care started for Isaac. The extra clothes she could do, which should've made her feel slightly better, except it didn't. Still, given this was the fourth time she'd been late for work in the last fortnight, Raymond had gone pretty easy on her.

'What was that all about?' Sally asked when she got back to her desk. Sally had never seen eye to eye with Raymond; she pushed all his buttons, but she seemed to enjoy the challenge and she loved her job, unlike Addie.

'I have to go and buy a new shirt.' She indicated the coffee stain. 'Raymond doesn't want me meeting my client like this. And I get it. It won't exactly give a good impression.'

Sally pulled open a packet of dry-roasted peanuts and offered them across to Addie who sat down, defeated, at her desk. 'Fair enough. But don't stress, you don't have to buy anything.'

'I don't?' She took a handful of peanuts. The teacake from earlier hadn't filled her up in the slightest.

'I have a spare shirt. And a bra, knickers and trousers.' She leaned closer to Addie. 'Remember how I stayed out all night a few weeks ago?'

'How could I forget?' It still made Addie smile, the tale of Sally's love life which was a riot compared to her non-existent one.

'No way did I want McTwat to know I'd been out all night,' Sally went on, 'so I bought new clothes on my way in and since then, kept a spare outfit here. You know, just in case. Ever the professional, me. Apart from my funny names for people.' Sally, a massive fan of *Grey's Anatomy*, was into labelling people with a 'Mc' prefix. So far there was McHottie for Allan who worked in accounts, McPerv for Bob who talked to your cleavage, McMisery for Chris, the security guard, who hadn't smiled once in the whole year he'd worked at the main doors to the office block they shared with four other companies.

Sally disappeared out of view for a moment as she bent down to open the bottom drawer of her filing cabinet. She sat back up again and passed across a shirt after making sure nobody had their beady eye on them.

'You're a lifesaver. Thank you. I really can't afford to buy another one. I'll bring it back washed and ironed.'

Sally popped a few peanuts into her mouth and swished a hand to dismiss any concern about the shirt.

Addie went off to the ladies to get changed and, being the only one in there, she lingered in front of the mirror.

What had happened to the Addie Rafferty who, despite losing her parents, had begun to find happiness on an island in the English Channel? What had happened to the girl who enjoyed baking and had once felt like it could be the start of an exciting journey for her?

Loyalty. That was what had happened.

Being loyal to her sister and sticking to the pact they'd made as young girls had cost her – she'd lost a closeness with their aunt that Susanna had never had, and she'd never followed her passion for baking since her aunt, like her sister, seemed convinced university and academia were the key to her future.

Losing all of that was worth it for the gift of her son, of course, but she greedily wanted it all – she wanted Isaac, her happiness, a job she loved and a place where she really felt at home.

But as she made her way back to her desk, she got the impression that asking for all that was asking far too much.

2

SUSANNA

Susanna Rafferty spotted the post on the side table when she came downstairs. She couldn't remember the last time she'd picked up the post from the mat, or answered the landline, because her husband, Alex, always got there first. It had led to her worrying about what he might be hiding. He insisted everything was fine, but it wasn't. In fact, things hadn't been right for a while.

Perhaps today would put her mind at ease. They'd both taken a day off with the express purpose of spending it together – no property solicitor tasks for her, no going into his dental practice for Alex. Simply a day as a married couple.

As she sifted through the post a pale blue envelope immediately caught her eye. Postmarked Anchor Island, this letter was from the place she'd left behind a long time ago.

'You ready?' Alex came up behind her, the cool box in one hand.

With his dark hair and tanned skin like he surfed the ocean every day rather than worked indoors, Alex was still good-looking at forty-seven. He hadn't changed all that much since their wedding day, aside from a few lines on his face and bits of grey in his beard when he didn't shave for a while. It wasn't fair. Women drew the short straw when it came to changes as they got older. Already she'd got a rounding in her tummy she'd never had before, it felt as though the muscles she'd once had in her arms had lost a lot of their oomph, and she had aches and pains at the end of the day that ten or twenty years ago she'd never felt.

'Almost,' she told him, the pile of post still in her hand. 'I'm just seeing if the quote for the driveway is amongst this lot.' Their driveway needed levelling, resurfacing and two potholes filling in, and she'd requested quotes for a new garage door because the existing one had damaged panels and rust – hardly surprising, given they hadn't touched it since they'd moved in.

The quote wasn't amongst the letters, so she decided to deal with the blue envelope first. But as she started to tear it open, Alex picked up his keys and made for the front door. 'I'll be in the car.'

The atmosphere was tense enough between them and she didn't want to add to it by making him wait, so she put the envelope down. She could take it in the car with her but she'd rather not. Whatever Aunt Gayle had to say would have to wait.

'I just need to use the bathroom,' she called after Alex's retreating back. She wasn't sure if he'd even heard her.

As she used the downstairs toilet, she wondered what was inside the blue envelope. It wasn't her birthday or any other special occasion that warranted correspondence. She tried not to think about the island much, but when a letter arrived, she was right back there, thoughts churning over and over in her mind.

Most likely the letter inside the blue envelope would be another request from Aunt Gayle for the sisters to go to the island and sort through their dad's things. They'd do it, eventually, but the thought of going back there filled her with dread.

Aunt Gayle had become their guardian when their father, Harry, passed away just three years after Susanna and Addie lost their mother, Cynthia. The sisters had had to watch as their semi-detached Edwardian house – just over a mile from the lively heart of the city of Oxford – had been packed up and emptied. They'd been driven down to Portsmouth by their grandparents where they'd met their dad's sister, their Aunt Gayle, and the three of them had boarded an enormous ferry to take them across the Channel to Guernsey where they'd transferred to a smaller ferry to take them to Anchor Island. Susanna had been fourteen, Addie only eight, and she could still remember the eerie silence between them all as they travelled from their old life to a new one, the wind whipping against their skin, and the assault of salt water which left its residue in their hair long after they'd stepped onto dry land again. As they'd docked, Susanna had whispered to Addie that this wasn't forever. And later that night at their aunt's cottage they'd made a pact to leave Anchor Island as soon as they were old enough.

The only time Susanna forgot her plans to flee was when she met Mateo Collins. Four years older than her, he had a maturity she was drawn to and all of a sudden she had someone in her life just for her. They had a passion she'd never expected and had never forgotten. She'd stayed out past curfew with Mateo, she'd got drunk more than once. Oh, how they'd laughed too, and she'd felt wild, free, like an entirely different person. But Aunt Gayle had soon put an end to the relationship and Susanna had never been able to forgive her for what she did.

She was about to head out to the car when she spotted the Post-it she'd slipped into the porch mirror as a reminder to pay the window cleaner. Alex usually took care of it, but a flustered call from their window cleaner this morning while Alex was taking his time in the shower proved that he hadn't.

She leaned out of the front door, held up a hand to Alex to indicate she was on her way, but he was sitting with his eyes closed in the driver's seat of his shiny Lexus.

She went into his study. He'd have the details for payment in the file in his desk where they kept all the bills.

She paused when she saw his doodles on the jotter pad next to his keyboard. Those drawings were one of his little habits that amused her and true to form there was a row of stick people of varying heights next to a doodle of a house with a chimney sticking out of its roof and smoke drifting upwards. She had no idea what the drawings meant but she'd always found it an endearing habit.

She was about to leave when she spotted the familiar logo of a posh restaurant poking out from a piece of paper beneath the jotter and out of curiosity, she pulled it out fully. They'd been to the venue for their last wedding anniversary, celebrating with a good bottle of bubbly and beautiful food. Except this receipt wasn't old. It was from a recent meal. The booking date was last week and judging by the total amount either Alex had eaten a meal fit for two kings by himself, or he'd had company.

She put the receipt back where she found it, went outside and locked up behind her. She walked towards the car, avoiding the pothole she'd been stepping over for as long as she could remember.

She knew full well her husband was hiding something now. It was hardly a trip to a Harvester, or Pizza Hut, that he'd neglected to mention. The restaurant was classy, only for special occasions, and it hurt that he'd clearly shared it with someone else. She felt sick at the prospect of who that person might be. *Was it someone from work? It had to be. Was it a patient? Why hadn't he told her about it?*

She looked across at him as he reversed out of the driveway. She should ask him outright.

But when he turned briefly to face her as he pulled away, she couldn't do it. She was scared, terrified of her whole world imploding.

As they drove towards the parking area where they'd access the river, the September sun was out in full force and there was absolutely no sign of rain. It should've been the start of a perfect day but how could it be now? Already she wished she could lose herself in a complex property dispute instead of having to face up to her own personal problems and the possibility that her husband was cheating on her. He'd been cagey for a while and she'd tried to tell herself she was imagining things, but now she knew she wasn't. If that dinner had been innocent, it's the sort of thing he would've told her about – he'd have detailed the courses he'd chosen, the fine wine he'd selected, baulked at the cost but said it was worth it. Just like they'd done together before.

She needed a distraction. She opened her banking app on her phone and paid the window cleaner. When she explained what she was doing Alex claimed to have forgotten and didn't flinch when she announced she'd been into his study to get the details. Maybe he hadn't ever expected her to be suspicious and that's why he hadn't hidden the receipt away. Or perhaps he wasn't that clever, maybe he'd made a mistake.

Why had he agreed to spend the day with her if he had someone else?

Unless he'd ended an affair to save his marriage.

She felt like she wanted to run far away, make it all stop, put a pause on her life. But no chance of that.

With Alex focused on the road and not making much attempt to talk she looked out of the car window, her mind back to the day she and Alex had gone to the same restaurant and toasted their marriage, their future.

Was he really having an affair?

Alex pulled into the car park and found one of the few remaining spaces before they took everything they needed down to the nearest patch of green space looking out at the River Cam. Peals of laughter from a nearby group clearly not used to punting along the river accompanied the gentle swish of water beneath the flat-bottomed boat that glided in the opposite direction. Mild days like this would soon be put to one side until the spring.

'You okay?' Alex asked after they'd laid out the picnic rug and weighted it down with the cool box at one end and their shoes at the other.

Did husbands who cheated still care whether their wife was all right?

'Of course.' She took the can of lemonade Alex passed to her. 'It's a lovely day,' she added. It was a pathetically bland exchange of conversation. If she had a friend in her position, she'd be telling them to come out with it, get the truth, and move on. But it was all too easy to give advice when it didn't directly affect you, and it was much harder to act upon it when it did.

Having Alex sitting so close made her realise how much she missed her husband. They shared a bed night after night, but there was a distance. She longed to be able to take his hand or lay her head on his shoulder and instinctively know that everything was okay.

Alex's can of Coke gave a satisfying hiss of release as he flicked it open. 'We got the best of the weather,' he said in response to her comment.

How had they ended up like this, with so little to say? Since when had time together become snatched and not the way it once was? Her job as a property solicitor was demanding and

Alex's work as a dentist left little opportunity to do things like this on a whim. Come weekends they both had to catch up with work, her especially, and then there were chores, or it was meeting up with friends, and before you knew it Monday had rolled around again. She'd tried to talk several times over the last couple of months about them both putting work before their relationship, but Alex's comeback had been to query why it was such a problem when that was how it had always been.

He was right. But it had worked before, and now, somehow it didn't feel as though it did. Before, they'd always found time at the end of the day to connect.

She almost wished she hadn't found the receipt, that her mind wasn't now heading in a direction she'd never wanted it to go.

Alex leaned closer and gave her an unexpected peck on the cheek. 'Time to relax,' he said, and lay back on the rug, reaching for her hand so she would lie back with him.

Did husbands who were cheating still kiss their wives? Or hold their hand?

Was it all a ploy to put the wife off the scent?

She tried to relax but she couldn't, and after a few minutes she propped herself up on her elbows. The same group of punters who had got Susanna's attention when they first arrived had their boat moving through the water, but they kept ending up towards the middle of the river rather than gliding majestically across the surface on the right-hand side as per the rules.

'We were better than that, surely?' Alex asked.

She hadn't realised he was looking too. '*So* much better,' she said, turning to grin at him. She remembered fondly when they'd first moved to Cambridge in their twenties and made a point of 'punting on the Cam'. They hadn't done it in a while. When had they stopped having fun? Somewhere along the line that had faded too and she missed the way they used to laugh, the way they worked hard but had so much energy outside their jobs that she hadn't wanted anything to ever change. They were married, neither had ever wanted kids, they were right where they both wanted to be. Or so she'd thought.

Did husbands who were cheating still reminisce like this about better times? Or was that a distraction technique too?

'We should book a holiday soon,' she said, before she could even think about how desperate the suggestion made her feel.

'I'll look into when is the best time.' His voice came from behind her, and when she looked he'd closed his eyes again.

The saying *actions speak louder than words* sprang to mind. They'd been all set to secure a gorgeous villa in Tuscany earlier this year for July, until Alex pulled the plug, and since then they hadn't discussed it again let alone agreed on anything holiday-wise.

She considered the stage of life they were at right now. She was forty-four, Alex was forty-seven. They weren't part of the sandwich generation – they didn't have kids and neither of them had a surviving parent so there weren't those additional pressures that some of their friends had. Maybe they were just going through a rough patch. She knew others who were – one friend had found out her husband was having an affair with another man, another friend had had a big health scare, and two of her and Alex's mutual friends were going through separate nasty divorces.

She and Alex had never really hit a rough patch before, not even when they spent a year travelling together around Australia and New Zealand on a budget in their early twenties. They'd stayed in hostels, been on the move often, and they'd watched the pennies – all of it would have tested even the closest of couples, but apart from the odd bit of bickering they'd got on well. They'd moved in together on their return to England when Susanna was in her mid-twenties and got engaged shortly after that. Both had understood the other's work ethic – they'd been well-matched from the start – and since they'd married almost eighteen years ago it had felt like plain sailing ever since.

Until recently.

She turned to look at him again. 'It's so lovely today. Should we barbecue later on?'

He opened one eye. 'Already got the steaks marinating.'

She felt tugged between the familiar Alex and the one who was so distant. 'When did you do that?'

'Before you even surfaced this morning.'

In this moment things felt normal, they felt good, and they felt right. 'We'll open that special bottle of wine my client gave me last Christmas,' she said, in an effort to make the feeling last.

But she couldn't put it off forever.

She had to confront him. She needed to know the truth. She needed to know whether her marriage was over.

3

ADDIE

It was the middle of September and although the underground wasn't as sweltering as it was mid-summer, Addie still felt the air contract as she took the steps down into London's deep belly. At least she'd nailed today's presentation and left the office on a good note.

The Tube whizzed her on her way and eventually she was back at street level and on the way to her flat. Her flat was affordable, and it had been the best out of a bad bunch when she'd landed a job and had to find somewhere quickly. The listing had certainly used a bit of artistic licence, which only became apparent after she moved in. 'Tree-lined communal areas' sounded beautiful, but once the sun came down those areas filled with undesirable characters and she couldn't let Isaac outside to play on his own. The flat itself had good locks on the front door and was just big enough for two, but that was where the positives ended. It came with stained carpets, windows that let in too much of the cold and damp when the seasons changed, a kitchen tap that wobbled and threatened to give up every time it was switched on, and eighties decor that was there to stay. On the plus side her landlord hadn't hiked the rent up too much over the five years that she'd been there. He said she was a model tenant – she never missed a payment, she didn't make noise, she looked after the place. She did, but not everyone else was as considerate. The neighbour above was loud and for some reason dragged furniture around at all hours of the day and night, while the next-door neighbour smoked – when Addie opened her windows for fresh air she very often had to close them right up again as smoke snaked her way. Then there was the man in one of the ground floor flats who yelled a lot, the sort of yelling that sent a shudder right through you. Isaac was scared of him and to be honest so was Addie, and usually gave him a wide berth.

An incoming text message eased away some of the melancholy Addie felt about working over the weekend rather than spending time with Isaac. It was a message from Maurie containing the single word *Lego!* and a picture of Isaac concentrating as he added another block to the boat he was building.

She replied with *Love it!* because she did and Isaac simply made everything better.

Almost seven years ago Addie had met a guy in a pub in central London. She'd skipped ahead of him in the queue at the bar without realising. He'd introduced himself as Jonty and said he would only be willing to accept her apology for pushing in if she agreed to go out with him. By his own description Jonty was nomadic – he wanted to travel the world, said that wherever he laid his cap was his home or some other phrase which meant he wasn't interested in settling down. It might have been fine with Addie had she not fallen pregnant and suddenly their lives were intertwined forever.

True to his word, Jonty hadn't stuck around for long. He'd taken off, but his parents – Isaac's Granny Maurie and Grandad

Jarrett – had remained a constant in her little boy's life, the son she loved with every fibre of her being.

Back at her block of flats, Addie hurried past the teenagers vaping by one of the trees, and upped her pace to avoid the shouty man as he came out of the front entrance with such force she was surprised the glass part of it didn't shatter.

At her flat – number six – she went through the familiar routine of pulling the door hard towards her so that the key would turn easier and let her inside. It was eerily quiet when Isaac wasn't here, but she was welcomed by the photograph of her on the wall with her arms around her son, his cheeks bright red following a day at the beach during the summer, his curls wild, his eyes full of excitement.

She looked at the other framed photograph on the same wall. In the picture her parents stood with their girls – baby Addie in their mother's arms, her older sister, Susanna, standing next to their dad, leaning against his leg as though she daren't let go. Susanna looked like she loved their dad as much as Addie did, and this photograph always prompted Addie to wonder why her sister seemed to forget that half the time.

Addie remembered very little about her mother but lots about her dad. He'd always championed her – when she got her grade one flute, he'd let out a whoop; when she had a small part in the school play, he'd been in the front row on opening night with a look that suggested he thought she was the star of the show. Her dad was lovely – she couldn't think of a single thing she hadn't liked about him, and she missed him every single day. He would've loved Isaac too. Isaac didn't have any grandparents on her side, what with her mother and father both gone, so it made Addie doubly glad that Maurie and Jarrett doted on him and always leapt at the chance to have their grandson to stay.

She put a glass beneath the tap in the kitchen, held her

breath when the stream of water slowed, but released it when the water thankfully flowed enough to fill her glass.

She gulped it down, thirsty with the heat of the day, her eyes falling to the pile of post with the blue envelope on top.

How different would her life have been if she'd never left Anchor Island? If she hadn't honoured the pact she'd made as an eight-year-old with her sister that they belonged in England and not on some remote island. At the time she'd felt as if she'd been torn away from everything – their home, the memories of her dad and the way he'd walked down the street with her on his shoulders on summer days as he took her to the park, her world as she knew it.

Over the years talking to Susanna, she'd pieced together the parts of her dad's life that she couldn't remember – his love for a family café he'd longed to keep but couldn't, how he'd retrained and moved into the travel sector instead. And these days she wondered whether her dad had been doing what she was doing now, working in a job she didn't really want to be in, just to keep bills paid and food on the table.

With the envelope in her hand, she thought about the island she'd promised to leave, but which she'd slowly begun to like. She remembered spending summer days by the water seeing what sea creatures lurked in rock pools, she had fond memories of skimming pebbles from one of the little coves, she remembered making friends, but most of all she remembered baking with Aunt Gayle and the Sweet Life Café.

When Susanna left the island to go to university on the mainland, Addie had grown closer to Aunt Gayle and she'd begun to work weekend shifts in the Sweet Life Café, a place dedicated to puddings of all kinds. At first, she'd cleaned up, swept floors, wiped down. Then she'd served customers, discussed the menu options if a customer didn't know what to choose, and eventually she'd started to bake with her aunt, particularly after hours. They'd chat, they'd laugh, and they'd eat whatever they made. They made all sorts – fruit crumbles, thick, delicious custards, chocolate brownies, profiteroles, lemon meringue pie. And even if the recipe didn't quite work, there was a joy in the process, and a sense of belonging Addie had found comforting.

For a while Addie felt like she'd found her place in the world, but then Aunt Gayle seemed to push her away and she began to encourage her to return to England to take up a place at university as if that was her only option. It had hurt when Addie realised that perhaps Gayle didn't really want her around after all. And she'd never admitted to Susanna that the island, by that point, had begun to feel like home.

She sat down at the table and tore open the envelope, which most likely contained a request she and her sister go and retrieve their dad's things from their aunt's attic.

But what was inside couldn't be from Aunt Gayle.

The words on the invite went blurry as her emotions took over. No matter what had gone before, no matter that she and Susanna didn't have much of a relationship with their aunt, the news was still devastating.

Aunt Gayle was gone, and it was too late to repair anything now.

4

SUSANNA

Back home, Susanna opened the window in the lounge at the front of the house to let the fresh air filter through while the weather was still so mild. She tried not to let her imagination run riot when Alex disappeared into his study to apparently deal with some paperwork. It was possible, of course, because not only was he a dentist, he owned his practice, the practice that over the last decade had grown exponentially.

She went into the kitchen and opened another window in there. She loved this house, their home. It wasn't far from the centre of Cambridge, and it reminded her a lot of the Rafferty home in Oxford before she and her sister had been forced to leave when their dad died. Cambridge, like Oxford, was thriving; it felt like real life here, not some back of beyond place like Anchor Island where they were miles away from the mainland.

If her marriage disintegrated, would Alex want the house? Would she fight to keep it?

She felt nauseous at the thought of what he was hiding as well as the confrontation she knew they needed to have, let alone what their future held.

She ran her hand along the mahogany mantelpiece. This home had been a labour of love. As she and Alex had put their own stamp on it with colour schemes and new fixtures and fittings, they'd kept its character. She loved the large rooms, the high ceilings, the fireplace that dominated the living room with its dual aspect windows. She opened up the rear doors on to the outside space they'd redone as a classic cottage garden with plenty of greenery at the borders, giving them privacy and a feeling of nature. There was a summerhouse in the far-left corner, a small seating area on the patio before the lawn began, and enough colour from the easy-to-maintain shrubs and flowers to feel special. They'd always wanted something that didn't require much upkeep – their focus had been on their jobs, and still was. But perhaps that focus needed to shift if they were to save their marriage.

In the upstairs bathroom, she pinned her dark hair up into a messy bun, hair that was – for now – devoid of any grey thanks to regular touch-ups, and climbed into the shower cubicle, closing the door gently behind her because of its tendency to wobble. They really needed someone to come and look at it – she'd mentioned to Alex about redoing the entire bathroom as well as the garage door and driveway because it was getting tired and worn. But like with so many other things, they hadn't talked about it since.

After her shower she pulled on a pair of jeans and a loose-fitting T-shirt and went downstairs to prepare a couple of salads, one with buffalo mozzarella, tomatoes and basil leaves, the other with salty halloumi, bitter rocket and thinly curled cucumber. Alex was still in his study, and she resisted the urge to listen at the closed door to see whether he was talking to another woman. He never used to shut the door. He'd always been able to focus with comings and goings, unlike her who needed quiet and to be away from everyone when she was doing anything work-related.

Once the salads were ready, she took out a couple of wine glasses. If Alex ever emerged from his study, they could open that special bottle, although right now it would feel a lot like drowning her sorrows.

She glanced at the photograph on the wall of Addie's son, Isaac, as he jumped through the sprinklers on the lawn. It had been taken last summer and captured his personality perfectly.

Addie and Susanna were still close. She loved that and her sister was a great mum but Susanna wished Addie had more in her life. She had a good job and said she was happy enough, but Susanna could tell something was missing. She'd always looked out for her little sister. And yet, she knew she shouldn't interfere too much. She'd once floated the idea of helping Addie to get on to the property ladder by lending her money, but it had been a categoric no from Addie, followed by a request that Susanna let her stand on her own two feet for once. It was the only thing that had ever come between them, apart from their difference of opinion when it came to their dad. The girls tended to avoid talking about him most of the time, otherwise it risked leading to disagreement and tension. Of course, Susanna had plenty of fond memories of their time as the Rafferty family before they lost their mum, but Susanna had also kept something from her sister for years, something that would easily explain her feelings towards their dad, and yet she could never speak of it. She really had loved him – she'd been devastated when he'd died – she just wished she'd kept the same innocence about their parents as Addie had.

Addie remembered only good things when it came to their family, which, as the protective older sister, Susanna was grateful for. She did her best to fill in the blanks about their parents where she could, especially facts about their mum that Addie would've been too young to remember, and as for the rest of what she knew? Well, she shielded Addie from more unnecessary hurt wherever she could. She'd done it for so many years she had difficulty switching it off when Addie reached adulthood. More than once she'd wished she had a mum to talk to, or that Aunt Gayle had been more of a mother figure. Susanna had never felt able to confide in Aunt Gayle and instead sought advice from the teenage magazines she read or from friends at school, or she simply got on with things. The lack of closeness with her aunt was partly her fault, she knew that, but Aunt Gayle had betrayed her shortly before she left the island for good, and she'd never been able to forgive her for what she'd done. Susanna had wanted to close that chapter of her life and never look back once Addie was also off the island.

She walked towards the study and was about to knock on the door, but her hand dropped as she changed her mind. The sound of a child wailing carried through the open window of the lounge, grabbing her attention instead as she went to sit down in the squishy armchair. She could just about see a young woman near their drive doing battle with a toddler. Her competence reminded her of Addie and how she'd taken to motherhood so effortlessly. Susanna had never had the urge to procreate, and it wasn't only because as the eldest she'd been thrust into a childcare role in her teenage years, watching Addie after school instead of hanging out with her friends because Gayle was busy with her pudding business. She'd just never seen herself as a mum. She wondered whether it had anything to do with losing her own so young, but she doubted it. She just wasn't wired that way. But she was definitely wired to be a doting aunt. She adored her little nephew. Whenever Isaac visited, he loved to help her water the shrubs and plants with the hose while Addie had a break relaxing in an outdoor chair, and he'd keep her amused with his quirks, laughter and funny chatter.

She wondered, if they'd had kids, would Alex have cheated? If he was cheating at all, that was. A fact she'd never know unless she asked him.

What was wrong with her? She wasn't this meek person who shied away from conflict. She wouldn't put it off any longer. They'd talk tonight and she'd be able to make a plan to move forwards.

Alex took her by surprise when he emerged from the study and it was even more of a shock when he came over and pulled her to standing for an impromptu hug. It felt so good, so safe, like nothing could ever come between them.

After things had ended messily with her first serious boyfriend, Mateo – who might well be living on Anchor Island with his family unless he'd sailed off somewhere exotic – Susanna had been put off getting serious with a man again. She'd been hurt, she was upset, and she'd vowed to maintain her independence. She liked making her own decisions, not needing a man to define her. She'd read an article in a magazine once and that exact phrase had stayed in the forefront of her mind ever since. It was partly why she'd kept her surname, Rafferty, when she married, as well as wanting to keep hold of the link to the family she hadn't had for very long at all. She'd always been *one of those Rafferty girls* on the island and she'd loved being thought of that way despite her desperate need to escape. She remembered once, when she and Addie were in the Sweet Life Café, overhearing someone talking about *those Rafferty girls* freewheeling on their bicycles down the hillier parts of the island, their legs outstretched and their hair flying out behind them in the wind. That person hadn't approved but Addie and Susanna had found it hysterical to listen to and vowed to keep doing it –

which they did, getting faster and faster, laughing louder and louder every single time.

When she took up a place at the University of East Anglia, Susanna finally got to leave Anchor Island and it was like a whole new world opened up to her, a world that was her own. She had a small amount of money that her dad had left her which, on top of the loans, saw her through. She finished her degree before moving to Cambridge to finish her studies and soon embarked upon her first job as a trainee solicitor. She had boyfriends but never anyone serious until she met Alex.

They'd met when she was on holiday on the Norfolk coast with friends. Despite the swimming lessons she'd assumed were enough to keep her strong in the water, and years of living on an island, she'd got into difficulty in the sea on the first day, a cramp in her leg making it near to impossible to stay afloat, let alone swim. She'd flailed around, desperately trying to move back to shore. Her head kept going under the water, but the next thing she knew, a strong arm had lifted her above the surface and another muscular arm had aided the first, and she was on a surfboard before she knew it. The rescuer had paddled her back to shore with her beneath his torso and when she finally stood up, she looked into the eyes of Alex Byrne, who worked at the beach as a lifeguard over the summer.

If it hadn't been for her cramp that day, they might never have met at all.

Alex Byrne. The man she'd finally let herself fall for.

And now, despite being so much older, the idea that Alex might be hiding something still hurt as much as when things ended with Mateo when she was only nineteen.

Alex pulled away and asked, 'Shall I open the wine?' He sounded so normal.

'That would be lovely.'

She stood to follow him and paused at the table in the hallway. She looked at the blue envelope. She'd been so focused on her husband she hadn't had the headspace for Aunt Gayle and what she wanted this time.

She picked up the envelope and tore it open, noting that the writing on the front looked unfamiliar. Aunt Gayle never put funny loops on the bottom of her fs in Rafferty.

And she was right.

It wasn't familiar at all.

Because it wasn't from Gayle. Aunt Gayle was dead.

Her chest tightened. They hadn't been close, but knowing that she was gone and the way they'd left things could never have a different outcome was unsettling.

Another part of their family was gone, and it was never coming back.

5

ADDIE

Addie hugged her sister hello. She'd arrived at the airport an hour ago, checked in her luggage and waited in the café for Susanna to arrive. Today they would fly to Guernsey where they'd catch a connecting ferry over to Anchor Island. It was the final connection of the day and would get them there shortly before the sun came down.

'I'm not really sure how to feel,' said Susanna as she unwound her neck scarf. As usual, Susanna looked far more together than she did. While Addie favoured jeans and sloppy cardigans when she wasn't at work and found most of her clothes at charity shops, bargain outlets or one of the markets in London, Susanna usually went for labels and always looked smart no matter whether she was wearing a suit for the office or was dressed in jeans and a simple top like she had on now.

'It's hard to believe she's gone,' said Addie, and after a beat, wondered, 'Who's arranging the funeral?'

'I don't know, but it was the most upbeat funeral invite I've ever seen. Not that I've seen that many.'

'To ask everyone to wear bright colours means that she must have had some input before... well, you know.'

'Before she died,' Susanna finished for her. 'Maybe she knew what was coming, asked someone who works with her at the Sweet Life Café to help. She must have appointed someone to deal with her affairs, given we're out of the picture.'

That fact didn't sit well with Addie. They'd all drifted apart, left it too long, and now it was too late.

Yesterday, when she'd spoken on the phone with her sister, she was glad of Susanna's decisiveness and ability to be organised. She'd half expected Susanna to refuse to even set foot on Anchor Island again – she'd been resisting the suggestion they go and sort through their father's things for long enough – but yesterday it was Susanna who had looked up train times, ferry schedules, and flights, and had them sorted out in no time. She was a lot like their Aunt Gayle; not that Addie would dare mention the similarity out loud to her sister.

Addie felt a sudden surge of panic. 'Do you think whoever is organising the funeral has already cleared out Gayle's house and the attic, including all of Dad's things?'

'Gayle wouldn't have let that happen.'

'We should've gone back a long time ago.'

Her comment was met with silence. She hadn't pushed Susanna to go and sort through their dad's things. Addie had wanted to go, to get it done, but she'd be the first to admit that she'd been waiting for Susanna to take the lead. Perhaps that was where she'd gone wrong. For years she'd wanted her sister to let her make her own decisions, jumped on her back if she tried to interfere. She should've been more forceful.

Instead of deliberating the fact that they hadn't gone to the island until now, she asked, 'Do you think Aunt Gayle made a will? I mean, I'd assume so. There's the house, the business, all her personal effects...'

'We've been gone a long time,' Susanna interrupted, as if she needed the reminder.

Addie closed her eyes. 'This all feels like such a mess.'

'We'll see what's what when we get to the island.'

'We're going to need somewhere to stay.' Addie pulled out her phone. 'I didn't even think of that.'

'The inn is still running, but it'll make more sense to stay at the cottage. We can sort things out better from there.' Susanna stirred her coffee once again. Addie had long since finished her second cup.

'The cottage?' Addie had to wonder if her sister had thought it through. 'It would be too weird. And besides, I don't have a key any more. Do you?'

'There'll be a spare key in the bottom of the stone tortoise ornament outside.' She smiled slightly. 'I came back drunk one night, barefoot because it was so hot, and I stubbed my toe on the thing trying to locate it to let myself in and sneak up to bed.'

'I suppose it would make it easier to go through Dad's things, if they're still there.' But Addie still wasn't sure about the idea.

Susanna finished her coffee, took the cup to the counter and brought them both back a bottle of water. 'How did Isaac take the news that you'll be away for a while?'

'Better than me. It's the longest I've gone without seeing him.' The plan was to go over, sort out what they needed to, attend the funeral and head back a couple of days after that.

'The time will go quickly, you'll see. There'll be a lot to do.'

'I cried last night at the thought of being so far from Isaac.'

Susanna's hand reached across the table and gave hers a squeeze. 'If it's all too much, you can nip home and see Isaac and then return to the island. I'll cover the cost.' She squeezed Addie's hand more firmly. 'And I won't take no for an answer on that one.'

She didn't argue. It was nice to know she had a get-out clause if she really couldn't stand to be away from Isaac for that long, but she wished her sister wouldn't assume she couldn't manage. She could scrape together enough to visit her son, but hopefully it wouldn't come to that. They'd be busy. Maurie and Jarrett were well versed at keeping Isaac entertained, and knowing he was in his element should be enough to keep her head straight.

When Susanna went off to call Alex, Addie let herself think about the island. Sometimes she didn't. Sometimes she pushed the memories away, as it felt easier.

Addie had lived on Anchor Island since she was eight years old and slowly she'd begun to settle and feel happy again. She made friends, got through school easily enough, but at the back of her mind was always the pact she and her sister had made the day they were dragged from their beloved home in Oxford, away from all that was familiar.

The day Susanna announced she had got the grades she needed to go to university back on the mainland, Addie had been heartbroken. She'd known the day was coming but she also knew how hard it was going to be living here without Susanna. She was twelve, almost thirteen, when she and Aunt Gayle took her sister and her bags to the ferry and waved her off. Addie had known then that Susanna would never come back, not properly anyway, and it felt like the Rafferty girls were disappearing like the rest of their family had.

Addie missed Susanna more than she could explain and one night a month or so after Susanna had left, she'd been missing her sister like crazy and was so upset that she'd run upstairs as soon as she got back from school and buried her face in her pillow. She'd howled. She couldn't remember crying that hard since her dad had died.

She'd been mid-sob when she heard the creak of the door opening, felt the sag of the mattress as someone sat down, and when she opened her eyes Aunt Gayle was there. She didn't say a word, just opened her arms. It was the first time Addie had really let herself be hugged and comforted by their aunt, the first time it felt like Aunt Gayle was there when she needed her rather than Susanna filling the role of their absent parents. That night Addie had been allowed to stay up past midnight. They'd had apple and rhubarb crumble with hot custard, they'd talked about school, about what Addie missed on the mainland, what she liked on the island. Addie had gone to bed full of the pudding but with something else too, the feeling of family.

The following day Addie had gone into the Sweet Life Café after school and asked if she could help out and she'd gone in every day since. If Susanna was on the island visiting, she spent time with her sister, but when Susanna wasn't there Addie was at the Sweet Life Café with Gayle, and slowly, things on Anchor Island began to subtly change.

As the days and weeks turned to months and years, Addie enjoyed her time at the café more and more, baking almost every day, sometimes to Gayle's recipes and other times her own, and she began to wonder whether a university place was what she really wanted.

'I love baking,' she said candidly to Gayle one day, as she washed her hands after handling pastry. She had offers from three universities, had accepted her preferences, both with courses in web design, and was set to go to the mainland in less than six months providing her results were good enough.

Gayle put an apple and raisin strudel in the oven. 'I can tell.'

She was smiling as she picked up a cloth to wipe down the surface.

'I'm not sure I'm doing the right thing.' When Gayle looked her way she explained, 'With university, I mean. I've applied, I've got offers, but is it what I really want?'

'Are you worried about the money?'

'No. I have some money from Dad, and on top of the loans I'll apply for I'll be fine.'

Gayle turned her back and continued to wipe the bench top, gathering flour and pastry debris in her opposite palm. 'You have a plan, Addie, a good plan.'

'But what if it's not the right thing for me?'

Gayle turned to face her. 'Have you talked to your sister about this?'

'No.' Of course she hadn't. Susanna would think she'd lost the plot if she told her sister that rather than a university place, she would prefer to see whether she could make it in the baking world. She hadn't looked into what that might entail; all she knew was that she had a passion for it and spending time here with Gayle had made her realise that perhaps her hobby could be a lot more.

'Did you feel the same way?' Addie prompted.

'What do you mean?' Gayle rinsed out the cloth under the tap.

'Did you have a passion for baking and find you couldn't imagine doing anything else?'

Gayle took a moment to answer. 'Yes, that's exactly how I felt. But I didn't have many options. I was never very good at school like you are. And I took a huge risk with this place. My parents did with their café and your dad struggled when he took it on, as you know. A café or pudding place or bakery means you're dependent on demand, on customer preferences and loyalty. It's not an easy business.' She left the kitchen abruptly, leaving Addie wondering what had just happened.

Addie had expected a different reaction. She couldn't believe Gayle hadn't embraced her joy of baking, told her exactly how it was for her, how delighted she was that Addie showed the same interest. They'd been getting on so well she'd imagined her aunt being excited, encouraging, considering her career direction seriously. But instead, Aunt Gayle hadn't been able to get out of the kitchen fast enough.

That day set the scene for Gayle putting a damper on Addie's enthusiasm, either changing the subject to England and university or the job market whenever Addie tried to bring up her passion again, or talking about the hard times she'd had trying to keep the Sweet Life Café going.

Soon Addie stopped mentioning it and she stopped going into the café to help out. She studied hard, she got great results, and by the time it came for her to take up the place at Loughborough University, Addie had all but pushed aside her love of baking to follow an academic route.

It was certainly what everyone else seemed to think was the right thing to do.

As Addie buckled her seat belt on the plane, she felt a sadness come over her that whatever they found when they got to the island, things were never going to be the same again.

6

SUSANNA

Susanna's thoughts had been all over the place on the flight to Guernsey. She'd closed her eyes on the pretence of being exhausted and Addie hadn't questioned it. Both needed time to process their return to the island and the loss of Gayle in their own way.

For the entire flight Susanna's mind was either on the island itself, Gayle or Alex. She'd called Alex from the airport but he hadn't answered, and so the questions began to churn over and over. Where was he? Who was he with? And when was he going to tell her what was going on?

As they boarded the ferry that would take them over to Anchor Island, Susanna requested they sit outside.

'Does it help?' Addie asked her as they found a seat in the open air.

'It seems to, at least a little bit.' It was Mateo who'd once suggested it to combat her seasickness. In her school days, getting the boat was a daily occurrence with the high school on Guernsey but she was well and truly out of practice now and already felt queasy at the thought of the rocking motions that would accompany the almost three-hour-long crossing ahead of them.

Addie noticed the wristbands Susanna was slipping on.

'Alex got them for me,' she explained.

While Susanna had been packing her things yesterday, Alex had nipped out and returned with a small package containing the funny little bands, each featuring a small plastic stud. 'Apparently the studs push against an acupressure point, and it helps avoid nausea.'

'Fingers crossed,' said Addie.

It was such a kind thing to do. Did husbands who were cheating buy their wives thoughtful gifts?

As the boat's engines started, Addie began to smile. 'There was a time, you know, when boats were totally your thing.'

Susanna laughed. 'How long have you been gearing up to drop that massive hint?'

'A hint at what?'

'Don't play innocent. You're wondering if I'm thinking about Mateo.'

'Okay, guilty. So... are you?'

'No.' She pulled a face. 'All right, a bit. I wonder if he's still there.' Mateo used to work at the marina adjacent to the harbour they would be sailing into today. He'd gone off to work elsewhere for a few years, but as Anchor Island had always been his home, was he back there now? She'd never bumped into him, not on any of her brief return visits to see her sister after she left for university, and she'd always been grateful for that. Things hadn't ended well, so the thought of facing him again had always filled her with dread. But now? Now there was a curiosity. She wondered what he was like. Had he changed or had time stood still?

Mateo Collins had taught Susanna what it was like to have a lover rather than a boyfriend. Up until she met Mateo, she'd had the odd date – she'd kissed boys, even gone a bit further than that – but Mateo was entirely different. Susanna and Mateo talked about a future together too, something she'd never seen coming. She always thought she knew exactly what she wanted – leave the island, never come back, but with Mateo's other love being the sea she had a lot of thinking to do. They talked about living near the coast somewhere, even if it wasn't on an island. They even talked about maybe setting up a business, something to do with boats or water sports. She didn't really care back then, as long as they were together. Mateo had fast become her world and she'd thought they'd go the distance.

'I wonder how much the island has changed,' she said to stop her thoughts going deeper and deeper to the first man she'd ever loved.

'I'll bet Bay Street still looks the same,' said Addie. 'The Sweet Life Café will still be in situ with its balcony that gets crazy hot in the summer and freezing cold in the winter.'

'The café was Bay Street's main attraction.' Back in the day, anyway. People had come from all over the island to try one of Gayle's puddings – some had come from even further afield. 'Have you ever looked it up online?'

'Bay Street?'

Susanna shook her head. 'No, the Sweet Life Café.'

'Never. You?'

She looked at Addie more closely. 'You've really never got curious?'

'Honestly, I haven't. You seem surprised.'

'Well, you were always a bit more attached than I was.'

Addie looked away, out to the water as the vessel began its slow departure.

'I wonder what will happen to the café without Aunt Gayle?' She wanted to distract herself from the crossing; she was sure that would be just as effective as the wristbands, or perhaps the two things would work together.

'I don't know,' said Addie.

'Did she ever say what she eventually wanted to do with it?'

'Susanna, it's been a long time. Mostly we talked baking, not business. I don't remember ever talking about long term plans.'

Was there a note of regret in Addie's voice?

'If the Sweet Life Café lasted through the pandemic, then Gayle did well,' said Susanna.

'I didn't think of that.'

'A lot of businesses went under.' She paused. 'I hope hers didn't.'

'Do you really mean that?'

'Addie, I never hated Aunt Gayle.'

They both looked out across the Channel as the boat chopped through the water, taking them back to the place they'd left behind.

Susanna had been very young when their dad was forced to give up the Cuppas and Treats Café in Oxford due to financial pressures, but she remembered the change in him – how he'd gone from embracing every day with an energy and vigour, to lacking much enthusiasm at all. From what she understood, Aunt Gayle was originally supposed to take on the family's café with Harry, but she'd gone off to do her own thing very early on. In later years, Harry had made it obvious that he resented the fact, and Susanna suspected that was why they hadn't seen their aunt for years while he was alive. It had made her wonder why on earth their dad had entrusted his sister with their care after he was gone rather than their maternal grandparents who they adored. They were both gone now, but Susanna and Addie had never forgotten how special they were, the grandparents who told them that going to the island to be with their Aunt Gayle was for the best, that they'd have a good life with all that sea air and Gayle's youthful enthusiasm. They'd waxed lyrical about the wonderful puddings Gayle created too, and the Sweet Life Café on the island.

The café had indeed been somewhere the girls loved, even Susanna, who had had to go there to babysit Addie so many times when her friends were off being young and free. The Sweet Life Café had some good memories, and it was there that Susanna first crossed paths with Mateo. The handsome, bronzed stranger had come in to fetch a pie, and she'd been unable to take her eyes off the tall guy with dirty blond hair, seaside-messy like he'd just been out on a boat. She knew that if she was close enough to touch it, it would be full of salt. She'd watched him as he waited at the counter, chatting to her aunt, who was putting the pie into a takeaway box for him. Dressed in shorts and a T-shirt, she'd immediately guessed this guy couldn't possibly work in an office given his casual attire and his strong physique, even before she heard him say something about working with boats and that he was taking the pie back to the yard for the other guys.

As the boat furthered its journey across the Channel Susanna thought about the Sweet Life Café and the other times she'd been happy to be there. Their aunt had always been generous with puddings. She'd let them choose whatever they wanted while she worked until closing time, and she'd always told them that they would do dinner in reverse – dessert first, main course later. The girls had thought it was heaps of fun. In fact, it was one of the times they'd both thought that maybe Gayle wasn't so bad. But she would never take the place of the mother who'd died when Susanna was only eleven years old, and Susanna had never forgotten what Gayle did to ruin the happiness she'd eventually found on the island with Mateo.

The fresh air felt good, but Susanna didn't feel entirely great on the boat. And they were nowhere near halfway through their crossing. Instead of silence and contemplation, she needed conversation. 'The attic will take a while to sort through,' she said to Addie.

Addie hooked her hair away from her face as she turned towards her sister. 'No doubt. Dad's things have been up there for so long. I'm quite looking forward to raking through old memories.'

'True.' She wasn't sure how much Harry-worshipping she could do, though – probably very little compared to her sister. She decided to add a practical suggestion rather than getting lost in the emotion. 'We should think about hiring a skip.'

'I don't think that'll be necessary. We'll want to keep some things.'

Well, that backfired – Addie no doubt thought she was about to chuck out as much as she could.

Harry had been a good father in so many ways and Susanna knew, much like Addie holding on to good things about the past, she was holding on to the bad parts.

'How's work going?' she asked Addie in an effort to avoid anything contentious. Everyone around them was chattering, kids were giggling, people clustered at the side of the boat eager to see their destination when it finally came into view.

Addie talked about her job, and the recent presentation she'd worked so hard on plus the extra hours she'd been putting in.

'Would you ever look for something different?' Susanna only asked because Addie hadn't seemed entirely happy, especially about the weekend work. Weekends were sacred for most people but particularly for a single mum.

'When would I have the time?' Addie smiled. 'And besides, sometimes it's better the devil you know. And my boss is quite nice really, at least when I'm not running late... again.' She explained her recent tardiness and the coffee spill on her shirt.

'Life happens, he should understand that. You aren't always late, are you?'

She pulled a face. 'A few times, in quick succession.'

'But he knows you're a parent, right?'

'He does.'

'Then maybe he should be looking at giving you a little more flexibility rather than making you feel bad about yourself.'

Addie began to smile. 'You're just like Dad was. He never took any crap from anyone.'

Susanna looked out at the white crests on the waves. 'I'm more like Mum than Dad.'

'Right...' she heard Addie say.

Susanna was beginning to feel unwell and the last thing she wanted to do was talk about their dad, not when it brought a whole lot of stress when their differing opinions and memories emerged. She shifted her gaze to the horizon to hopefully quell any more nausea.

She wondered whether she should talk about Alex, confide in her sister some more but when she turned to face Addie her sister was looking out across the water.

Perhaps silence was the best thing for them both right now.

And as the land mass of Anchor Island became visible, they stayed quiet, both sisters looking in opposite directions, waiting for the inevitable moment when they stepped onto dry land.

Back to the island they'd both left behind. Back to memories of the woman who'd been their last remaining connection to family and who had hurt Susanna so much that Susanna had never forgiven her for it.

She wondered if, were Gayle still alive, she would have been able to find forgiveness towards her aunt. And would her aunt really have wanted it, or had she been glad to get her life and her café back to herself?

7

GAYLE

When Gayle Rafferty decided to plan her own living funeral, she hadn't expected it to backfire quite so spectacularly.

'Oh, you're in trouble.' Nancy, her second in command at the Sweet Life Café on Anchor Island, put a dollop of cream on the side of a big triangular slice of cherry pie and pushed the plate closer to Gayle.

This café, conveniently situated only a short stroll away from the front door of Gayle's cottage, was her life. She'd built the business herself and knew that it would be with her until the day she died. She hoped that would be later rather than sooner, but over the last month she'd begun to get a bad feeling that something sinister was brewing. A couple of weeks ago she'd fainted at home, and came round, terrified, when nobody else was there. She hadn't told a soul what had happened, but she was always waiting for a repeat performance, especially as she'd had other symptoms. She often had tummy pains and she felt sick; she got through the days with a smile and the same air of control she'd always had, but inside she'd been breaking with concern about her health and whether her time would soon be up.

Her spoon hovered over the golden shortcrust pastry with cherries oozing from its centre. She didn't need Nancy to tell her she was in trouble. 'Susanna and Addie are not going to be happy with me,' she told her employee and very good friend, before a small smile tentatively formed on her lips. 'But at least this way they'll come.'

Nancy collected Gayle's latte from the espresso machine. 'They said that?' When Gayle didn't respond, she prompted, 'You did call each of them to let them know your mistake, didn't you?'

A reprieve came when Nancy was needed by a customer at the other end of the counter, and Gayle put her spoon into the cherry pie, catching a nice bit of pastry and a cherry as well as a scraping of cream.

As she'd got older, Gayle had noticed that her writing wasn't as good as it once was, which was why she'd had Louisa, the newcomer to the island and to her life, write out all the names and addresses onto envelopes for the invites.

Louisa Miller had come looking for Gayle a few weeks ago and had stayed on the island for almost a week. During that time, they had been getting to know one another. Gayle knew it was probably down to not having family around her that made her so receptive to Louisa, but more than that, she enjoyed the young woman's company as much as when a fresh wind blew in off the English Channel to cool you down and remind you that you were still alive. For now.

Gayle had never been one to be bossed about, but once Louisa knew some of the intricacies of Gayle's relationship with Susanna and Addie she'd said to Gayle, *you can't leave things the way they are.* The words had struck a chord. She wasn't getting any younger. And her health, like anyone in their eighth decade, wasn't what it had once been. If she didn't do something and soon, those girls would never return to the island, they'd never know her regrets, they'd never know how much she wished things had turned out differently. She was sorry for what she'd done to Susanna, and she was sorry for what she'd done to Addie too.

Louisa had gone on to apologise for overstepping, but in the days following, Gayle had come to realise that Louisa had said what needed to be said. And when she saw a piece in the local newspaper about the passing of Jeffrey Sutton, the man she'd once been married to, she realised that time wasn't on her side. Jeffrey had been the love of her life, and she would have given anything for one more conversation with him if only to know that he was happy. It sounded like he had been. The piece in the newspaper honoured the work he'd done at the school he'd worked at for almost five decades. He'd made a mark on others' lives as much as hers.

Nobody had forever – she certainly didn't – and that day she knew she had to do something.

By mere coincidence she'd picked up the magazine insert that came with the same newspaper that day and inside was an interesting article about a lady in France who had organised a living funeral. Gayle had thought it a rather peculiar thing to do, but the idea began to grow in her mind when she read about Jeffrey. She'd started to wonder whether maybe it was a way to get the Rafferty girls back on the island and maybe, just maybe, they could try to salvage their family.

She'd looked into the idea further online, found examples for the wording she could use, and had utilised cut and paste and tailored invites to her taste. Louisa had written out the envelopes for her and between working at the Sweet Life Café and trying to get the invites out as soon as possible, Gayle had somehow missed a close proofread of the wording.

The envelopes and the legibility of the addresses had turned out to be the least of Gayle's worries because she'd made a mistake. A big one. One very small, but *very* important word had been left off: 'living' should have preceded the word 'funeral'.

Gayle felt some comfort from the cherry pie Nancy had served her, although not as much as usual because her appetite these days was nowhere near what it used to be and she'd hardly made a dent in the pudding.

She basked in the soundscape of the business she'd built – the staff chattering, the laughter of customers, the clattering of utensils and pots and pans as puddings were baked, served and enjoyed. She inhaled the sweet smell surrounding her that always had a calming effect, and looked around at the inviting space she'd created. She'd wanted the Sweet Life Café to be a little retro and different. Stools were positioned at intervals in front of the long counter, each with a turquoise leather seat and chrome body. A few booths were dotted along one wall beside an enormous window, and each one had a table in the middle with turquoise leather upholstery on the seats. Round tables and chairs were dotted across the chequerboard tiled floor of the café, and wide glass shelving behind the main counter held vases of flowers and a host of certificates the Sweet Life Café had earned over the years. Gayle had kept it the same way as it had been when she first opened the café's door to the public, with just a little spruce here and there.

As she overheard a gentleman excitedly order a passionfruit cheesecake to take away, Gayle thought about the hours she'd spent in the kitchen, not just here but at her cottage and back in Oxford as a young girl. She'd adored baking ever since she could remember. At first, she'd helped her mother as she made puddings for the family, but her mother had soon left her to her own devices when Gayle's enthusiasm and capability proved she didn't need to be supervised.

The feeling she got when she baked hadn't changed at all over the years. Pulling out ingredients, taking a big mixing bowl, sieving, stirring, pouring and beating, all of it delighted her and soothed her. Gayle needed to bake like some people needed to go on a run or do a yoga class or have a holiday. If ever she felt stressed or that things were getting too much, she baked. It didn't matter that she did it all day long in her job and had done for the last five decades, it didn't matter that she had no one at the cottage to enjoy the fruits of her labour... She'd do it anyway.

She remembered being caught by Susanna once, baking ginger steamed pudding in the middle of the night. It was a couple of months after the girls had come to the island and Gayle had felt particularly stressed that her nieces were never going to feel at home. Susanna had come downstairs and when Gayle looked up her niece was watching her from the doorway. Gayle had claimed she was baking the pudding for Nancy to sample and decide whether it would go on the menu, but she'd told her eldest niece that she could spare some and handed Susanna a fork before picking up one for herself. They hadn't talked that night, but there'd been a companionship in their silence, and Susanna had even thanked her before she went back to bed. *Thank you* wasn't a phrase her eldest niece used often. Gayle had sat at the table a while longer before going to bed herself and she'd realised it wasn't only Susanna's determination and her resistance to settling in here, the poor girl was being held back by something so much deeper, the hurt that had scarred her forever losing her parents so young. She'd thought that night might have been the start of getting to know each other, and for a while it had been. Things had never been what Gayle would call rosy, but they'd been calm, she'd really thought they'd turned a corner. Perhaps they had right up until Gayle ruined things by telling Susanna's boyfriend, Mateo, that he needed to put a stop to the relationship if he really cared about Susanna and her future. Susanna had fallen for him, she'd stopped working so hard at school, and Gayle had worried she wouldn't get into university with Mateo as such a big distraction. And university, life on the mainland, had been what Susanna had wanted for a very long time. She'd never said otherwise.

Warning Mateo off that day, however, had been the thing that came between her and Susanna once and for all. After that, they'd not talked about it, but she knew Susanna was only being cordial and visiting for Addie, and that once Addie left, Susanna wouldn't be back again. It turned out she'd been right, and Addie had stayed so loyal to her sister that she hadn't come back either.

Nancy was back and Gayle admitted, 'I haven't called them.'

'You haven't told them? Gayle... Those poor girls.' She was looking at Gayle so intensely that Gayle began to shuffle in her seat. She pushed her hands into the front pockets of the turquoise gingham half-apron all the staff wore over dark-coloured bottoms teemed with a white shirt.

'Those girls wouldn't be coming otherwise. You and I both know that. And I need them to. I don't want them coming for my funeral some day and clearing out my house before I've had a chance to talk to them. I need to make my peace.' And she might not have long to do it, not with the way she'd been feeling lately. She suspected her fate was creeping up on her like a thief on her tail down a dark alley, and she wasn't going to go out before she'd put the past to rest. This gathering would be her chance to feel alive while she still was, to see friends on the island smile and enjoy themselves with her as the host and see the business she was so proud of, but most of all she wanted to see the Rafferty sisters who had always had her heart even though they might not have realised it. She hoped she still had a little piece of theirs too, but she wasn't so sure that was the case.

She was definitely playing with fire where Susanna was concerned. Susanna had her father's tenacity, and while Addie was determined, she was gentler, a lot like her mother had been. She hoped that both girls would be relieved that she was alive. She suspected they'd be furious too, but when she'd realised her mistake she'd seen it as the best way to get them here.

Over the years she'd written to the girls a few times asking them to come and sort through Harry's things. She'd contemplated making it easy for them by sending it all back to the mainland, but she knew that keeping her brother's belongings meant she still had a tie to the girls, a tie that might mean they would come back some day. Perhaps she should've added in those letters that she wanted to see them too rather than hiding behind the pretence that it was all about their father's things. Maybe that would've made them come. But instead, she'd left things alone as much as possible. Addie had replied once to say they would arrange a date. Susanna hadn't responded to any of the requests, and so over the years Gayle had thrown her energies into running the Sweet Life Café, her pride and joy, and what remained between them all was a simple exchange of Christmas cards, or birthday cards, the contents of which grew more sparse as the years rolled on. In between those times it was radio silence.

As she tried to eat a little more of the pie so Nancy wouldn't pick up on anything being wrong, she gazed over to the large window at the front of the café. Customers took up space in the outdoor seating area and as she'd approached earlier she'd noticed that plenty of people were still taking advantage of the mild September weather by sitting on the balcony upstairs, accessed from an internal door at the rear of the café. On a clear day, weather permitting, you could just about make out the Jurassic Coast from the edge of the balcony. She hadn't been back to the mainland for years. What was the point? She was happy here, she had plenty of people around her, and she had the local news. Okay, so it was a bit blinkered, but the world could be a bitch of a place sometimes, and at her stage of life she'd seen enough doom and gloom. She wanted to spend her twilight years with nothing but the island, her friends and pudding for company. At least that's what she'd thought. But she'd been kidding herself. As soon as she'd suspected her health was deteriorating it was Susanna and Addie she'd thought about more than anything. Her heart skipped a beat now thinking of the real world she'd closed herself off from. The real world where the Rafferty girls lived. Would they actually come back? Would they give her a chance to talk things through with them when they saw she was still alive?

Maybe they wouldn't. Maybe they'd be so angry they'd jump straight back onto the ferry and that would be that.

She set her cup on top of her plate along with the serviette, but before she could take it out to the kitchen herself Nancy appeared.

'You all done?' she asked as Gayle got down from the bar stool she'd just about been able to shuffle onto.

'It was a big slice,' said Gayle when Nancy noticed she hadn't eaten all her pudding. 'I'll see myself out.'

Outside, she looked up at the little sign which hung from two short chains and swung slightly on the breeze. She could still remember the day it went up, telling everyone who passed that this was the Sweet Life Café, and it was open for business. The name was written in fancy lettering on the menus too, on the aprons the staff wore, on a blackboard detailing daily specials and placed outside in the sunshine on dry days, or beneath the canopied wide porch if it looked like rain. The tarmacked surface of the street today, like on other days, had a light layer of sand that had either been blown up from the beach or brought up by foot passengers or the minibus that transported visitors to their accommodation and Bay Street.

The Sweet Life Café had kept its character so well over the years. She wondered whether Susanna and Addie would see any joy in it at all. She doubted it. Susanna had been desperate to escape the island, and when Addie began to mellow and show signs of wanting to hang around and perhaps even bake like her aunt, Gayle had almost got excited until she remembered her promise. She'd pushed Addie away after that, not abruptly, but subtly over time, and it had been one of the hardest things she'd ever had to do.

In the hours before Harry had died, he'd asked Gayle to make sure that Susanna and Addie never fell out like they had, that his girls would always be there for each other. And with Susanna having never given up on her plan for them both to leave the island, how could Gayle have done anything other than take a step back so that she didn't come between the sisters?

Back at the cottage she sat in the armchair for a while, fresh air floating in through the open window. Fatigue plagued her these days and necessitated frequent rest.

Her mind ran through the possibilities of what might be wrong with her. Heart problems? Those had killed her sister, Bernice, aged nine, the details of which they'd never known. Or maybe she had what Harry had died from – pancreatic cancer that had taken him quickly.

She couldn't put off going to the doctor forever, but she had to for now.

Bad news could wait.

She sat a while longer until she had the energy to go upstairs and make up the girls' beds in the hope that they might come. She wanted to be prepared if they did, even though there was every chance they might not. She hadn't done anything with the girls' bedrooms since they'd permanently left the island. The truth was she'd been devastated at her own shortcomings, her failure to make them happy enough to stay here, and so she'd left the rooms exactly how they were. She barely came up here unless it was to open the windows and get the air circulating a bit, because when she did it made her too sad.

In Susanna's bedroom she finished sorting the bedding and pushed the last of the pillows into its case and sat down on the edge of the bed. She'd tried so hard to make the girls happy, but had she tried hard enough? The Sweet Life Café was her joy, and she knew the girls thought she was there an awful lot, but it was how she kept a roof over their heads, and it was how she was able to take care of them all. Financial commitments sprang up when least expected: a new school uniform if one of the girls outgrew theirs; a school excursion to pay for; Addie wanted to play piano and lessons weren't cheap; Susanna asked for a hamster as a pet and whilst a hamster wasn't expensive it was at a time when money was incredibly tight. Gayle had forked out for all the accessories because saying no to Susanna would be just another thing to come between them. Gayle had only been thankful that the girls didn't want to get a dog. Maybe they did, but they just knew it would be a big ask. Some days she waited for Susanna to make the request just to see what she'd do because Susanna, unlike Addie, seemed more determined that this arrangement of theirs was not a long-term solution. If Gayle told her the sky was blue on a gloriously sunny day, Susanna would've told her it was purple.

Gayle knew it was harder for Susanna to settle more than it was for Addie because in order for Gayle to work, she needed someone to watch Addie before she was at an age where she no longer needed it. Gayle had tried to find a childminder but hadn't had any luck, and it was also something she could barely afford.

And so she'd had to ask Susanna to help out a lot. It had been just another thing to come between them.

Addie had always been a little more amenable than her sister and it became more noticeable when Susanna left for university. Addie had been so upset that day and for the first time Gayle had been able to give her the comfort a mother might have done, the sort of comfort Susanna had been providing until she was no longer there.

After Susanna left, Gayle and Addie had jumbled along together, they'd laughed and joked in the cottage, they'd watched television, and they'd baked. Gayle had started buying baking accessories for Addie's Christmases and birthdays, and if Susanna thought she was trying to model Addie into another version of her, thankfully she never said so. One year Addie had made the Christmas pudding and Susanna had been so proud of her sister, she'd even had three helpings.

Addie's love of baking became more apparent when she started experimenting – a different type of sponge cake, a new flavour of icing, varieties of dried fruits in place of what Gayle used, ingredients Gayle might not have considered. But every time Susanna came to the island to visit her sister, Addie backed off a little and she wouldn't set foot in the Sweet Life Café for days. Her change of behaviour never failed to remind Gayle of Addie's loyalty to her older sister and the promise that she had made to Harry.

She looked at the walls of Susanna's room – still blue, but not the wonderfully aqua shade they'd once been, rather a faded version with a number of cracks and chipped paint in parts. She went into Addie's room and made up her bed. In here the lip-gloss pink of her walls was less vibrant with every day that passed in her absence. Her gaze fell to the little vase of pink asters she'd put on the bedside table. An identical vase was filled with blue asters in Susanna's room. They were little touches that would likely go unnoticed. If they even came.

Being a parent to those girls – if only for a short time – had been hard, but it had given her joy too. She wondered whether they remembered any of it. Would they remember playing in the garden at the cottage, making a den out of cardboard boxes Gayle brought home from work? Would they remember shopping trips where they'd buy new clothes for the season and have a fast-food lunch as a treat? Would they remember cycling around the island, carefree and smiling and laughing so much that locals began to call them *those Rafferty girls*?

She went downstairs and without enough energy to make a proper dinner she settled for a ham and cheese sandwich, which she didn't even finish.

She remained at the kitchen table until the room grew dark.

And at nine o'clock she gave up.

The girls weren't coming today.

Maybe they weren't even coming at all.

8

ADDIE

Susanna was as quiet as Addie as the boat drew in to the harbour at Anchor Island. Already Addie got the impression that not much would have changed on this island, with little to no traffic, the only transportation allowed being the minibus from the harbour, deliveries or bicycles for residents. She wasn't sure why she thought that, she just did.

'Ready?' Susanna asked as they joined the queue to get off the boat.

'Not really.' It felt so monumental, it felt as if Susanna should be taking her hand so they could leap together.

As her feet stepped onto the solidity of the island, lights twinkled in the darkness from the roadside and from up the hill and beyond. Some of those lights would belong to Bay Street, she was sure of it.

Despite the darkness, Addie could tell the island, the place they'd once called home, had never lost any of its prettiness. She looked around to take in everything that she possibly could. A small boat was coming into the visitor moorings marked out with yellow buoys and enough light from the marina to guide them. A couple of holidaymakers hurried past with their suitcases in a quest to get on the minibus first, while someone else rushed towards them to greet a fellow passenger. As they reached the road where the minibus waited, a trio of young boys cycled past. Their lights warned of their presence and illuminated their legs going ten to the dozen, in a gear too low for the flat ground after the hill had brought them down to the harbour. A couple of gulls pecked at something discarded on the ground beside them as they walked, and smiles on faces suggested this wasn't such a bad place after all.

It was the end of another day on the island. This life could've been theirs if they'd wanted it to be, and the thought made Addie sad that things hadn't turned out differently.

She had a sudden thought as a man called out from the boat that had come into the marina. 'I wonder if Mateo is over there.'

Susanna made a face and didn't turn her gaze in the direction of the boatyard. 'Who knows. He left, remember? I've no idea if he came back. He always used to talk about sailing boats across the world. He could be in France, Italy, America, the Canaries, the Caribbean... anywhere.'

Addie wondered whether Susanna really believed that. His family were here, or at least they had been, and it was quite likely that would've drawn him back.

'I'd rather walk than get the minibus,' said Susanna.

'Me too. It's packed already,' she said, watching another holidaymaker squeeze on board. The doors would soon close and everyone else would have to fend for themselves unless they had a second minibus these days.

'Actually, would you mind if we went and sat down near the fish and chip place? I don't think I'm ready for this either. I just want to grab something to eat after the crossing.'

'Good idea.' They started to walk. 'Hope it's still as good as it used to be.' They could see it was still there, like a beacon for anyone arriving by sea or for locals coming down from the surrounding streets.

The girls both ordered grilled fish with large chips and sat for a good hour or so while they ate, as they adjusted to how it felt to be back here. They chatted, remembering some of the little bays around the island they'd visited during their summers here. They also began to ponder who else would be at the funeral.

'We've been away so long we might not recognise anyone,' said Addie.

'I'm kind of dreading it.'

'Nobody likes funerals.'

Susanna gathered up their rubbish. 'Come on, we can't put it off any longer.'

As they deposited their trays and wrappings in the nearby bin Addie at least felt a bit better for eating. She'd needed the food but also coming for something to eat first had helped her adjust a bit to being on the island. In a way it felt almost normal to be here.

They began the walk back past the harbour to the foot of the hill and turned left to make their way up to Bay Street.

Addie stopped midway up the hill out of puff.

Susanna stopped briefly too before they both picked up their luggage and carried on. 'We'll rest at the top,' she called out as Addie trailed behind her.

Addie had quite forgotten the steepness of the hill. Had they really cycled up and down this as young girls? She didn't have the money or the time for a gym in London, but she walked a lot, and she ran around with Isaac in the park whenever she could. But, here on the island, you'd be in training every time you set off from your front door.

They paused at the far end of Bay Street, catching their breath, knowing the Sweet Life Café was about to come into view. And then, the mouth of Evergreen Close would be in sight too.

'Are you sure going to the cottage is the best idea?' Addie quizzed. 'I know we're almost there but I'm worried. What if a neighbour thinks we're breaking in? The neighbours must know she's gone.' She also wasn't sure how she felt about staying in their dead aunt's house. What if Gayle had died in the kitchen where they would make their breakfast, or on the sofa in the lounge where they might sit and talk about what happened next? The thought made her shudder. And it was dark, which really didn't help.

As they drew closer to the Sweet Life Café, they stopped again.

'Closed,' said Susanna, as if either of them might have expected the lights to be on and a crowd to be gathered on the balcony, laughter and chatter carrying on the wind the way it once had.

'It's late,' said Addie. 'And…' She didn't finish her sentence. Gayle was gone. And perhaps the Sweet Life Café would never open again.

'It doesn't look much different,' said Susanna.

'The sign has been redone.'

'Has it?'

'It used to be faded pink, remember?' Now it was a lovely shade of sea-blue which they could see despite the fading light. Addie wondered whether the leather seats in the booths and on the other chairs and stools were still the same turquoise blue as before.

'Wonder if the leather seats are still there,' said Susanna, almost reading Addie's mind.

'I bet they still stick to your bare legs when you're wearing shorts.'

Susanna let out a gentle laugh. 'I remember.'

'It'll be weird going inside, won't it?' Addie didn't need to add that she meant when they went inside to attend the funeral due to be held in eleven more days. It wasn't like they were going to go in there before then. They'd be busy sorting the attic and any formalities, unless someone else had been named as responsible for that now. They wondered whether Nancy had been named as Gayle's next of kin since they'd been gone.

As they carried on towards the cottage, Addie turned once more to look over her shoulder, back at the Sweet Life Café, back at what might have been.

And then suddenly there they were, in front of Gayle's cottage, and the sight of it swept Addie back in time. Her gaze went straight to the upper dormer windows, one beside the other, her and Susanna's rooms beyond the glass.

'Maybe we should go to the inn for the night,' she suggested quickly. Now they were here she really didn't want to go inside. It gave her the heebie-jeebies. If Gayle had died in her home, what if her ghost was still hanging around? She shuddered, over-thinking it all. She didn't believe in ghosts, not really, and yet...

'No point,' Susanna said decisively. 'We need to be here, we need to sort through things in the attic and Gayle's things too, now she's gone. No point being elsewhere.'

'I might knock on the neighbour's door,' said Addie.

'Don't be chicken, we'll see if we can find the key. No burglar is going to put all the lights on and move in, so if someone sees us doing that, they can come ask whatever questions they like.' Susanna took the lead down the front path and to the side.

Addie reluctantly followed her past the front windows and to the gate which wasn't locked. She couldn't remember it ever having been. The cottage was achingly familiar, with the ivy that she could see creeping up the wall even in the dark, and the stone pavers that lined the way. When they reached the back, however, as well as the little lawn and borders that Addie remembered, the shed had been moved to one side and at the rear there was now a fancy garden room like the sort some people installed as a home office. Now there was an industry that had probably done well since the pandemic, when people's work arrangements had changed. She wondered why Aunt Gayle had needed one, though.

Susanna bent down near the rockery and stood up with a stone in her hand. On closer focus Addie could see it was the tortoise, mostly unaffected by the passing years, with a little coating of moss, and gleefully Susanna undid the bottom of it to reveal a key.

Addie shivered. She thought she'd heard something rustling in the bush. 'Let us in, then, I'm getting cold.'

Susanna tried the key in the back door and smiled when it clicked to open up. 'Hey presto, we're in.'

They took themselves and their luggage inside.

Addie hadn't been prepared for seeing the cottage from the outside, but that was nothing to the nostalgia that flooded her as they passed through the narrow utility room and into the kitchen. They were met with a sweet aroma that had always hovered in the air the whole time they'd lived here. It was unlikely to really be the same and yet somehow it was.

Susanna grimaced. 'I meant to grab some milk and tea and coffee at least so we'd have provisions for the morning.'

'I didn't think of that. And I don't suppose we can do an online order around here.'

'Better check nothing has gone rancid inside.' Susanna

opened the fridge but quickly turned to Addie. 'That's odd... It's really well stocked.'

Addie peered inside for herself and sniffed. 'I'm surprised it doesn't smell. It must have been a while since—'

She was silenced when they heard the back door open and a voice yell out, 'I've called the police! Get out unless you want to be hurt!'

'I told you we should've informed the neighbours!' Addie hissed in a panic, grabbing Susanna's arm as she yelled back, 'We're not burglars, I promise! We are family. Gayle's family.' She wasn't about to confront the person – who was female, given the voice – because if they had a weapon, she didn't want either of them to get injured.

Footsteps drew closer. Clumpy boots, bronzed legs and then the face of a young woman with the craziest blonde curls all the way down her back appeared. 'You must be Addie and Susanna.'

Addie nodded, relieved this person seemed more friend than foe. 'I'm Addie, this is Susanna.' She pointed at herself then her sister. 'You must be a neighbour?'

But the woman didn't answer because they heard movement from another part of the cottage.

What was going on?

'Louisa, is that you?' came a voice.

Addie shook her head. She was hearing things. It sounded so much like Aunt Gayle it was uncanny.

And when the owner of the voice came into the room Susanna spoke first, with a word beginning with 'f' that she'd never been allowed to utter under this roof.

Addie stumbled back into a chair at the shock. She didn't believe in ghosts, but she didn't believe in people coming back from the dead either.

She looked at Aunt Gayle and her eyes filled with tears.

'What is this?' Her voice trembled. 'Is this some kind of sick joke?'

Susanna fixed their aunt with a stare that could have turned a person to stone. 'You'd better have one hell of an explanation.'

9

SUSANNA

Susanna slumped down at the table next to Addie. In situations like this, when it was clear that someone was playing games, she usually walked away, refusing to be a part of it. Like the time a group of girls she hung around with at school decided to invite everyone to a house party but not her. She could tell by the way they were looking at her in the classroom that they wanted her to beg, to find out why she wasn't invited, but she'd packed up her books and left them to it. She'd got an invite in the end, but she hadn't gone. She didn't need the drama. And she definitely didn't need drama now. She wanted to walk away, out of this cottage and back to her life, but this was such a shock it kept her right where she was.

At least she hadn't lost the ability to demand answers. 'Are you going to explain?' She looked her aunt right in the eye but her voice almost wavered as she said, 'You're supposed to be dead and you're not.'

'I'll leave you to it, Gayle,' said the neighbour, who had put down the broom she was holding, which was presumably intended to be her weapon. Clearly the neighbours knew their aunt was alive. Were she and Addie the only ones who didn't?

Gayle sat at the table in a long, bright floral nightdress with an equally vivid pink dressing gown wrapped around her shoulders. She hadn't always worn bright colours but now the wording on the funeral invite made more sense. She must have changed over the years. They all had.

When the back door clicked shut Gayle settled her elbows on the tabletop, her fingers steepled in front of her. Susanna remembered her doing that exact thing when they lived here. She'd do it when she had bills to pay, when Susanna had stayed out late and not told her where she was going, coming back only when she was ready. Susanna had always been waiting for Gayle to explode, yell at her, except she never really did.

'I made a mistake,' said Gayle into the eerie silence that had fallen over the kitchen on Evergreen Close.

'How can you accidentally plan your own funeral?' Even to Susanna's own ears her tone felt mild, when all she should be feeling was rage. She shivered. It was chilly in here without the sunshine that usually streamed through the windows.

'It was supposed to be a living funeral. I—'

'What on earth is a living funeral?' Susanna wanted the facts and fast.

'It's a celebration of life... but obviously nobody has died.'

'Glad we've cleared that up,' Susanna snapped.

'I didn't mean it to happen.'

'Really.' It wasn't a question; the remark dripped with sarcasm. She looked at Addie who was so in shock that she wasn't talking. Susanna looked at their aunt, the person who had tricked them into coming back to the island. She was the same Gayle, except now her hair was more white than grey, and the sun had left deep creases in her face and brown spots on her forearms.

Gayle still sounded the same as she had done the last time they spoke, decades ago, with the same caution in her voice, mixed with regret and wariness that Susanna remembered from when they'd first come here as young girls.

'I used online guides to work out what to write,' Gayle went on, as if an explanation would ever make this any better. 'My concentration span these days isn't the best. I was toying with what to call the gathering. I could've called it a celebration of life, or a pre-death party or a pre-funeral. I'd decided on "living funeral" but I'm afraid I lost focus and ended up forgetting to add in the word "living" entirely. I didn't do a check before I folded the invites and popped them into the envelopes.' She looked at the girls very briefly over the top of her fingertips before she tore her gaze away.

Addie finally found her voice. 'Why not just have a party rather than anything to do with a funeral?'

'It's not my birthday for ages. I don't have anything else to celebrate coming up.'

'Then you should've made something up.' Susanna's voice rose like her fury.

'We can't be the only ones who got invites,' Addie chipped in.

'Well, no, there were plenty of other guests.'

'Your neighbour?' At the puzzled look on Gayle's face, Addie added, 'The woman from before. She obviously didn't think you were dead.'

Susanna sat straighter in her chair. 'Hang on, when did you realise you'd made the mistake?'

Aunt Gayle looked deflated. 'Soon after the invites went out in the mail, I had a knock on the door from Nancy... You remember Nancy?' Her brief uplift of demeanour sank again when she realised neither of her nieces were going to embrace a bit of nostalgia. 'We'd only seen one another a few hours before she got home and found the invite. She came over to see what was going on.'

Susanna crossed her arms in front of her chest. 'And what did you do next?'

'I had to call around and spread the word.' Her composure faded when she realised what she'd admitted.

Addie took her by surprise when she shouted, 'So basically, you told everyone apart from us!'

Susanna stood up. 'This is so wrong. Come on, Addie. We're leaving.'

'No, please...' Gayle stood up too, hands firmly on the table, but when she wobbled she sat straight back down. As the girls retrieved their suitcases from the side of the room she begged, 'Please don't go, not now you're finally here. I know I should've told you. But tell me this...' Her voice followed them to the door as Susanna tried to wrangle her suitcase between the chairs and head out the front, which was closer to the kitchen than the rear door.

'Tell you what?' Addie asked.

Susanna kept her back to them both; she didn't want Gayle to see her weak, to see that her eyes had filled with tears, from the shock, the audacity, the cruelty of the situation.

Aunt Gayle's voice shook as she said, 'Tell me, would either of you have bothered to come for a party?'

Susanna turned round. 'Probably not.' Her words delivered a sting she hoped Gayle felt as keenly as the one delivered to them as the only people not to know the truth, the same cruel sting Susanna had felt when she realised Gayle had told Mateo to end things with her.

Gayle's eyes implored Addie to give a different answer to her sister. But Addie didn't say a word. She slumped down at the table again while Susanna stayed where she was in the doorway.

'You girls left and never came back,' said Gayle. 'There are things I need to put right before it's my time to go, whether that's soon or not for a number of years.'

'Are you sick?' Addie immediately asked.

Susanna harrumphed. 'That's it. You're not well and you want us here to look after you.'

Gayle shook her head. 'That's not it at all. I'm getting old, nothing surprising there. When I realised my mistake I thought I would test the waters, see whether either of you came. I thought you might if it was for a funeral, if only to clear out your father's things.' She managed a small smile. 'And you came together. You've no idea how happy that makes me.'

'Don't you dare say that!' Susanna roared. 'It's not our job to make you happy!'

'Susanna…' Addie had always been softer than she was; Susanna could tell she was going to be lenient despite the circumstances.

'You're right,' said Gayle. 'It isn't your job.'

Addie was looking at her the way she had as a kid, as if she was torn between two opposing sides and didn't know which one to take. Susanna had seen it enough times when she returned to the island to spend time with her sister, the way her sister had pretended to have zero interest in the Sweet Life Café when Susanna could tell she'd settled into a different life without her there.

Susanna felt her chest tighten. She couldn't be here. 'I've got to get out of this house.' She didn't even look at either of them. She heard Addie say, *let her go,* and she left her suitcase behind in the middle of the kitchen doorway.

She took off. She left the cottage, turned right, followed Bay Street all the way along until she came to the footpath she knew so well, even after all this time, even in the dark. She'd never not felt safe here. Guided by the light of the moon she paced all the way along, the route familiar, the views the same. She sat at a bench, the same bench she'd sat at so many times when she felt troubled. The view took her gaze out across the water, sideways to the silhouettes of rooftops, upwards towards the stars.

She needed Alex. No matter what was going on between them she really wanted to talk to him, grasp at some semblance of normality.

Her hand shook as she pulled her phone from her coat pocket.

'Susanna?' He sounded groggy when he answered.

'Were you asleep?'

'Yeah, it's been a long day.'

'I'm sorry. I shouldn't have called. I'll call back tomorrow.'

She heard rustling as if he was shifting back the bed sheets. 'I'm awake. I'll go downstairs and get myself a glass of water.'

She waited until the sound on the other end of the line calmed. 'I miss you.' The words sounded desperate even to her ears.

'Miss you too.'

Was he saying it because he meant it or because he thought he should?

Oh, she was questioning everything. How she wished they were back to the way they'd once been, when she hadn't questioned their relationship at all.

She heard a tap go on for a few seconds, water splashing into a glass, followed by a few glugs as he drank. 'How are things there? Did you let yourselves into the house without having the police descend on you?'

This was better, better than her launching into asking what was going on with him. This big news would be a distraction. 'You're not going to believe this...'

It felt so good to talk to him. While he'd been distant and secretive lately, now he indulged in conversation in a way he hadn't done for a while. It felt intimate, she felt their close connection even from so far away.

'Of all the things you could've told me tonight,' he said, 'that definitely wasn't one of them. What the hell?'

'Yeah, add in a decent expletive and that was pretty much my reaction.'

They talked until Alex yawned yet again and she let him go back to bed. Alex never went before eleven; it was another thing about his behaviour that was off lately, and she hated that it made her so unsettled.

The wind picked up a little as she began to make her way back towards Evergreen Close.

As she approached the cottage, she wondered what Gayle and Addie had found to talk about. Addie had always got on better with Gayle than she had, it was one of the things that had tilted Susanna's world. They'd promised each other in the still of the night so many times when they first came to the island that they would stay together, that they would return to the mainland and the world that was theirs.

They'd lost their mum and their dad and neither of them ever wanted to lose each other.

10

ADDIE

After Susanna had stormed out of the cottage, Addie had got up and left the front door on the latch. She'd then texted her sister to let her know she could come back in that way. Funny – she'd been away for twenty years and some things were still second nature to her. She knew to turn the door knob and secure it, she knew the cold tap in the utility room ran colder than the one in the kitchen, she knew there was a dip in the bathroom floor upstairs near the sink, and that the windows on this side of the house always rattled in a storm.

Addie hadn't known what to say to Gayle, who had apologised repeatedly when it was just the two of them, so she'd taken herself off as well and gone for a walk up to Bay Street. She knew Susanna would've gone towards the track – she'd done that a lot when she was meeting Mateo because it was another way of getting down to the marina – and she wanted to give Susanna a bit of space to think because that was what she needed herself.

Addie had reached the Sweet Life Café and stood opposite it for a while, fifty metres or so from the entrance door, not too close, and just stared. And then, ten minutes ago, she'd come back to the house to find Gayle sitting in the same place in the kitchen. Gayle had made her a cup of camomile tea and they'd sat there in silence, waiting for Susanna.

When Susanna came back to the cottage, Gayle was rinsing out their cups. She turned around from her position at the sink and announced, 'Your rooms are made up.'

Susanna shook her head. 'We'll stay at the inn.'

Without looking at them again Gayle simply said, 'If you like. But your rooms are ready, they're free, and you have fresh sheets and towels. There's shower gel in the bathroom, bath salts too.'

'You were that sure we'd come?' Susanna demanded before Addie could even get out a *thank you.*

'I wasn't sure at all,' Gayle said defeatedly, finally lifting her gaze. 'I'm going to turn in. You girls will want to talk. And I've got—'

'An early start,' Susanna finished for her, turning away to face the window that looked out over Evergreen Close.

Aunt Gayle had always been an early riser. Even if she didn't immediately go over to the café, she would be doing something related to the business, whether it was talking to one of her staff on the phone about supplies or baking puddings here at the cottage to transport over there. Addie suspected operations still worked in much the same way – nothing but raw ingredients brought in, every pudding made from scratch, just the way the customers liked it.

'Goodnight,' said Aunt Gayle.

'Goodnight,' said Addie in return.

Susanna said nothing, and when Gayle had gone, she sat down at the table.

When they heard the groan of the pipes as Aunt Gayle used the bathroom at the end of the corridor, she asked, 'What did she have to say for herself when I was out?'

Addie didn't want to admit it, but even with the silence between them it had felt wonderful to sit in front of this woman who had tried so hard over the years. Addie wasn't sure Gayle ever stood a chance with two sisters who had lost so much, who'd agreed they would one day leave, and one of whom pushed against being here right up until the day she left. Addie had followed in her sister's footsteps when she hadn't had to. She'd done it partly out of loyalty but also because she was scared to do anything else. It had always been the two of them, sisters together, united, who could take whatever was dealt to them.

'We didn't talk,' Addie explained.

'But you must have talked a little.'

'No, we just waited for you.'

'I'm surprised she didn't want to talk about her death.' Susanna harrumphed.

'You're angry—'

'Aren't you?'

'Sshhhhh…' Addie kept her voice low. 'Yes, I'm annoyed. But—'

'But what?'

Aunt Gayle's bedroom was downstairs, and she didn't want their voices heard through the walls. 'Why don't we go upstairs out of the way and talk there?'

'So we're staying?'

'It's late, the rooms are right there, and they're free.'

'I guess we might as well then.' Susanna led the way, hauling her suitcase and bags up the stairs, Addie behind her.

'I'll put my things in my room and come into yours,' said Addie. It was the way it had generally worked when they were younger. Addie's bedroom was above Gayle's, and they'd been well aware of making too much noise so they usually met in Susanna's. Addie had slept in there for a while when they'd first moved in, and Susanna had let her. Her big sister had comforted her every time she'd had a bad dream, like the recurring dream about their parents being out of reach on a bridge, with her below calling up to them. Even now, thinking about that dream made her feel nauseous and scared of it happening again. But it hadn't happened for years. Instead, every once in a while she had pleasant dreams about their parents, mostly about their dad, and sometimes woke smiling like she'd seen him for real while she was asleep.

On the way up the stairs, Addie wondered whether her room would have all sorts of paraphernalia dotted about, things Gayle didn't know what to do with. Everyone had one of those rooms or cupboards, didn't they? She had one at the flat, a big cupboard with shoes littering the bottom and five or six deep shelves. She called it her no-bloody-idea cupboard, which Isaac had picked up on, and she had to admit that although it wasn't good to teach him naughty words, it always sounded so hilarious when he said it with an air of seriousness as if that was its real name.

She pushed open the door to her old bedroom. It was as though time had stood still in here. The furniture was all in the same spot, even the wicker chair in front of the small dressing table still had its blue and white checked gingham seat with the small area of out-of-place stitching from a part of it that Gayle had had to sew up for her more than once.

It was oddly comforting to know that in all this time Aunt Gayle hadn't wiped away the last traces of the Rafferty girls.

She hung up her coat and got out her pyjamas and washbag, both of which she put on top of the chest of drawers, and then she went into Susanna's room. Her sister was taking her make-up off in front of the same mirror that had always been on the back of the door. It was full-length and Addie had often come in to check her reflection as she only had the mirror on top of her dressing table and so could only see herself in it if she stood on the bed.

Susanna looked into the mirror to meet Addie's gaze as she wiped an eyelid gently with a piece of cotton wool. 'Sorry I'm so grouchy.' She smelled of the same Diptyque perfume she'd used for years, a scent fragranced with water lilies and another floral bouquet. Addie usually stole some when she was visiting, it was so luxurious compared to her cheaper supermarket-bought versions.

'It's understandable. I'm a bit all over the place myself.'

'You handle it better than I do.'

'Finally, something I can do better than my big sister.' Addie grinned.

Susanna turned to face her. 'You can do a lot that I can't do – be a mother, for a start. You're wonderful at that. My nephew is living proof.'

Addie took a deep breath. 'How desperate must Aunt Gayle have been to not call us and let us know of the mistake?'

Susanna turned back to the mirror to do the other eye. 'She should have done though, that wasn't fair.'

'She seems lonely.'

'Lonely?' Susanna wasn't convinced. 'She was never lonely. She had her business, her staff and friends… She was always so busy.'

'It's not the same, though, is it? We both know that.' Just like living with Aunt Gayle wasn't the same as being with their mum and dad. 'She's our family, Susanna. And we don't have much of that left.'

Susanna put the top back on the make-up remover and came to sit down next to her sister on the bed. 'I'm not sure where we go from here.'

'I say we sleep on it and tomorrow is another day.'

'Part of me wants to walk out of here and never come back,' Susanna told her.

'Usually, you know exactly what to do.'

'Are you implying that I'm bossy?'

'Yes, and I'm happy for you to be – takes the pressure off me.'

Susanna adjusted the headband that was holding her dark hair away from her face. 'Mind if I do my teeth now?'

'Go for it.' The main bathroom was downstairs but up here there was another one with a toilet and a sink. 'Mind if I steal some cleanser?'

'I brought extra, I knew you'd want to use it.'

Addie hugged her sister tightly. 'Things will be all right, you know.'

'Yeah.'

But Susanna didn't seem all that convinced as Addie left her to it.

11

GAYLE

Gayle was up early, the habit of a lifetime. She'd already called Nancy to ask if she could cover for her for a while, and Nancy hadn't asked questions. Maybe she already knew it was because of the Rafferty girls.

She made a cup of tea and sat at the table. She hadn't expected the girls to stay the night, even though she'd told them their rooms were ready. She'd spent the first couple of hours after she left them in the kitchen lying in bed looking at the clock, waiting for the slam of the front door. Eventually, she'd fallen asleep and when she surfaced – much later than she'd intended – she could hear someone in the bedroom upstairs and the toilet flush on the upper floor.

She couldn't believe they were both under her roof once again and she wondered whether today the tension would be as palpable as it was when they arrived last night, or even when they first stepped over the threshold thirty years ago.

As Gayle stirred her tea, she thought about her life then and her life now. There were things she would change if she got her time all over again, but she wouldn't change everything.

Gayle had worked at her parents' café in Oxford on weekends and during the school holidays when she was a teenager. Harry already worked there full time and sometimes they would talk about taking on the Cuppas and Treats Café together when their parents retired. Harry raved about having a family business, proud as punch that their parents had started the café and made it into such a success. Having no idea of what she wanted to do once she finished school, Gayle had gone along with the idea, which sounded like it could work.

Gayle started to take charge of introducing puddings to the menu at the café – she'd suggested it to her parents, given they mainly made soups, sandwiches and other quick snacks, and they'd been happy for her to experiment for a while. The experiment turned into so much more when customers returned over and over again to see what the pudding of the day was. Gayle was in her element. She'd only ever baked at home for herself and her family, never for strangers, and slowly an idea began to form. What if she stepped out on her own? What if she could do what she loved for a living?

It was the first time she'd ever felt a flush of ambition and suddenly, she could see nothing else in her future other than starting her own pudding business. When she was alone in her bedroom, she'd sketch out rough pictures of what a pudding business could look like: she'd make up menu choices, think about customers' faces when they got to eat what she baked. She had no idea of the details, how or even *if* it would work, but that was the thing with ambition – it rarely stopped in its tracks once it gained momentum.

For a while she didn't admit her thoughts to her brother. Whenever he brought up the notion of them taking on the café, she simply stayed quiet or at least didn't contradict him and carried on with what she was doing. Eventually, however, she hadn't wanted to lead him on and so she'd admitted to both Harry and her parents the vision she had for her future. All of them had urged her to think very carefully before taking a leap.

After her admission, she didn't take much of a leap at all, not in any aspect of her life, until Jeffrey Sutton started to work at the café one summer. Jeffrey was working to fund his university studies and Gayle won him over with her chocolate self-saucing pudding. His love for the pudding had led to a love for her, and when she'd shared her dreams of running a place solely dedicated to puddings they'd put their heads together and he'd helped her make a plan. Harry took it better than expected when he realised her dream might actually come into fruition. He simply said that he would run the café by himself. No big deal. Everything seemed sorted.

Jeffrey, who was studying to be a teacher, found his first job on the island of Jersey and Gayle didn't hesitate to leave Oxford and go with him. Her dream of starting her business was some way off, so in the meantime she found work as a typist, which was good pay and long hours, but it helped her with her living costs and allowed her to save.

Life on Jersey chugged along steadily for a while until Gayle saw an advertisement in the local newspaper for a premises on Anchor Island. The potential site for a pudding café was perfect. It was spacious enough without being too huge, it was in a great location and a suitable commute from Jersey for the time being, it had an attractive frontage and even had a balcony. Within seconds of seeing the advertisement, Gayle imagined herself inside, in a kitchen with every piece of equipment she needed, with a counter she would stand behind and pass the time of day with locals as they chose what pudding they wanted. That day she'd run all the way from work to Jeffrey's flat and showed him the advertisement. It felt like serendipity, and the sale price wasn't sky high either, not like it would have been back in Oxford.

She bought the premises and slowly, with Jeffrey's help and the loan she'd secured with some of his backing, she'd made her dream a reality.

The pudding business, which she'd chosen to call The Sweet Life Café on account of what she intended to sell and the feeling she got at this new-found existence, wasn't an overnight success by any means. It took ages to turn a profit. It was a slog. Gayle rented a small flat prior to the launch of the business and as it was on the other side of the island, like many of the locals, she bought herself a bike to get to and from her place of work. To be fair, she loved the bike from the moment she got on it for the first time. Cycling everywhere made her feel so free and filled her with more energy than she'd expected.

Gayle worked hard. Her days often melded into the night. She rarely took any time off, but with Jeffrey by her side, albeit some distance away, life was going in the right direction. And when Jeffrey proposed, Gayle didn't hesitate to say yes. It felt like she had everything she ever wanted. She called Harry and he'd been delighted at the news. He was happy, so was she. Brother and sister had gone in different directions and that was okay.

Gayle and Jeffrey looked at a few houses on the island but the second they saw the cottage on Evergreen Close they fell in love, particularly Gayle. It was the smallest cottage and stood out because it was neglected, but the first time she walked through the front door she hadn't seen the dilapidated insides, nor the damaged tiles in the kitchen, and she hadn't seen the overgrown unkempt garden either. She'd imagined her and Jeffrey moving in and their children growing up within its walls. Their children – maybe a boy and a girl if they were lucky enough – could play in the garden, make daisy chains from the patch of daisies on the front lawn, chase each other with water pistols in the summer, just like she and Harry had done, or build snowmen in the winter. She would bake in the kitchen, meals as well as puddings, she would call her children downstairs from their bedrooms at the top with the dormer windows. She and Jeffrey could live out their future here on Anchor Island, him as the headteacher of the local primary school so he no longer had to commute to Jersey – because he'd get a position there eventually, she had no doubt of that – and her with her successful pudding business.

Not all of their dreams came true, though. The Sweet Life Café began to get regular customers and started to make a decent profit, they bought the cottage and it had taken no time at all to get it looking like a home, and then Gayle found out she was pregnant. They were over the moon. They married quickly, but their dream was shattered when she miscarried at ten weeks. What had followed was heartbreak after heartbreak with the pain of never being able to carry a baby to term, and it had ripped them apart in the end. The cottage on Evergreen Close wasn't occupied by a young couple head over heels in love for very long at all. Gayle and Jeffrey divorced. He returned to Jersey, the cottage became Gayle's, those two bedrooms at the top stayed empty, and she never found love again. She put all her energies into the Sweet Life Café; it made it easier to forget everything else.

By the time Gayle and Jeffrey divorced, Gayle and Harry's parents had fully retired from the café and Harry took over the full running of the place. He was in his element, happily married with two daughters. But then over the coming months every time she spoke to her brother Gayle could detect an underlying stress in his voice. Eventually he told her that the café was struggling but he made out the problems were minor and temporary.

It was only after their parents died a year later that Harry admitted quite how bad things were. He was in real trouble, struggling to make ends meet. The café had real competition, he wasn't getting people through the door as easily as before, and he was trying to do the job of three people, so he didn't have to employ anyone else.

To make matters worse, at the same time as Harry was having problems, the Sweet Life Café started to gain momentum and become a real success, earning Gayle write-ups in the national press, radio coverage, and an award for Women in Business. It had taken a long time for her café to get on its feet and even longer for it to thrive, and she'd worked so hard to get it to that point, but her brother resented it. She tried to keep in touch, to talk to him, but every time she did, she would hear the regret in his voice that they weren't doing this together, the worry in his tone that he wouldn't be able to turn things around, the blame that she had left him on his own with it. It wasn't long before his finances took another blow due to a rent hike on the café and rising costs of supplies, and while his business slowly sank, Gayle's forged ahead even more. It was the start of the irreversible tension between them both and they never recovered from it. They stayed in touch for a while, but over the years that contact faded away. Gayle knew he'd had to take a job in the travel industry to make ends meet when the Cuppas and Treats Café was sold, and shortly after that he stopped taking phone calls from her altogether. The only contact she got was when Harry's wife, Cynthia, died. She went to the funeral, she watched her brother, a broken man, a widower. She reached out but he didn't want her help, and she retreated. She hated that it had come to that.

Over time she often thought about going to Oxford, showing up on Harry's doorstep, and she might have done if she didn't think he'd close the door in her face. And so she'd stayed on the island. She occasionally sent Harry letters, but she never got a reply. She always remembered his birthday and the girls' but again, she never had anything in return.

In fact, she never heard from him again. Not directly.

Thirty years ago, her world was knocked sideways when she got a call from the hospital in Oxford to say that Harry had been admitted, and that she should come immediately. The doctor didn't want to give details over the phone and so Gayle asked Nancy to step in for her and run things at the Sweet Life Café, packed her suitcase, and off she went to the mainland.

The first time she'd seen Harry lying in that hospital bed, sick and vulnerable, had been incredibly confronting given how long it had been since they'd seen one another or even spoken. Prior to that moment she'd only even seen him full of life, whether happy and excited or moaning about her not wanting to run the family's café with him, or that his life hadn't turned out the way he'd planned. He'd woken up and smiled at her, and to be honest she hadn't been sure that was the reception she would get, but when she saw not just the man but the boy she'd grown up alongside, free of the worries that came to you as an adult, she'd smiled right back and known that this was the moment they made their peace.

She'd covered his hand with hers. 'How are you doing?'

He'd grunted a bit, then tried to speak, but she couldn't make out the words.

She stood so that she was much closer. 'Can you say that again?' she asked him, hoping that lip-reading might work.

'Louisa...'

'Is she one of the nurses?'

'Not here,' said Harry.

Gayle smiled. She wanted to help. 'Why don't I ask around, find out when she's in?'

'Find Louisa,' he said.

'All right. Let me try.'

She went over to the nurses' station but none of them had heard of a Louisa. Apparently, there was a cleaner called Louise, a midwife called Loulou but no Louisa on this ward.

She went back to Harry's side but he was asleep. Maybe he was mistaken about the name.

As the days rolled on and her visits continued, Harry spent much less time awake. The beeping of the machines and the garish lights in the hospital made Gayle think how impossible it must be for the patients to get any sleep at all. Harry slipped in and out of consciousness. He wasn't saying much, though occasionally he squeezed her hand back and she reassured him that she was there at his side.

'Keep talking to him,' a nurse at her shoulder encouraged during one of her visits. 'When his daughters come in, they chatter away. They'll be here again soon.'

His daughters. The girls she would have trouble recognising given how little she'd seen of them since they'd been born. It saddened her that Harry hadn't shared that part of his life with her.

'I don't really know what to say,' she told the nurse.

'Some people talk about the weather; others start spilling their deepest, darkest secrets.' The nurse's forehead rose up and down suggestively before she added, 'You'll think of something.'

She started talking about Anchor Island. He'd been hellbent on resisting her business success and too preoccupied with jealousy to ever come and visit and see what it might be like.

'It's so windy on some days,' she shared with him as she wittered on. 'It's still beautiful, don't get me wrong, but when that wind whips up it's not so pleasant. I don't like going out on the balcony, I think I'm going to get blown away. Do you remember the terrible storms when we were little and on holiday in Brighton, how we begged Mum and Dad to take us closer to the beach so we could see the sea?'

Before she could go on, she watched his mouth open slightly and out came a murmur. 'Waves,' he said.

'Yes!' A tear pooled in the corner of her eye. He had heard her after all. 'Enormous waves! Oh, they were so big, weren't they, Harry?' She felt like she was that little girl again, him that little boy, that none of their conflict had ever happened, like this was all that mattered now. 'As tall as skyscrapers, we reckoned. Or maybe that was the way it felt when we were three-foot nothing, or four-foot in your case. Mum didn't like it; she only relaxed when we were back at the campsite wrapped in blankets and sipping on hot cocoa.'

She rambled on about the seasons, talked about the crowds in the city come summer, how they'd have extra ice-cream from the café and be allowed to stay out long past their usual bedtime with their parents working later than normal.

Her memories stalled when she saw her nieces coming into the ward along with their maternal grandparents.

Gayle went over to them. They'd grown, but they looked so much like Harry and Cynthia, Adeleine with Harry's curly hair he'd never liked, Susanna with Cynthia's smile.

'You're both getting so big,' she said, addressing Adeleine, a dainty eight-year-old who barely looked up from beneath her fringe, and Susanna, the fourteen-year-old whose gaze darted from her dad to the machines, her dad again and then finally to Gayle.

Susanna reached for her sister's hand. She led her past Gayle and closer to their dad.

Gayle picked up her bag from the chair. 'I'll let you have some time with Harry,' she told the girls and Harry's in-laws. Gayle hoped her beautiful nieces brought them some comfort, although she suspected nothing could really take away the pain that their daughter died before they did. It wasn't the natural order of things, was it?

The next day when Gayle returned to the hospital, Harry was still drifting in and out of consciousness.

'Promise me...' he said all of a sudden when Gayle was almost dozing off herself. He hadn't said a word in the last hour, and she'd found her eyes closing as she sat at his bedside.

She stood, got closer to work out what he was saying. 'Harry, I'm here.'

'Promise me...' he said again.

'What, Harry? What do you need me to do?'

'Girls...' he said. And then he opened his eyes wider than he had in days. 'Susanna... Adeleine... They can't fall out.'

'Oh, Harry, they won't. Of course they won't.'

'Like us...' he said. 'My fault...' he added, his voice croaky with dryness.

She shushed him, told him not to worry. Her bottom lip trembled, and she tried not to burst into tears. 'Your girls will be together forever. I'll see to that.'

'Promise...' His eyes were closed but he was determined with his request.

'I promise. I will do whatever I can to make sure Susanna and Adeleine are the closest they can be.' She felt a sense of relief when he squeezed her hand back in response.

He stayed quiet for another hour as Gayle sat processing what he'd said. She wasn't sure she had the power to steer two girls' emotions, but she would do her very best. Things should never have gone this far with Harry. She wished they hadn't, but all she could do was be here for him now and let him go peacefully, knowing his girls would be okay.

A few days later, Harry passed away. Gayle lost a brother, Susanna and Adeleine lost their only surviving parent, and what she'd never realised was that rather than his daughters going to live with their maternal grandparents, Harry's wish was for Susanna and Adeleine to live with her. In all those years she'd thought he resented her, and yet his wish had always been for his girls to go to his sister if he died before they reached adulthood.

Gayle finished her tea when she heard footfall coming down the stairs in her cottage.

If she could change the past, she would have tried harder with Harry, even though he was stubborn. She'd have turned up on his doorstep, forced him to listen to her and see that just because she didn't want to run a café with him and just because her business was a success, it didn't diminish what he'd done with the café. Circumstances had played a part, she knew that, but she wondered had he ever realised it for himself rather than shouldering all that dreadful blame?

She wouldn't change her pudding business if she had her time again – she loved everything about it – and she wouldn't change meeting Jeffrey, either. Their time together was special, and he'd been her one true love. She wouldn't have wanted to miss that, even though sadness ended up breaking them apart.

When Susanna came into the kitchen she rose from the table and took out another mug from the cupboard. 'Tea?'

'Yes, please.'

It was only a two-word response, but it was a start.

Today, wearing what looked like exercise clothes, Susanna looked a little more relaxed, but Gayle knew her mood could change in an instant. The smile, however, was golden because it reminded Gayle of the girl she'd seen emerge every now and then over the years, in the moments when she went with the flow, or when she forgot to put up a front. All those years fighting being here must have taken a toll on her oldest niece, but a moment ago when she smiled she'd looked so pretty, it soothed her seriousness as well as her features, showed off lovely straight teeth from those braces she'd hated so much in her teens, and it lit up her eyes too.

That was another thing she wouldn't change – being a guardian to Harry's girls. As hard as it had been all round, she was glad he'd entrusted her. What she would change, however, was the way they'd left the island and how she'd played a part in it, even though she'd felt she had no choice.

12

SUSANNA

Susanna had thought Gayle would've gone to work by now and, not ready for a confrontation, was caught by surprise when she went into the kitchen to find her aunt sitting at the table.

'Did you sleep okay?' Gayle asked, flicking on the kettle and finding a tea bag to drop into the awaiting mug.

'Fine.'

'I thought you'd sleep in,' she said, as she passed Susanna the mug of tea.

'I wanted to get outside for some fresh air.' Rather than shower straight away she'd slipped on yoga leggings, a T-shirt and a zip-up hoodie. She wanted to get out of the confines of the cottage before she had to deal with any of it. Unfortunately, the fact that her aunt was still here had ruined that idea.

'I'll get the milk for you,' said Gayle.

'No need.' Susanna opened the fridge before her aunt could do it for her. 'I thought you'd be at the café by now.'

'Nancy is the early bird these days; the arrangement suits us. Mind you, I'm still up before most. It's just a habit I suppose.'

Susanna reluctantly sat down at the table.

'How are you this morning?' Her aunt watched her cautiously.

'Apart from the shock of finding you alive?'

Gayle didn't flinch; she'd likely expected the terse reply.

'You wouldn't have come if I'd have invited you to a party.' Gayle waited but Susanna wasn't going to deny it. She was right. 'It's nice that you and Addie came here together.'

'You already said that last night.' She was being pedantic, but she couldn't help it. 'And why wouldn't we come together?'

'I wasn't sure how much you saw of each other.'

'We both have our own lives, but we're still close.'

'Sometimes siblings drift apart, that's all.'

'Like you and Dad?'

Aunt Gayle declined to answer and instead asked, 'Is your sister up and about yet?'

'She used the toilet then went back to bed.'

'She always slept well here. I think the sea air helps.'

'Maybe.'

'Do you ever see the sea?' Gayle asked.

'I live in Cambridge,' Susanna sniped, then immediately felt petty in her rudeness. It was the same way she'd been the day she arrived on the island, waiting for Aunt Gayle to put a foot wrong, waiting for her to say something she could latch on to and criticise.

The sound of the post dropping onto the mat took her aunt from the kitchen to the hallway and gave Susanna a brief reprieve, although it didn't stop her memories from flooding back.

She could still remember her first day here. She'd sat in her bedroom – well, a room anyway – at the top of a ramshackle cottage far away from the mainland, her school, her friends. She and Addie had lost everything – their mum, their dad, their home. It was just the two of them now. No matter that Aunt Gayle was their guardian, she would never take the place of either of their parents. She was fourteen years old, she was here, but she had a plan. When she was eighteen, she could do what she liked and she was going to get far, far away from here, from a woman who was a stranger, a woman her dad hadn't seen eye to eye with, from the place she'd never wanted to come to.

That day she'd opened the little velvet pouch she'd kept in her rucksack and took out her mother's brooch. Her dad had given it to her, and another brooch to Addie, when their mum died. Susanna could still remember the first time she wore it, long before it belonged to her. Her mum had given it to her to wear when her nerves were frayed one night when she was about to perform with the school orchestra. She played the violin, usually well, but not with an audience and that night she'd been convinced that she would mess up. Her mother had simply unpinned her brooch from her blouse, pinned it on Susanna's school shirt, and told her she could never mess up in her mother's eyes. The day she arrived on the island she'd held on to the brooch like a talisman as she curled onto her side and let her tears soak into her pillow.

Susanna had stayed in her bedroom a lot when she first came to the island. Inside its blue walls at least the room was a place of her own, a place she could be herself. She'd started school, she'd begun to make friends and she started to try to find some sort of happy, even though it wasn't the same here as it had been in Oxford.

One morning, a few weeks after their arrival on Anchor Island, Aunt Gayle summoned the sisters downstairs and into the kitchen. On some days Susanna found herself tempted to reach out to her aunt for a comforting hug, to know that she was safe;

on other days she thought of Aunt Gayle as the devil and wanted to keep her distance.

'I have something for you both,' Gayle announced.

The girls followed her to the back door and out into the sunshine. Addie's hand slipped into Susanna's; she'd been clingy since they lost their dad. She'd only just started sleeping in her own bedroom, having been sneaking into Susanna's in the middle of the night ever since they'd arrived at the cottage. They'd curl up together in the little bed and fall asleep that way and whisper that they'd always be there for each other.

With Addie's hand still in hers they followed Gayle to the shed at the side of the cottage. In front of it were two bikes, one red, one blue.

'Everyone cycles or walks on the island,' Aunt Gayle told them. 'I think bicycles are a lot of fun.'

'Do you have a bike?' Addie asked their aunt.

'I do, and I ride it when I can. I love the way the wind rushes past me if I go fast enough.'

Addie giggled. 'I like going fast. But I have to wear a helmet.'

'Right... Do you each have a helmet?'

'I outgrew mine. So did Addie,' Susanna informed her.

'Then I'll order some from the mainland,' said Gayle.

'They might not fit,' Susanna told her.

'Then why don't I take you both to Guernsey tomorrow and we can shop for them there?' their aunt suggested.

Susanna kept Addie's hand in hers. 'We have school.'

'Right.' But then her face brightened. 'I'll bring Addie after school to meet you in Guernsey and we'll get the ferry back together. How does that sound?'

Susanna felt Addie let go of her hand, and she watched as her sister went over to admire the smaller of the two bikes, the red one. She pushed one leg over the crossbar so she was straddling her bike.

Aunt Gayle opened the door to the shed. 'I have a spanner I can use to adjust the saddle and handlebars.' She briefly disappeared inside.

Susanna put her hand out for the spanner when Aunt Gayle joined them outside again. 'I'll do it. Dad showed me how.'

That day, Susanna had barely raised a smile, and she hadn't looked happy when they went shopping for helmets either. And when Addie climbed onto her bike for the first ride and said thank you for about the twentieth time, Susanna's mouth went dry and she couldn't speak.

'Stick to the trails,' Gayle told the girls that day. 'Avoid the roads, even though there isn't traffic. The trails are better to start with.'

'Okay,' said Addie.

'I'll look after her,' Susanna muttered, hitching her bottom onto her saddle, her bike slightly tilted, with one foot on the ground.

'Is your saddle the right height?' Gayle asked.

'It's fine.' Susanna edged closer to her sister. 'You can go in front of me, Addie.'

'I'm the leader?'

'Yes. I need to see you to make sure you're safe,' she said. 'But don't go too fast.'

'I won't speed.' Addie grinned and turned to Aunt Gayle. 'Why don't you come with us?'

Aunt Gayle hesitated but then reminded them she had work. 'Another time, I promise. Now I need you two to promise *me* something... I need you to come to the Sweet Life Café in one hour, so I know that you're both okay.'

'Yes, Aunt Gayle,' Addie chimed.

'We will,' said Susanna, looking at the ground beneath her feet. 'Thank you for my bike.'

She looked up to see an expression on her aunt's face that she had never forgotten.

In the weeks and months to come, when she found herself wondering what it might have been like for Gayle to come out with them on bikes that day or any day after, she squashed the thought or perhaps the hope right down. Good job, because Aunt Gayle never did come on a bike ride with them, and Addie eventually gave up asking. Aunt Gayle had the Sweet Life Café and her life, and the girls had each other. It was the Rafferty girls against the world. Just the two of them. And if they stuck together, they would be just fine.

Gayle came back into the kitchen, snapping Susanna out of her reverie. 'Just a bit of junk mail and a couple of bills,' she said, placing the pile of post on the bench near the sink.

Susanna attempted a smile. Her aunt had been trying to get a conversation going about the seaside before she was rescued by the sound of the post landing on the mat, and now Susanna was reminded of the look on her aunt's face the day she'd thanked her for the shiny new bike. It wasn't the look as such, but the fact that in that moment fourteen-year-old Susanna had realised that it was an incredibly tough time for Gayle as well as them. She'd tried to remember that over the years, she thought she'd managed to be a lot more pleasant, and there were moments when she felt happier. But then Aunt Gayle had interfered in her relationship with Mateo, and any bond that had begun to form between aunt and niece had been broken once more.

'You asked if I saw the sea,' said Susanna, just about managing to lift her gaze. She and Addie had to sort through their dad's things, and they had to decide if they were staying for the living funeral despite the deception, but she could be polite to make things easier all round.

'Yes.' The hope on Aunt Gayle's face was almost too much to bear and conjured up all sorts of emotions for Susanna.

Matter-of-factly she told her aunt, 'I like to visit the coast in Norfolk. Me and Alex love it there. It's where we met.' She checked herself as if she'd said too much and took a sip of tea. That was the way it had been as a teenager here – sometimes she'd let herself relax, smile, feel at home, and other times she'd remember that this wasn't what she wanted, it wasn't her life, and the emotional barriers came up.

'How did you and Alex get together?' Gayle asked.

'I got into trouble in the water and he saved me. He was a summer lifeguard.'

'Well I never. That's some meet-cute.' But her upbeat tone fizzled out when she saw that Susanna wasn't smiling back. 'Where do we go from here, Susanna?'

Susanna toyed with the sleeve of her hoodie. 'I honestly don't know.'

'I really am very sorry that I inadvertently tricked you and Addie.'

'What's done is done.' She knocked back the rest of her tea. 'I have to go.' She set the cup in the sink and went upstairs to retrieve her trainers.

'Will you stay?' Gayle's voice was small but loud enough to follow Susanna. 'For my living funeral, I mean.'

Outside the kitchen, she replied, 'I don't know.' But then she turned round and went back to where Aunt Gayle was sitting. 'I meant to ask about the young woman who was here when we arrived.' It had been puzzling her in the night.

'Louisa? Oh, she's my tourist.'

'Your tourist?'

'She's renting the garden room out back. I put it on that Airbnb site people use nowadays.'

'Right.' She turned to leave again but Aunt Gayle's voice stopped her.

'I needed to generate some more income,' she said. 'The business suffered during the pandemic.' She continued to ramble as if she wanted to delay Susanna's departure for as long as possible. 'I got the idea from someone else who'd done the same. Accommodation is in high demand here on the island. I decided I'd get an outside room installed with a small bathroom and kitchenette to make it liveable, and I'd give it a go. I decided if I didn't like it then I'd have a lovely place to do my paperwork or sit when it rains.'

Gayle looked down at the mug in her hands. 'Susanna… I'd really like it if you stayed for the living funeral. I know I'm in no position to make demands, but it would mean a lot. If not, then I respect your decision. Yours and Addie's.'

'I'm just not sure,' said Susanna before she walked away. The thought of staying here for another ten days and having to face a party, which after all was what the event really was, was almost impossible to imagine. It felt like such a farce given the state of their relationship.

But then she remembered how she'd felt when she opened the invite back at her house in Cambridge. She hadn't been filled with satisfaction that her aunt had gone, and she hadn't blithely thrown the invite away; she'd been upset that they had never worked things out between them.

Aunt Gayle had destroyed her confidence when it came to men, and it had taken a long time to recover from that. Could she really forgive Gayle when she'd been head over heels with Mateo, planning a future with him?

13

ADDIE

Being back on Anchor Island was weird enough, but waking up in the cottage this morning had been a whole new level of odd. She'd slept better than she'd thought she would, wiped out from the emotions of the last forty-eight hours since finding out Aunt Gayle was dead, organising for Isaac to stay with his grandparents for a while longer, packing and making the journey here, feeling all over the place without her son for an extended period of time, and then finding out her aunt was actually alive.

She could hear murmurings downstairs but not enough to make out what was being said. Still, at least it meant her sister was talking to their aunt.

When her phone pinged, she picked it up. It was Isaac sending a message via Maurie.

> Miss you, Mummy... Is it good on the island? Was the boat fast or slow?

> I've built a boat out of Lego, but Grandad says it might fall apart if I put it in water. Will it?

> Love from Isaac x

She picked up her phone and dialled Maurie's number for a video call, and sure enough Maurie picked up within four rings.

'You're in your pyjamas,' said Maurie with a smile.

'Guilty.'

'Isaac is busy right now,' Maurie said more quietly. 'Can we call you later on? He's been baking and once that's done – if it ever gets done – we're off to the swimming pool before my dentist's appointment.'

'It sounds like you're busy.' And they were baking? All of a sudden, she wished she was right there, helping her son to tie on his apron, making him wash his hands and watching how excited he got at the prospect of turning raw ingredients into something special.

'Wait a minute,' said Addie, 'I didn't pack his swim things.'

'We'll buy him a pair of trunks and some goggles at the pool. They aren't expensive and he'll have a spare set then. Mind you, he'll probably outgrow them soon enough.'

'Thank you, Maurie. You're really so good to him. You could've said no about the swimming.' She didn't have to ask to know how it had likely gone down. Maurie and Jarrett probably asked what he wanted to do that day, and baking and swimming were likely top of the list.

'We just love having him, Addie. Any time. You know that.'

'I do.'

'Are you all right?'

Addie thought she'd hidden her longing for her son behind her smile well enough, but clearly not. 'I just miss him, that's all.'

'Of course you do.' Maurie knew her so well.

'I think I'll be all right. Seeing him and talking to him helps.' Video calls would hopefully keep her going until it came time to return home, although that might come sooner if they decided not to hang around for the living funeral.

'Addie, I'll have to get Isaac to speed up or by the time we leave the traffic will be abominable.'

Maurie had used the word 'abominable' in front of Isaac a few weeks ago and Isaac had latched on to it. He'd wanted to know all about the abominable snowman and Addie had had to resort to Google as she had no idea what to tell him.

Isaac's voice rang out in the background, asking whether it was Mummy on the phone. There was some rustling and shuffling around until Maurie finally angled the phone in front of Isaac who was wearing an apron and had flour on his cheeks.

'What are you making?' she asked her excited little boy.

'Pie!' Isaac declared.

'What sort?'

'Apple.'

'And blackberry,' Maurie added in the background.

'Well, it sounds delicious.'

'I'm allowed to eat some, but only after swimming.'

'That's fair enough.'

'After that I'm going to kick my ball in the garden, Granny got me a net.' In true Isaac fashion he flitted from one topic of conversation to the next with barely a pause.

'A net?'

'A goal,' he said, eyes widening, hands demonstrating and no doubt flicking mess everywhere.

'Well, that was very kind of them.' Yet another thing she couldn't give him – space to play outside, room to kick a ball and run about and be a kid. When his grandparents came to collect their grandson from the flat, they never hung around long and always held get-togethers at their place rather than hers, which was absolutely fine except it only reminded Addie that she and Isaac didn't have the sort of home she wanted long term.

But beggars couldn't be choosers, right?

She remembered his question about the Lego boat. 'I think the Lego boat should be fine in the water,' she told him. 'And if it falls apart, you'll just have to rebuild it again.'

He grinned. But then he was onto something else. 'Are you going to the beach, Mummy?' A little frown formed on his brow.

'I'm still in my pyjamas but I might venture down there later, yes.'

He looked pained. 'Will you explore the rock pools?'

She could honestly say, 'No, I'll save that for when you're with me.'

'I wish I was coming.'

'You'll have too much fun there with Granny and Grandad to even think about me.'

Maurie leaned into the picture with a face that suggested it was time to wrap up the call. Addie waved at the screen and blew a kiss.

She lay on her bed, looked across at the tiny vase with the pink asters Gayle had placed there. It gave her a jolt of sympathy for the aunt they never really contacted and certainly never saw. But it had worked both ways. Aunt Gayle could've encouraged her to stay on the island, to bake, yet she hadn't.

Her gaze moved to take in the sky beyond the dormer window. She'd loved looking up at the vast expanse when she was little too.

Addie was eight years old when she first came to live here, clutching a pile of her birthday cards, each with a big number 8 on the front. The cards had still been up at her dad's house, on the windowsill in the front room, where all the birthday cards went and stayed for at least a couple of weeks.

After their dad died and the girls were coaxed to pack up their things in their bedrooms with their grandparents' help, Addie had told Susanna that she wanted to be called Addie from now on. Her dad had never called her that – it was always Adeleine – but she no longer wanted anyone else to use her full name now he'd gone. She was Addie to her friends at school, occasionally she was Addie to her big sister, so that was the name she wanted to keep.

Later that morning after they'd finished their packing, Aunt Gayle had come to get her and Susanna from Portsmouth where they'd travelled to with their grandparents. Addie didn't know much about Anchor Island, and she hadn't ever wanted to leave Oxford, but she'd hugged her grandparents goodbye, listened to Aunt Gayle thank them for taking such good care of the girls, and then Addie, Susanna and Aunt Gayle had boarded a ferry to Guernsey where they met another connection to the island that would be their home from then on.

Addie remembered how much she'd cried when her grandparents told them that they would be going to live with Aunt Gayle. She couldn't understand why they couldn't stay with them. Her grandpa said that they were old, that the girls would have a good life and so many adventures with their dad's sister, but Addie wasn't so sure.

'What do you think?' That day Aunt Gayle had stood beside Addie in the doorway of one of the two bedrooms upstairs in her cottage. Susanna had already been shown to her bedroom, next to Addie's, and all Addie would have to do was tap on the wall separating them if she needed her sister.

'It's nice,' said Addie. She looked over at the small glass vase of little pink flowers next to the bed and she wanted to go across, put her nose to them and see if they smelt real. They looked real. Susanna had had blue ones in her bedroom. She wondered if they smelt the same.

Aunt Gayle's words galloped along with, 'This is your

bedroom. I'm downstairs. The upstairs is yours – there's plenty of space. It's nice and bright too.'

Addie knew what it meant when adults talked fast and seemed to be finding anything to fill the silence. It meant they were uncomfortable, awkward. Well, so was she. She wasn't sure this was ever going to feel like a home, no matter how nice the colour of the walls or the little cluster of flowers or the view of the sky when she looked up and out of the window.

She had two windows, just like Susanna, and on the one that looked out over the Close she started to line up her birthday cards, the card from her dad closest to the bed and where she could reach it and trace her fingers over the words he'd written.

'Let me help you, Adeleine,' said Aunt Gayle, reaching out and taking the pile of cards. She had flour up one arm and a bit in her dark hair, even though she hadn't even been at work. Or maybe she had before she came to meet the girls and bring them to this new life.

Susanna appeared in the doorway and came into Addie's room. 'I can help her do that,' she instructed. And to Aunt Gayle she said, 'She calls herself Addie now. Not Adeleine.'

Addie looked at the carpet.

'Oh, right,' said Aunt Gayle. Addie was glad she didn't ask why.

To Addie, Susanna said, 'Want me to help you arrange the cards the way they were before? I think I can remember.'

Addie nodded.

Gayle handed Susanna the pile of cards in her hand. 'I'm sorry, I was just—'

'I know what she wants,' said Susanna in the tone their dad had used if either of them was in trouble.

Aunt Gayle retreated, saying she'd be downstairs when they were ready, and pudding would be served if they were hungry.

Addie wondered whether Aunt Gayle would hug her goodnight like her dad and her grandparents always had.

'I hope she makes proper dinners, not just puddings,' said Susanna the second they were on their own and she'd put the cards out. She wrapped her sister in a hug. 'We can't live on sugar for the rest of our lives.'

The rest of our lives. That's what was happening now, wasn't it? She was going to be here on this island, away from her school and her friends, the familiar places such as the corner shop, the library, the city of Oxford not far out of reach. She wouldn't even get to take their grandparents' dog, Freddie, for a walk either.

Addie wished Freddie was here now, to make a fuss of and hug. Freddie was old, he had a limp, and he didn't want to play with the ball so much when she threw it for him. Granny said he couldn't help slowing down. Addie had cried saying goodbye to Freddie because she knew she probably wouldn't get to see him again. She'd even asked to bring him to the island, but Granny had explained he was settled in his own home and besides, he needed taking out to the toilet a lot and sometimes he didn't make it and went for his wees and number twos inside. Addie didn't suppose Aunt Gayle would have the time to sort him out, Dad always said she was obsessed by her pudding place, and she didn't have time for anything else.

Addie wondered if she really had time for her and her sister.

Susanna still had Addie in her arms. 'We'll be all right, you'll see. We don't need anyone apart from each other. And we *don't* need pudding forced on us either.'

Susanna always knew what to do. Addie didn't know what she would do without her big sister. But she hoped Susanna wouldn't stop them from having the pudding even if it was forced on them because the smell was filling her room already and it smelled good.

'I like my room,' Addie admitted timidly.

'It's your favourite colour,' Susanna approved. With a white bedspread dotted with tiny pink flowers and a bright pink colour on the walls, it was similar to the colour of her room at home, the room she'd had her whole life until their dad got sick.

Addie, still in her pyjamas the morning after they'd arrived back on Anchor Island after decades of absence, knew she couldn't gaze out of the window and reminisce for ever.

She crept down the stairs quietly and past the kitchen in case Gayle and Susanna were still in there. She needed a shower, time to wake up – she always worked better once she was ready for the day. Then she would be able to tackle whatever was thrown at her.

She took her time, washed her hair and lathered up creamy shower gel from what looked like a brand-new bottle purchased especially for their visit. Once she was done, she opened up the bathroom window to let some of the steam escape. It wasn't the best shower in the world, with pretty dire water pressure, but the heat and scented products had made up for it and she was ashamed to say she'd stayed in longer than she should. She'd forgotten how matted your hair could get from the sea air on a ferry crossing, and although she'd tried to brush the salty residue out last night it was still in need of a good wash this morning.

She was about to head back upstairs when she noticed movement beyond the bathroom window, and as she peeked outside, she saw the young woman from last night emerge from Aunt Gayle's garden room. Whatever was she doing there? They'd thought she was a neighbour and Aunt Gayle hadn't said otherwise. At least not to her.

Once she was dressed and her hair was dry, she came back downstairs. Susanna was in the hallway putting on her trainers and Aunt Gayle was coming out of the kitchen.

'Why is the woman from last night in your back garden?' she asked their aunt.

Susanna looked up only briefly and as Aunt Gayle explained, Addie realised they'd already had this conversation. She supposed that was a positive – they were talking.

'I need to get to the Sweet Life Café,' said Aunt Gayle, who was dressed already in a lemon blouse and navy trousers. 'I'll leave you girls to your own devices. I've told Susanna you can go into the attic space whenever you're ready. It's crammed full of my things, but you'll easily find your father's belongings – they're all still boxed up and labelled.'

'We should've taken them earlier.' Addie, hovering on the bottom stair, felt bad that they hadn't.

A look passed across Gayle's face and Addie knew exactly what it meant. If they'd taken them all already, there would be nothing left to hang around and sort through.

When Aunt Gayle picked up her bag and left the cottage, keys in hand, Addie said to Susanna, 'Do you think renting out her garden room was more about her being lonely than needing the money?'

Trainers on, Susanna stood up. 'No idea.' She said it in a tone that suggested thinking about Gayle and whether she'd been lonely or not wasn't high on her priority list. 'What I do know is that if we're going to get through the things in the attic, we need to make a start today. See you upstairs in an hour?'

'Sure. Enjoy your walk.'

Addie suspected this was less about getting some exercise and more about escaping the walls of the cottage she'd never ever wanted to be restricted by. She felt much the same in some respects, but in others, it almost felt like coming home.

Not that she'd ever admit that to Susanna.

14

GAYLE

Gayle hated lying to the girls. She hated lying full stop, and there had been enough tension between the three of them that yet another fib felt like it could be the straw to break the proverbial camel's back if she wasn't careful. So careful she would have to be, because now wasn't the time to tell them the rest.

In the kitchen at the Sweet Life Café, she poured cake batter onto the fruit lining the tin for a berry upside-down cake. She scraped the remnants with a silicone spatula until the bowl was almost clean. She'd learnt in the early days not to waste ingredients, and the habit had never left her.

With the berry upside-down cake in the oven, she sat on the stool at the side of the kitchen and reached for the notebook she'd slotted behind a bread bin. It contained all her notes, her planning for the living funeral. She had a sketch of how the Sweet Life Café would look once all the tables were rearranged, and she'd selected an array of puddings to cater for everyone, noting their accompaniments – custard, ice-cream, whipped cream, pouring cream. She'd even worked out a timetable for the day when it came to further cooking as puddings disappeared, what would go into the warming ovens and when, how much crockery and utensils they'd need, the guest list and, of course, how she wanted the place to be decorated. This was a celebration rather than the funeral her nieces had thought they'd be attending, and so with the invite specifying bright colours, she had gone for the same theme. She had silver and white helium balloons arriving, which would look great against the café's blue colours, and she'd ordered some special blue and silver bunting to loop around the interior and really make it look like the event of the year.

Louisa poked her head around the kitchen door. 'I know you said I wasn't needed until later, but—'

'Come in – there's plenty to do, don't you worry about that.'

Louisa, her tourist as the girls had been led to believe, had volunteered to help out at the café when it became obvious that with an event coming up there was just too much to do. Gayle had leapt at the opportunity and paid her, despite Louisa volunteering to do it for free. Louisa wasn't much of a baker, but there were plenty of other things she could do, including tidying up and sweeping, taking things out of the oven, washing up, or driving the delivery van to take puddings to customers on the island. Louisa brought a delightful young vibe to the kitchen, with her laughter and her chatter that Gayle absolutely adored and which reminded her of the days when Addie had been at her side.

Installing her garden room had turned out to be serendipitous. She'd thought it might be a way to generate extra income, and she'd thought she might enjoy the company of holidaymakers and probably bore them silly talking about the Sweet Life Café. But then came the pandemic, and although her room was installed and she was ready to list it on Airbnb just like she'd told the girls, suddenly she couldn't do it. Rules meant she couldn't take guests and so the room just sat there for a while until a year or so later when the world opened up again. By then the owner of the inn had told her that they would pass guests they couldn't accommodate her way, and it had worked well ever since. Then when Louisa showed up looking for her six weeks ago the garden room had been the perfect solution so that they could get to know one another. And when she said she'd return for the living funeral, Gayle hadn't even hesitated to offer her the garden room again for her stay.

Louisa Miller was like a breath of fresh air. At thirty-two, she had bouncy blonde curls that cascaded all the way down her back, golden skin which Gayle had learned was largely due to her mother's complexion, and a way of smiling that made Gayle feel like she wasn't completely out of touch with the younger generation.

As Louisa pulled on a pair of marigolds ready to wash up a big mixing bowl and whisk left next to the sink, Gayle confessed, 'I still haven't told them the truth.'

She turned on the taps and put in the plug. 'Gayle, you can't put it off forever.'

'I think after the living funeral would be the right time. They've already had a big shock.'

Louisa paused, soap suds falling from the fingertips of her marigolds as her hands dangled over the sink. 'They both looked so upset the night they arrived.'

'Seeing a dead person alive and kicking would do that.'

Louisa let Gayle sit with her thoughts, and when she picked up the notebook again Louisa wanted to know what else she'd added to it. She shared the order of balloons and the bunting.

'The café will look amazing on the day.' She set the washed whisk down on the drainer.

Gayle wasn't sure how long it was before she felt the young

woman's eyes on her, and realised she'd leaned her head against the wall and began to drift.

'You need some fresh air,' said Louisa. 'You're overdoing it.'

'Piffle. I need to bake. I need to plan.'

Louisa tugged off her marigolds. 'Come on, I've cleaned up in here and Nancy said there's nothing pressing. We'll walk to the end of Bay Street and back.'

Gayle supposed a walk might make her feel more alert and less sleepy. And the end of Bay Street was about as far as she wanted to go these days.

Louisa slipped her arm through Gayle's once they were outside. They went to the end of the street and down the trail that led to the first bench. Whatever else was going on in her life, it felt good to be here, making the most of every day she had left on this island. The second she'd moved here she'd been unable to imagine living anywhere else.

As they walked, they chatted about the living funeral, the decorations, the recipes, the guest list. Gayle was excited and nervous in equal measure, but she was glad she'd organised it, not least because the girls were here on the island again. And if the event hadn't been planned, with or without her mistake, that definitely wouldn't be the case.

They sat on the bench as soon as they reached it and it felt good to get off her feet.

'It's so pretty here,' said Louisa. 'Does the novelty ever wear off?'

'It hasn't with me. And I'm not lying when I tell you that I love it in all seasons.' She chuckled. 'Mind you, the winter winds are so strong they can almost knock you off your feet some days.'

'A warm treat at the Sweet Life Café must take the edge off,' said Louisa.

'There's nothing like a hot pudding on a freezing cold day.'

'With a dollop of ice-cream...'

'Or custard.'

Louisa giggled. 'Always ice-cream for me. My mum's the same.'

From what Louisa had told her it sounded like she'd had a wonderful relationship with her mother, who was fully supportive when Louisa decided she wanted to come to the island to get to know more about the Raffertys.

She looked out across the Channel. This wasn't the best spot, but you could see enough as the bushes swayed and parted, giving glimpses of the water. She hoped she got to do a lot more of this before her time was up.

'I walked all the way round the island this morning at sunrise,' said Louisa.

'Oh, I used to love doing that.' And it made her happy to know Louisa was embracing the island's beauty.

They fell into conversation about the island, the little bays, the marina and harbour, the shops that had stayed on Bay Street and what had changed over the years. She'd got to know Louisa so well over this visit and her last that now, chatting with her was less pressured, with fewer questions and answers, and more of a two-way conversation about the minutiae of life – the weather on the island compared to the mainland, puddings of course, local eateries, life experiences both good and bad.

'I'm happy to do more deliveries later.' Louisa took her arm as they set off to walk back to the café. 'I enjoy driving the pink van. I think it's the colour.'

Gayle laughed. 'It's bright, that's for sure.'

Delivering puddings was another thing she'd introduced during the pandemic – with customers unable to come to her, she wanted to ensure puddings came to them, and the van had been a solid investment. Now there were plenty of events she catered for – engagement parties, christenings, birthdays, weddings.

Gayle realised she'd never asked Louisa the ultimate question. 'Do you have a favourite pudding, Louisa?'

She thought hard. 'If I had to choose, I'd say the rhubarb crumble and cream with a generous scoop of vanilla bean ice-cream.'

'I love crumble. Then again, there's not much I don't love in the way of puddings.' She stopped for a beat.

'Are you okay?'

'Just a bit stiff after sitting.' Really, she felt a little light-headed but she didn't want to admit it. And hopefully it would pass. It usually did.

'Do you ever wonder what life would've been like if you hadn't come to the island?' Louisa asked.

'Sometimes. I suppose it's natural to wonder *what if*?'

'I often wonder how my life would've turned out if I'd studied horticulture rather than drama. Maybe I'd have a steady job rather than doing whatever work I can lay my hands on.'

'You'll find your way, don't worry.'

'Mum would like to see me settled.'

'I can understand that.' Despite them not being close, it was what she'd always wanted for Susanna and Addie.

'Mum thinks I could do a course, perhaps start my own gardening business.'

'She has faith in you. She obviously knows you well, so grab some confidence from that.'

'How did you know the Sweet Life Café would work?'

'I didn't. No business owner is ever 100 per cent sure. But you do your research, you keep on doing it as time goes on. There's a certain element of luck too.'

'The location for the café is perfect. Did it take you long to find this place?'

'I wasn't even looking at the time – I was saving, waiting to feel ready. But then I saw an advertisement and the pictures grabbed me. I was hooked, even more so when I came here in person. I made an offer the same day as the viewing – the owner, who was French, wanted to return to Paris to be nearer to her parents. I think I got a bargain, she got a very speedy sale, and we were both happy.'

Gayle lost herself in her own thoughts of those days, those crazy weeks getting the business ready to open and then trying to get it off the ground.

'Did the girls never want to join you in your business?' Louisa asked.

'Addie loved to bake with me when she was little, but I'm afraid to say I kept her interest at arm's-length.'

'Why?'

'I didn't want to come between her and her sister. They were close and I didn't want to ruin that.' She left it there. Some things she hadn't explained to Louisa. She knew Gayle didn't have the best relationship with the girls, but didn't need to know all the ins and outs.

'Do you know if Addie still bakes?'

'I'm not sure.'

'Maybe that will change if you get to know her again.' Louisa oozed a positivity Gayle didn't feel.

'If she gives me a chance, then maybe.'

The girls were here, they were going through their dad's things at last, but after that? Who knew what would happen when they found out what else she was keeping from them.

It might just push them even further away.

15

SUSANNA

Susanna was getting used to these morning walks. She'd been doing them since the first day she woke up back here on Anchor Island.

It felt good now to be out and about. The drizzle from earlier had passed, the mist had lifted, and although the leaves on the trees clung to drips of rain before releasing them to the ground, the sunshine gracing the skies now acted as if it had been out in force the whole time.

Over the last couple of days Susanna and Addie had hauled boxes from the attic and stacked them against the wall in Susanna's bedroom, ready to sort through. It had been an unspoken agreement, but Susanna suspected Addie felt much like she did – that after the shock of Gayle dying then coming back to life before their very eyes, as well as being on the island after all these years, they needed to get their heads around things before they plunged into all their memories that those boxes no doubt contained.

In between the sorting out, Susanna had got some work done and also walked a bit with Addie. They'd shared the cooking of the dinners at the cottage too and there'd been an unspoken peace under Gayle's roof, with all of them taking it one step at a time.

Today she turned the same way as she usually did onto Bay Street. She joined the track that went all the way around the island, her intention being to do the full walk which would take around three hours. But as she passed the top of the steps that cut down to the harbour street below, she found her feet taking her in that direction before she could change her mind. This would be the first time she'd been near the harbour or the marina since the evening they arrived, but she doubted anyone would recognise her with her sunglasses on, and more likely because of the decades that had passed since she was last here.

She bought herself a coffee from a little venue near the fish and chip shop and headed towards the green space near the marina. She was glad she had a jumper on, although she suspected she'd need another layer if she was back in Cambridge. Despite the sea breezes, the island's more southerly location meant that it was often warmer than England. She could recall some beautiful summers here. When they'd first arrived, they'd been heading into winter which added to the gloom she'd felt, but despite her resistance to the island she'd never forgotten her first blast of warm weather with the island's gloriously long days, the blistering sun, and what it had felt like to finally get into the clear waters and have a swim.

Aunt Gayle had watched them like a hawk that first summer and the girls were never allowed to go down to the bay without her. The water was dangerous, she'd told them. Both girls had had swimming lessons, but by their own admission they'd stopped going to those as soon as they could stay afloat. Addie had treated Isaac differently, or maybe that was what kids did nowadays – they didn't just learn to swim, they got strong in the water. But if she'd done that, she may never have met Alex.

Triggered by her memory, she picked up her phone to call her husband but changed her mind as she reached the green space. She had her eye on one of the picnic benches, most of which were empty this morning. She'd spoken to Alex last night, so she'd leave it until later – she didn't want to be the source of more tension if he thought she was checking up on him.

The gulls soared overhead, and she watched one go for a man's food. He waved his hands at the gull and yelled at it to get away. She almost laughed, but knew those gulls could be vicious – she remembered one knocking her sandwich right out of her hands one day while she was sitting on one of the island's perimeter path benches. She would've cried if it hadn't been for friends laughing and making her see the funny side. She'd gone to the Sweet Life Café after that, and when Aunt Gayle asked what was wrong, she'd burst into tears. It was the first time she showed the vulnerability she'd done her best to hide. Aunt Gayle had sat her down and given her an enormous serving of steamed sponge pudding with honey butterscotch sauce, and even sat there with her despite how busy the café was.

She'd totally forgotten about that moment until now.

She stepped onto the grassy bank to head towards a picnic bench, but somehow she didn't judge the gradient too well and the next thing she knew, her feet went from under her. Her coffee and phone went flying, but two arms grabbed her from behind right before she hit the grass.

And when she turned around, she came face to face with her past.

Mateo Collins. Her first love and the man she hadn't seen in over two decades.

Since the first day she saw Mateo at the Sweet Life Café when she was the tender age of seventeen, Susanna had been unable to get him from her mind. Every day she'd linger down near the marina and try to spot him, but she never seemed to have any luck. She didn't see him again until a couple of weeks after their initial encounter, when she was returning to the island after school. The ferry crossing had been the worst she'd ever experienced – it was the first time she'd had seasickness, and he'd seen her walking away from the busy harbour. He'd led her over to a picnic bench, sat her down, and ran to get her a bottle of water.

When he came back to her side she smiled. He'd gone to the fish and chip shop for the water, and she knew he was trying to hide a cone of chips behind his back because she could smell them. He also had a grain of salt on his bottom lip that she waited for him to lick off.

'You don't have to hide them,' she'd said.

He pulled a face. 'Thought they might make you more queasy.' He gestured for her to drink the water. 'I had to get something. I was about to head there anyway until I saw you looking wobbly and as if you might puke at any second. I've been working on boats all day and I'm starving.' He pulled the cone into view. 'I'm Mateo, by the way.'

'Susanna.' She didn't say that she already knew his name, and had remembered it ever since the first day she heard it.

'Your aunt owns the Sweet Life Café, doesn't she?'

Did he remember seeing her in there? Her tummy was doing somersaults just thinking about it, and she didn't know what else to say. 'She does.'

He ate more of the chips, and she tried to take some calming breaths, sipping slowly from the bottle of water.

He offered her the last chip. 'Might make you feel better,' he said.

'Might make me actually be sick,' she replied.

But he still held the cone in her direction. She took the chip, and it went better than she thought because she managed to keep it down.

'They're good,' she said. 'Not too greasy.'

'Fluffy,' he answered.

She began to laugh.

'What's wrong with saying *fluffy*?'

'Nothing.' It just sounded funny coming from someone so manly as him – she expected gruff outbursts and confidence, not talking about the inside of a chip in such a delicate way.

'Feel like having chips again with me tomorrow?' he asked.

Suddenly, she wasn't sure. 'How old are you?'

'A bit older than you, probably.'

'You're avoiding the question.'

'I'm twenty-three.'

'I'm seventeen. Almost eighteen.'

'So do you want to meet up?'

'Okay. But can we do later? I have to look after my little sister until closing time at the café.'

'Is that who you were with when I saw you in the café that time?'

So he *did* remember the details about that day. 'Yes, that was my sister, Addie.' Had he thought about her as much as she'd thought about him? Especially when she went to bed, hoping she'd fall asleep and dream about him.

'Meet me 7 p.m.?' he suggested.

And that was how it had started. She'd fallen for him more and more as the days went on. Each day after school she'd get her homework done and he'd either come into the Sweet Life Café to meet her or she'd run down to the marina to surprise him. They'd talk and talk, laugh hard, go on walks and kiss whenever they could. They'd sneak onto boats and have little romantic picnics as if they were the owners of a vast yacht and sailing around the world together. They got serious really quickly and Susanna couldn't imagine it any other way. She'd even started to question whether she wanted to run far away from the island and go back to the mainland. The thought of leaving Mateo was almost incomprehensible.

One morning, Susanna had skipped school. She knew it was bad, but it was gloriously sunny and she hadn't seen Mateo for a few days. Sometimes she worried that she wasn't mature enough for him, that with her still going to school he might decide he wanted someone older. But he'd told her he loved her many times, and she'd said it back. Nothing was going to come between them; she just had to be careful Aunt Gayle didn't find out about her coming here rather than to school. She'd have to make up a cover story because the school would be sure to get in touch with her aunt, given her absence.

She reached the marina and her heart lifted when she spotted Mateo, but as she quickened her pace around the boats on dry land to reach him she came to an abrupt halt when she saw her aunt standing near him. She hadn't been able to see her from further away, her view being obscured by the other boats.

She hid so neither of them could see her, her cheek catching a coldness from the body of the boat she was hiding behind. She wondered why her aunt was here. Was she looking for her?

'She's so much younger than you,' she heard Aunt Gayle say.

'I'm not going to hurt her,' Mateo had replied. 'I told you before that I wouldn't do that.'

So they'd had a conversation before? Mateo had never told her, and neither had Aunt Gayle.

'Well, you are indirectly hurting her because she's started skipping school,' said Aunt Gayle.

'That's news to me,' Mateo replied. He was being so polite. If it was her, she'd tell Gayle to mind her own bloody business.

'She's also not doing her homework – she's rushing it all, she's distracted.' Silence until Gayle spoke again. 'You know she wants to go to university, don't you?'

'She hasn't mentioned it for a while.'

'That's because you're all she's thinking about these days. She has a plan, or at least *had* one. She wants to leave the island, and if she is after a decent future she needs some qualifications.'

Susanna's heart thumped as she froze on the spot, waiting to hear what her boyfriend replied. It was true, she did want to go to university – at least, she thought she did. But she would still want Mateo. Why couldn't Aunt Gayle work that out?

'Gayle, I'm not out to hurt Susanna. I love her.'

Susanna let a smile form. He loved her and she loved him. Aunt Gayle could never take that away from her.

'Has she been down here this morning?' Gayle demanded.

'She's at school,' Mateo answered.

'She isn't. They called me.' Her remark was met with silence. 'You're in your twenties, you're too old for her. You don't want the same things.'

Mateo didn't say anything and Gayle added, 'If you see her, send her home. Please.'

Susanna made to leave at the sound of their voices drawing slightly closer, but not before she heard Gayle add, 'Think about what I've said. Don't stand in her way of having a decent future.'

Susanna had managed to run between a couple of boats on dry land at the marina and weave her way out without her aunt seeing her. She wasn't going home. Instead, she headed past the fish and chip shop and up the steps, because she knew Aunt Gayle would go the other way to Bay Street and her precious workplace.

She hid out for half an hour and then returned to the marina, but there was no sign of Mateo. She asked after him and one of his colleagues said he'd taken a boat over to Guernsey. She hung around for almost two hours, but by then she was getting cold, and with no sign of her boyfriend she went back to the cottage. She called Aunt Gayle at the Sweet Life Café and told her that she had been sick on the boat on the way to school, that she'd missed a connection back but was on Anchor Island now.

When Aunt Gayle came home to check on her, she dived beneath her duvet, pinched her cheeks so she looked a bit red and – hoping it could pass for sickness – pretended to be asleep.

She felt better by dinner time and her aunt agreed that it was okay for her to go out for some fresh air. She left the cottage, went down to the marina and saw Mateo bringing a boat in. He must've delivered one to Guernsey and brought another back. She hoped someday she'd have a job she loved so much. Perhaps he could sail and she could do the business side of whatever venture they tackled together.

She beamed a smile his way as he spotted her, but he didn't return it – he simply jumped off the vessel and then secured the thick rope around its mooring.

'Where were you today?' he asked her as he stood up from his kneeling position.

'Well, I was planning to come and see you until I saw Aunt Gayle got here first.' Instead of him sharing a conspiratorial smile his expression was hard to read. 'I'm sorry she said those things to you.' She reached for his hand, but he pulled it away.

'Don't tell me you're listening to her,' she said jokingly, until she realised that was exactly what he was doing.

'She's right, Susanna.' He carried on securing a rope at the other end.

'No, she isn't.'

'You've not been working so hard at school since you met me.'

'Well, maybe I want different things now. We talked about it, remember?'

'You've wanted to leave the island ever since I've known you.'

'And we can do that. Together.'

He said nothing. He got his bag from the boat he'd brought in, and they walked side-by-side out towards the street.

'I don't want to be responsible for ruining your future,' he said.

'You're not. Why are you listening to Aunt Gayle?'

'Because she is looking out for you. And she's right. I'm a lot older.'

She wanted to cry, and perhaps she might have done if she didn't think it would illustrate his point perfectly.

'I'm not academic,' he went on. 'Give me a boat and the open water and that's all I need. You deserve a whole lot more.' He put a hand on her shoulder.

She shrugged him off, crossed her arms. 'How can you seriously be listening to her? Don't you want me any more?'

He said nothing until he delivered a blow that shocked her beyond belief. 'I've got a new job. It's taking me away from Anchor Island, so ending things is probably for the best.'

'You're lying.'

'It's been on the cards for a while, and a couple of hours ago I accepted it. It's a contract for a few years. I'll be sailing boats to different places around the world. I need to do it for me, Susanna. Like you need to go to school, do university, find your career. It's what you always planned.'

'So that's it?' she cried after his retreating back as he walked away.

He said nothing. She slumped down onto a picnic bench and sobbed her heart out.

She could remember that day so clearly and she'd never forgotten the hurt and the feeling of betrayal.

And since that day, she hadn't seen him again. Until now.

She caught her breath, watched him reach down to pick up her phone off the ground.

'Coffee's gone, I'm afraid.' His voice fell over her the same way as it had all those years ago.

Mateo was almost fifty now. He still wore shorts and a T-shirt very well and his hair, slightly dishevelled and longer than it had once been, suited him. Tanned forearms and muscled biceps evoked memories of lying next to him on the deck of a boat he was fixing, pretending it was theirs and nobody else's. They'd been besotted with each other until Gayle ruined things. But somewhere amidst her anger at her aunt, perhaps Susanna had always known that Mateo would inevitably want to settle on Anchor Island. He belonged here, and she didn't.

His smile still made her feel slightly weak at the knees when he said, 'It's been a long time.'

She gulped. 'Yes, it has. You're back.'

'As are you.'

'I'm here for the living funeral.'

'I've been invited too. Bit morbid, if you ask me.' He leaned slightly closer when he said the last bit, as if he didn't want anyone to overhear.

'It doesn't feel as morbid as her letting us think she was dead.' She recapped the mistake on the invites. 'It seemed word got around the island that she'd made an error, but the truth didn't reach me or Addie.'

He paused. 'I know things were always a bit rocky with you and Gayle.'

'A bit rocky? That's an understatement.' Immediately she was right back there, just yards from here, listening to her aunt warn her boyfriend off, and she felt the hurt all over again.

'I'm sorry, you know.'

'For what?'

'The way things ended.' He didn't take his eyes away from her. He rarely had until that day Gayle had come down here and put doubts in his mind.

'You took the job to get away from me, didn't you?' she said. Even a metre or so apart it felt as if there was a magnetic pull between them. Or maybe she was just remembering when all he'd had to do was take her hand and she'd felt her insides ignite.

'I had to. I knew it would be the only way I wouldn't be tempted to keep things going between us. I knew my job would be here when I got back.'

'And that I wouldn't be.'

'It wasn't as callous as it sounds. I didn't want to get away from you because I didn't want you – it was the opposite. I loved you and wanted you to have the future your aunt talked about, the future you once talked about. I hadn't realised until Gayle pointed it out that you and I were so into each other that you'd forgotten what you even wanted.'

'Maybe I'd changed my mind.' And hearing his feelings spilling out after all this time had a strange effect on her. It made her question leaving here, forging a different life. Or maybe with Alex and her having problems she was just looking for answers, a way to rewrite everything so that it was perfect and she couldn't be hurt.

'You were so young. So was I.'

'None of that mattered. It wasn't her place to say those things to you.'

'It was. You were under her care and she did what she thought was best.' He looked at the ground momentarily, scuffed a stone beneath the toe of his shoe. 'Can you honestly tell me you regret doing well at school, going to university, becoming a hotshot solicitor?'

'Wait, how did you—?'

He smiled. 'Gayle talks about you. She has regrets, but she never stopped caring.'

It took Susanna by surprise. It shouldn't have, but it did.

'Do you regret leaving the island when you did?' Her question turned the tables on him.

'I did for a while, but the job was great, I won't lie. I was sailing much more than I would've been here and got to see parts of the world I hadn't known existed. It was a lonely life in many ways, and in others...'

She wanted the conversation to stop, it had to, she needed to walk away, get her head straight. 'I need to go. I have an attic to deal with.'

'I'll see you around.' His words drifted over her as she turned and left.

She took a faster pace up the hill to Bay Street than she otherwise might have done when she didn't have something hefty on her mind.

She was still thinking about Mateo when she reached the Sweet Life Café for the first time since they'd arrived on the island, when she noticed Gayle's visitor – or tourist, or whatever – Louisa, disappearing inside. Maybe Gayle included puddings in her tourist's holiday package, who knew. Or perhaps as Addie said, Gayle was lonely and she liked the company.

If she had been lonely, then why hadn't she fought harder for them to stay?

Aunt Gayle could've asked her and Mateo to slow things down for a while rather than warning him off. She could've let things unfold with him, see what Susanna wanted to do long-term.

Then again, if she hadn't left would she have regretted it?

She turned into Evergreen Close. Mateo's voice was in her psyche still, deeper, more matured over the years, but with the same notes as before. Seeing him felt like a pick-me-up in the gloom of her marriage troubles, but she also felt guilty for the way it made her feel.

She needed to speak to Alex.

Alex. The man she'd married. The man she thought she would be with forever.

The man who was keeping something from her.

As his mobile rang out, followed by the home phone, she wondered, if she found out that Alex was cheating, would she seek revenge and do the same?

She was here on the island and the man who had been the first one to show her what real passion, tenderness and understanding was, had looked at her in the same way he always had.

Did they have unfinished business?

16

ADDIE

'You were quick. I thought you were going all the way around the island this time,' said Addie when Susanna came through the door. Addie had been taking some time for herself, reading a book after baking a batch of oatmeal and raisin cookies.

'Changed my mind.' Susanna took off her shoes and left them in the hallway before following the aroma into the kitchen. 'Something smells good.'

'Help yourself.'

She reached for a cookie, still nice and gooey having not been out of the oven long and closed her eyes when she bit into it. 'You, my girl, have talent.'

'I haven't done any more sorting.'

Susanna spoke carefully through her mouthful. 'You deserve a break too.'

'This is the first time I've had a decent chunk of time to read a book, and I couldn't resist baking something too.' But she felt guilty. There was still a ridiculous number of boxes to go through. They'd already got rid of so many bits and pieces, which she supposed had all been lumped into boxes because nobody had had the time or the inclination to sort through what should be thrown and what should be packed. When Harry died everything had been so rushed with sorting the house and moving the girls so suddenly.

'Aunt Gayle had all the ingredients?'

Addie nodded. 'Fully stocked pantry.'

'We'll do more sorting after I've had another one of these yummy cookies,' Susanna declared.

They were getting there with the boxes and she expected they'd be through the rest of them way before the eight days prior to the living funeral were up. She wondered how they'd fill their days then or whether Susanna would push more to leave.

After Susanna finished the final mouthful of her second cookie she licked her fingers. 'I called Alex.'

Addie plucked a cookie for herself. 'And how is he?'

'He didn't answer.'

'I'm sure he's busy. Don't read too much into it.' She led the way upstairs. 'Just because he didn't answer it doesn't mean he's up to anything untoward.'

'Maybe.'

'It doesn't.' She popped the rest of her cookie into her mouth. They really did taste the best when they still held some of their warmth from the oven. As she'd made them, she'd wondered whether Gayle would mind her baking; she hadn't asked, after all. Was she crossing a boundary when she shouldn't be, perhaps?

They'd reached the upstairs when Susanna said, 'He's back on the island.'

Addie paused briefly in front of the attic door. 'Who?' But it took seconds to realise exactly who she meant. 'I thought he might be. Mateo is as much a part of this island as the sand on the beach. So… did you talk to him?'

She grimaced, then explained how she'd fallen, and he'd been the one to catch her.

Addie burst out laughing. 'Well, I suppose it beats being paranoid about when or if you'll bump into him. It's over and done with now.' She looked at her sister. 'So… what's he like after all this time? How did you feel?' Whenever her big sister had stayed out late Addie had come up to her own bedroom, but she'd kept a torch near her bed and always tried to stay awake until Susanna got home. She didn't always make it. Sometimes she fell asleep, but on the times she didn't, in whispers Susanna would tell her all about what she'd been up to. As she got older, though, Addie sensed the conversation had been somewhat filtered for an eleven-year-old's ears.

'It was odd. It was nice. It was like no time had passed.'

'I used to love hearing about your love affair. I wasn't even a teenager and boys were a long way off for me. So, will you see him again?'

'I'm a married woman.'

'That doesn't answer my question.' Addie knelt, ready to tackle the next box.

'If I'm on the island, I might not be able to avoid him.'

'Especially if you're down by the marina.' But she stopped with the teasing. Things with Alex were a little rocky, apparently, although Susanna hadn't gone into much detail about what was going on. Addie only hoped that her brother-in-law and her sister would work things out, and that Susanna wouldn't do anything stupid with Mateo around.

'Come on, let's get going with all this.' Susanna dragged a box nearer.

So far, they'd found plenty – a doll's house, some Lego Addie had put to one side to take back for Isaac, a collection of old books Susanna had read in high school. The memories slowed down the sorting, but to Addie that wasn't a bad thing. They'd gone on to find their dad's gold watch with the brown leather strap – Susanna had claimed it, and Addie took the cufflinks he'd worn when he got married. She thought maybe she'd give them to Isaac someday to wear on his wedding day.

Addie pulled off the tape from the box. The seal and Gayle's address, along with the removal company's logo on the boxes, spoke to how neglected all of this stuff had been.

'Look what I've found.' From inside the box, Addie pulled out a leaflet. It was the information the estate agent must have handed to prospective buyers, including their parents. The typed sheet of A4 looked so different to estate agents' listings these days, which were mostly trawled through online.

'That's our house,' said Susanna, scooting closer and losing interest with the box she'd selected to go through.

They glanced over the leaflet, deducing that bedroom three would've been Addie's – she could tell by the irregular measurements with its funny L-shape at one end, like it had its own entrance hall. She'd stuck plastic hooks on the wall as if she would have many visitors who could hang their coats there. In reality, she'd used the hooks for her thin dressing gown, scarves in the winter, sunhats in the summer. They weren't strong enough for much else. The one time she'd hung her towelling robe on one it had fallen straight down.

'Bedroom four was mine,' said Susanna, pointing to the picture of the house. She sat back on her heels, adding wistfully, 'I loved that house.'

'Me too. I was so sad to leave. It felt like losing the only thing we had left of Mum and Dad.' She felt Susanna's arm snake around her shoulders briefly before she shuffled back over to the box she was going through.

'What's in yours?' Addie nodded to Susanna's box.

'Boring stuff. Bank statements, old energy bills and a bag of old buttons. Random.' She looked across at her sister. 'We should've done this ages ago.'

'In hindsight, yes, we should have.'

'At least this takes our minds off the fact that Aunt Gayle pretended to be dead.'

'She didn't pretend to be dead...' When Susanna cast a doubtful gaze her way she said, 'Well, all right, she kind of did, but she wanted us here, and you know we wouldn't have come for a party. We all seem to have been getting on well enough for the last few days. I thought you were less angry.'

'I am... maybe. But I'm still not sure I'll stay for the event.'

Addie sat back on her heels. 'It'll be weird going to it.' But would it be even weirder to leave now?

She left the subject alone as they finished going through another half a dozen boxes and stacked them against the wall in her bedroom once they were done, with a pile to keep and another pile of things to be got rid of.

Susanna's eyes misted as she pulled something from the 'to keep' pile. She held up a wooden frame painted blue, but a blue that allowed the grain of the wood to show through. 'I still can't believe he kept this.'

'It looks very old.' To be honest, she'd been surprised when Susanna didn't drop it onto the discard pile.

'I made it at school in our woodwork class when I was about eleven, I think.'

Addie realised it wasn't just the frame, it had a picture inside and when she looked it was a lovely one of the girls together in the snow standing in their front garden. 'That was on a snow day when school was closed.'

'No wonder we look so happy.' Susanna chuckled.

'The frame and the picture have stood the test of time.' Addie smiled. 'So have we, I think.'

'Of course we have,' said Susanna.

They unearthed more of the relics their dad had kept at home or at work: the pen pot Addie had made out of half a washing up bottle before painting it bright yellow and sticking orange spots to it; the pottery Susanna had bought and painted for Father's Day one year, making a raw-clay coloured bowl into a striped accessory that looked like an old-fashioned humbug sweet.

'Didn't he use that to put crisps in?' Addie asked.

'Yes, I'd forgotten that. He'd fill it with salt and vinegar flavour on a treat night.'

'I don't remember him eating any himself.'

'I think they were more for us,' said Susanna softly.

'What's this?' Addie had pulled out a long piece of wire with a frog on the top.

Susanna gasped. 'That was Mum's.'

'Mum liked frogs?'

'She did.' Susanna chuckled. 'Dad didn't. I think it was her little joke, putting a pretend one in the flower bed. I don't remember the day he found it, but I do remember them talking about it, him admitting he'd thought it was real.'

'Poor Dad.'

'Keep it?' Susanna checked.

'Yes, keep.' She put it into the appropriate pile, but when she looked up again Susanna's face was pale. 'What is it? What have you found?'

Susanna sat down on her haunches, a delicate bracelet with tiny blue flowers in the palm of her hand. 'This was Mum's.'

'It's gorgeous.'

Susanna paused. 'Me and Dad argued about it.'

'Argued?'

'Oh, it was nothing, really.'

'No, come on – if you argued, it must have been something.'

'I just freaked out when I couldn't find it in Mum's things, that's all.' She found the little box it must have fallen from and put it inside before depositing it onto the keep pile. 'It's here now, that's what matters.'

Addie was convinced there was more to the story, but when Susanna didn't want to talk about something, there was no getting her to change her mind. She'd been the same discussing Alex and whatever was going on with him. She'd told Addie the bare minimum.

Susanna got back to raking through the rest of the box but didn't find much else worth keeping. She held up an old, empty washbag. 'I think this might have held Mum's make-up once upon a time.'

'You want to keep it?'

'No, it's all stained now.' She put it in the discard pile. 'She went far too soon.'

'They both did.' Addie gulped. 'I often wonder whether what Dad had is in our genes. Do you?'

'Pancreatic cancer?' Susanna always looked so together, but not in this moment. 'I worry about that sometimes. It's one of those things that's hard to detect early.' She stood up. 'I don't know about you, but I could use a break.' She brushed her hands together. If they were anything like Addie's, they were sticky with dust and old belongings, and held on to that musty smell that had developed on these old things over time.

'Me too,' said Addie. 'Tea?'

'Sounds good.'

'And a third oatmeal and raisin cookie?'

Susanna grinned. 'Now we're talking.'

As they both enjoyed yet another cookie, they decided that was quite enough sorting out for one day.

'I've got a bit of work to do,' said Susanna. 'I know it's boring, but it's better I keep up with it.'

'Go for it. I'll head out for a walk.'

With only eight days to go to the living funeral, her and Susanna were going to have to decide whether they were staying or not. But should they make the decision together? Or was this one of those times when Addie needed to do what was right for her? She hadn't always done that, and she'd had to live with her regrets.

Addie headed out and walked to the trail that led around the island to the point which gave a decent view. Without the rush of a commute and getting Isaac to and from childcare, the days here seemed to stretch endlessly. Or perhaps that was because she was out of her routine.

She stayed in her viewing spot for a while, absorbing what it felt like to be here once more, thinking about the day she left, contemplating how her life had turned out since she moved to London.

Ready to move on, she decided to do a loop. She took the steps down to the road with the harbour, walked all the way along and stood to watch another ferry coming in with holiday-makers and probably locals on board. She walked past the minibus waiting for passengers to cram themselves on board and save the effort of a walk up the hill. And then she walked up the hill just like they had the night they returned. Her legs were burning by the time she got to the top and made her way along Bay Street. London was relatively flat; the hills here were a reminder that not everywhere was.

She stopped walking when the Sweet Life Café came into

view. She was yet to go inside, and she knew Susanna hadn't either.

Addie and her sister had differing views when it came to their dad, and although they didn't discuss it, they had differing views when it came to their aunt, her café and this island.

Addie hadn't wanted to leave Oxford, but slowly she'd begun to feel a little more settled here despite her sister resisting this as being their home. She settled into the school and had some good friends, all of whom got the ferry together each day to the high school on Jersey. The first time Addie had made the trek she'd felt so grown up, so free. And being able to go to the beach without a chaperone was another inch of freedom she'd grabbed with both hands. She went with her friends to the pebbly beach on the island and the natural swimming spot, she tried fishing with her friends although she wasn't any good, and she gradually realised she could be happy here on Anchor Island.

While Susanna remembered Gayle being obsessed with the Sweet Life Café and working all hours, Addie remembered Gayle taking her shopping, taking days off here and there to spend time with her. Susanna remembered having to babysit her younger sister after school, but Addie remembered being at the café together and Gayle doing her utmost to see to her customers yet with one eye on Addie and a look of regret that she couldn't let Susanna go off with her friends when she had to go to work. Susanna remembered Aunt Gayle splitting her and Mateo up, a fact she'd never forgiven their aunt for, but Addie remembered Aunt Gayle talking to Susanna about school, pointing out the importance of not skipping classes and keeping up on homework to give herself a decent future. The future she had always wanted and never kept a secret.

What Addie most remembered, though, was baking. The day Susanna left for university, Addie and Gayle had seen the ferry off from the harbour. Addie had cried, Gayle had wiped away a tear and they'd both waved as the boat got further and further away. By that time Susanna was speaking to Gayle, but it was never a flowing conversation. Since she stopped seeing Mateo it seemed her sister was angry with the whole world. Addie would never tell Susanna, but when she left it had come with a little feeling of relief.

'Right, Addie, what shall we do?' Gayle had asked brightly as they left the harbour that day. 'Nancy says I can take as long as I need. I know this is tough for you.'

'I'm okay. She's going to be happy.'

Gayle gripped her hand firmly. 'Yes, I do believe she will be.' She cleared her throat. 'So come on, what's it to be? We could go for a walk around the island, or we could catch a ferry across to Guernsey or even Sark if you fancied it.'

'There is something I want to do, Aunt Gayle.'

'You name it.'

She smiled, shared her wish, and they spent the rest of the day in the Sweet Life Café, Addie in the kitchen helping out and waiting on tables when she was required, even mixing up some cake batter with Gayle. She got to sprinkle crumble mix on top of stewed apples, she rolled out pastry to make the top of a berry pie, she helped wash up and she served her first customer. And at the end of their day, she even had time for a big serving of lemon and elderflower drizzle pudding with a big blob of cream on the side.

Addie itched to go inside the Sweet Life Café now, and yet somehow her feet just wouldn't take her there some twenty years after she'd left it behind. Instead, her feet took her all the way home where she found Susanna getting dinner underway. This evening would be roast lamb, a proper family meal. Addie jumped right in to help and between them they prepared the vegetables, peeled potatoes and laid the table. And when Aunt Gayle came home, they ate together. And Gayle wasn't at all put out that Addie had baked the oatmeal and raisin cookies. She simply slotted the pie she'd brought home for pudding into the fridge and declared that tonight's second course would be cookies. If there were any left.

They'd had a laugh at her remark, the fact Susanna had now eaten four cookies, but conversation was still strained the way it had been since they'd arrived. Nobody wanted to address the past nor look at the future – it was as though they were all too afraid at what they might say or hear.

Eventually Gayle said she'd had a busy day and with her looking undoubtedly tired, Addie and Susanna insisted they would wash up and Gayle went off to bed.

Perhaps tonight had been another small step in the right direction for them all.

At least, that was what she hoped.

17

GAYLE

At the Sweet Life Café the next morning, Gayle lifted a slice of lemon meringue pie from the tin and set it on a plate next to the portion she'd already prepared. She took the plates over to the couple ensconced at the booth the girls had sat in so frequently. They looked so in love. It reminded her of how she'd once been with Jeffrey in her parents' café; it also brought back memories of Susanna and Mateo when they'd first started dating. After she'd interfered with their relationship and she and Susanna had fallen out spectacularly, Gayle had had visions of Susanna doing the opposite of knuckling down and passing her exams just to spite her. But she hadn't. And for that Gayle was glad. The only thing she regretted was that they'd never been able to work through their problems.

Last night's dinner of roast lamb had been wonderful and every time they sat together to eat it felt like a tiny step in the right direction. She hadn't been able to eat that much of it, unfortunately – her appetite hadn't allowed her to. She'd had a few pieces of the juicy meat, but struggled to have any of the caramelised carrots or the roast potatoes, perfectly golden and smelling like true home cooking – the sort of cooking that felt like she finally had family wrapped all around her. She'd shuffled her food around her plate, tried to squish down some of the food so it looked like she'd eaten more than she had, and a couple of times when her nieces were distracted, she'd hidden small bits in tissue that she pushed deep into the pockets of her multi-coloured cardigan and discarded later. The cookies had been good, though, and hearing that Addie had baked in her kitchen? Well, that had spread a warm feeling right through her.

Conversation had been lacking last night, as usual – much like her appetite. But she'd told herself at least they weren't at each other's throats, because that would be worse. She'd longed to ask the girls whether they were staying for the living funeral. She really wanted them to, Susanna knew that, but with just seven days to go, she was still none the wiser.

'Let me know if you need anything else,' Gayle told the couple as she left them to enjoy the pie.

The couple seemed besotted with each other, just like Mateo and Susanna had been.

Soon after her niece had started seeing Mateo, he'd come into the café while Susanna was minding Addie, and Gayle had overheard their conversation while she offered to take a break and sit with Addie for a bit. Addie was struggling with her homework, and Gayle didn't mind doing her best to help to give Susanna some time with Mateo.

Susanna and Mateo moved over to the next table and began to talk about seasickness. She wasn't even aware Susanna had an issue with boats.

'How do you handle going to school by boat when you get seasick?' Mateo had asked her.

'The other day is the first time it's ever happened. I was trying to get my homework done and then when I looked up the boat was rocking more than usual and my stomach rolled.'

'Er... maybe stop doing that on the boat,' he suggested. 'When you're on board, try to be outside in the fresh air, and keep your gaze on the horizon. That'll help.'

'Don't you ever feel sick?' Susanna had asked.

'I wouldn't be in the right business if I did.'

Hearing about his job when Susanna asked something about boats was a jolt that reminded Gayle of how much older this boy – man! – was than her niece. He was nice enough, but this wasn't right. Susanna needed to focus on her studies right now. It was such an important time.

A couple of months later, Gayle got a call from the school about Susanna's effort and attainment as well as her attendance, and that was when Gayle had felt a pressure to step up, do what she suspected Harry would've done, do it because she had her niece's best interests at heart.

She'd hated every minute of the day she'd gone down to see Mateo and had a talk with him. But she'd felt trapped, like she had no other choice.

But the way she felt was nothing compared to how she felt later when Susanna came home and revealed she'd overheard the whole thing.

'Are you happy now?' her niece had roared at her after coming into the house and slamming the front door. 'He's dumped me. He's going to another island to work! I hate you, you hear me, I hate you!'

And she'd left Gayle in her wake, the only sounds Gayle's thudding heart and the stomping of feet going up the stairs, followed by the slam of a bedroom door.

Gayle had tried to go in and talk to Susanna later that evening.

'I want you to focus on school,' she'd said to Susanna. Face down on her bed, her niece refused to acknowledge her presence. 'Once your exams are finished, then—'

Susanna turned over, eyes red from crying, puffiness beneath showing just how upset she was. 'Then what? Mateo is leaving! You've ruined *everything*!'

'I'm only thinking of you.'

Susanna harrumphed. 'Yeah, well now I really can't wait to leave this shitty island.'

'I'm sorry you feel that way.' She stood to go, but with her hand resting on the door handle she turned to Susanna. 'I know I've made mistakes, and I keep making them, but Harry trusted me to look after you and Addie. I think he'd have similar rules to me, especially when it comes to boys, schoolwork and curfew.'

But Susanna said nothing else and Gayle left.

Whether that had been the right thing to do that day, she had no idea. There was no guidebook when it came to parenting, never mind being a mother figure to two nieces who'd lost so much.

Gayle finished wiping down the table next to the couple with the pie.

'We need more custard,' Nancy told her as she passed by with a stack of dishes and cutlery in her hands.

'I'll be right on it,' said Gayle.

But as she turned, her gaze went out of the window. Her heart leapt for a moment at the sight of two young women on the other side of the road, one with blonde hair, the other dark hair. For a minute she'd thought it was Addie and Susanna.

Her spirits sank when she realised it wasn't.

Were they ever going to come into the café?

If they couldn't do it now, was there even any chance they would hang around for the living funeral? And if not, when should she tell them the other thing she'd been keeping to herself?

Life was complicated. Life was hard.

So she went into the kitchen and did what she did best: she pulled out ingredients, made another batch of her signature custard, and then baked another enormous apple crumble.

18

SUSANNA

When Addie came downstairs, she took one look at Susanna with her laptop on the kitchen table and frowned. 'You work too hard.'

'I'm not working... at least, not any more.' Not like last night, when she'd used the work excuse to escape the dinner table. Aunt Gayle had barely touched the stew Addie had made for their evening meal and when she'd started talking about the living funeral, the bunting, the food, and the arrangements, Susanna had wanted to avoid being asked the direct question of whether she was going, and even more so, she didn't want to hear that Addie had decided she definitely was.

Now, with six days to go, they were going to have to make a decision about the event sooner rather than later.

Susanna had also wanted to escape the dinner table last night because her head was all over the place thinking about Mateo and their encounter after all these years. It had been on her mind ever since she'd fallen into his arms at the marina. Last night, she'd dreamt about him and when she woke, she'd felt terribly guilty, as if she'd cheated on Alex. In the dream, Mateo had kissed her just like the first time. It was almost as if last night in her dream she'd been able to feel exactly the way she had back then as their bodies had drawn closer, arms around one another, and they'd had a kiss so tender she'd thought she might pass out.

'What are you up to if it isn't work?' Addie pulled the box of bran flakes from the cupboard and tucked it under her arm, before reaching for a bowl and then a spoon from the drawer. She brought everything over to the table.

'I'm trying to find this cottage on Airbnb,' Susanna explained. 'I'm just being nosy and wondering how it's being advertised.'

'And...?' Bran flakes tumbled into her bowl before she added milk from the fridge.

'And I'm not having much luck. No matter what search parameters I put in, I still can't find it.' Addie didn't seem all that interested, so she closed down her laptop.

'Where's Aunt Gayle? Is she at work?' Milk dribbled from Addie's spoon and splashed a few drops onto the table.

'I assume so. Did she mention the living funeral again last night after I left the table?'

'She told me about the colour scheme and the guest list and how she's drawn up a schedule to ensure it all goes smoothly.'

'So she didn't ask us whether we are going?'

Addie shook her head. 'I think she's probably too scared to.'

'I doubt that.'

Addie began to smile. 'You know, you and she are quite alike.'

'Really?'

'You're both determined, a little bit on the bossy side, and you're both headstrong too, just like Dad must have been with his café business until he lost it.'

Susanna sighed. 'Maybe he didn't fight hard enough to keep it.'

Addie bristled. 'I don't remember it, obviously, but by the sounds of it he did everything he could.'

'Sorry, I'm just ratty. I need to get outside for a bit.'

Clearly Addie hadn't finished. 'Dad told me he had to let the café go because he couldn't afford to run it. We talked about it. I remember even though I was really young – it stuck in my head how sad he seemed. You never gave him the benefit of the doubt.'

'He was our dad and I loved him, Addie. We both did.' She changed the topic. 'So, are we going?'

'Going where?'

'To the living funeral.'

Addie put down her spoon. 'I think we should. And I think I want to.' She hesitated. 'How about you?'

If Addie wanted to go, she didn't want to let her sister down. 'I still can't quite get my head around the idea, but I'll try.'

They left it at that, and Susanna headed out, closing the door to the cottage behind her.

As she walked, she thought about the different way she and her sister viewed the island and their time here. She thought about their difference of opinion when it came to their dad too.

Over the years she'd been tempted to tell Addie the truth about their dad more than once, but she'd always held back so she didn't cause her younger sister any more pain. And Harry hadn't been a terrible dad. Far from it – he just wasn't perfect. Nobody was. Least of all her with her marriage possibly in trouble and her thoughts about another man that had risen to the surface ever since she came back here.

She made her way along the coastal path and as she caught sight of the stunning view her phone pinged, bringing her back to reality and away from the refreshing autumn breeze.

It was Alex, returning her text from this morning. By the time he'd answered her call last night she was already tucked up in bed, so he'd sent her a text rather than phoning and in the message, he'd apologised for being so busy.

She texted him back, said she'd call tomorrow as he had mentioned he was heading into the practice early this morning. She wondered, was it another excuse? Was he putting off talking to her? She wished he would just tell her what was going on, she wished they'd have a massive row, and the truth would come out. At least then she'd know what she was dealing with.

She looked out across the sea, but it wasn't long before her feet took her down the steps all the way to the street, where she turned left and made her way towards the marina and the harbour beyond. She knew there was a high chance of seeing Mateo, and it took only moments to spot him. She hoped it wouldn't look like she'd gone down there on purpose, but they had a history and after the way things had ended she wanted to at least make peace. That way, if they were staying for the living funeral, there would be no awkwardness, nothing left unsaid.

Mateo jumped down from the edge of a boat, turned back to rest a tool on its body, and came over. His once shaggy mop of dirty blond hair was mostly grey now, and his skin showed more weathered creases from the harsh sunlight he was so often under out on the water.

'It's good to see you again,' he said, squinting against the sun until he pulled his sunglasses down over his eyes. His smile hadn't changed one bit.

'You too.' But she wished she couldn't remember how good it had felt to be in his arms, she wished he'd lost any appeal, that he'd stacked on the weight or something – anything to make him completely unattractive. But his physical fitness and muscular forearms – as well as the way he looked at her like she was the only person who mattered – were just as alluring as they'd always been.

'Where are you off to?' He pulled out a rag from his back pocket and wiped some grease from his fingers.

'I'm having a wander, that's all. We've been sorting out boxes from the attic, and it's a big job.'

'Always is. Attics are where you lob everything you don't know what to do with.'

She tugged her hair behind both ears, but it didn't stay put – the wind had other ideas and blew it right back again. 'We're really going through our dad's stuff rather than our own old memories.'

'Your dad's stuff?'

'I know, it's been up there a while.'

His gaze flitted over to a colleague and he held up one hand, fingers spread out to indicate he'd be five minutes. 'I thought you and your sister would've had everything sent to the mainland a long time ago.'

'That's probably what we should've done. I expected Gayle to send them, to be honest, have a clear out.' When he hesitated, she asked, 'What was that look for?'

'There was no look.'

She smiled. 'There was definitely a look.'

'She missed you, you know.'

'I thought she'd be glad to get her freedom back.'

'If you really believed that I don't think you'd be here in the first place.'

His words stung because he was right. And it was a reminder that this had never been black and white. It had never been all Gayle's fault, even though as a teenager that was exactly how she'd seen it. All that time she'd blamed Gayle for everything, and it was only after she left that she realised some of it had been her fault.

'Tell me something,' he said.

'Okay.'

'Does it feel good to be back here?'

She took her time answering, but with a small smile that came naturally she said, 'It feels better than I thought it would.'

He leaned against the bow of the boat. 'You always did appreciate the hidden parts of the island.'

It was a long time since anyone had made her blush, but she felt her cheeks colour now. Coyly, she looked down at her feet and went back to what he'd said about their aunt. 'Did Gayle actually tell you that she missed us?'

'Not in those exact words, but she'd drop your names into conversation. Often. She'd share things. She told me you were training as a solicitor, she told me Addie had graduated, when Addie had a kid, when you got married.' The word *married* hovered in the air between them. 'Sometimes I'd go up to the Sweet Life Café and she'd be standing on the balcony, looking into the distance. I always wondered whether she was thinking about you both.'

They carried on chatting about the island, what had changed and what was exactly the same, including the owners of the marina and his job, as well as some of the shops on Bay Street. All the while they talked, Alex kept popping into her mind. He knew all about Mateo. Not long after she and Alex met, conversation had turned to first loves. She'd told Alex how she and Mateo had been inseparable for a while, how the only reason they split up was because her aunt had interfered. As she and Alex became more serious, he'd brought Mateo up once more and asked if she thought they'd still be together had she stayed on the island. Her only answer had been that she'd left that world behind and she'd fallen head over heels with somebody else. Him.

Mateo waved over to a guy on the deck of a big white boat

that looked more expensive than some houses. 'Duty calls,' he said. 'I should get on.'

'Well, it was good to see you again,' she said as they walked back down the path.

'Really good to see you too. You haven't changed.'

She laughed. 'I'm totally different.'

'Not really, not deep down.' He said it as if he could see all the layers of her, as if all the years that had gone by had fallen away altogether.

'I'll see you around,' she said.

But he made her turn back when he called out, 'So are you staying? For the living funeral?'

'Maybe.' She left it at that.

And as she turned and walked away and up the hill towards Bay Street, her smile faded. She felt terrible. She was married, and here she was enjoying another man's company and finding herself wanting more of it. She wondered whether her agreement to stay for the living funeral was for her sister, for Gayle, or was it a desire to see more of Mateo that she hadn't even admitted to herself? It took the edge off her confusion when she saw Addie at the end of Evergreen Close.

Addie held up a hand to wave as she crossed over to meet her sister. 'Walk some more with me?'

'I can do that,' said Susanna. The good thing with Addie was that if you ever had words, she let it go pretty quickly and didn't hold grudges. Susanna was always relieved for that.

They made their way to the coastal path and stopped to take in the view and the first vantage point that Susanna had already enjoyed once today.

'I'm really getting my steps up,' said Susanna. 'My body feels better than when I spend a day at my desk.'

'Mine too. And the fresh air helps. I can see why Gayle moved here.' She waited a beat. 'You know, I thought I remembered how pretty this island was, but being here is something else.'

Susanna stood next to her. She couldn't disagree. 'We can just about make out France. Look.' She pointed.

'I remember when we first realised we could see it. We were fascinated. We never did go over there like we said we would.'

'I suppose life happened.'

'Life, work, the daily treadmill.'

Treadmill wasn't the word she'd used exactly. 'Have you thought any more about buying a place?' she ventured. It was a sensitive topic ever since she'd offered to lend Addie some money to help her get on the property ladder, and Addie had flatly refused.

'I think about it all the time. And I've got a good amount saved for a deposit.'

'That's good. Although I feel like there's a "but" coming.'

'But... I live in London, and you don't get much for your money. My job is there but I don't know that I want to buy a tiny flat, even if I could.'

'You'll work something out.'

Addie smiled and Susanna knew she appreciated her big sister not trying to leap in and save the day. She'd done that for so long that even now, with Addie in her late thirties, Susanna found it hard to stop.

They didn't walk too much further before they conceded that it was time to get back to the boxes.

They'd just turned onto the street from the end of the track when Addie collided with thick strings across her path. She waved her arms as if she was stuck in a giant cobweb.

'Sorry!' came a male voice as Susanna helped Addie disentangle herself.

The man came to help too, and he was joined by a little boy.

'No harm done.' Addie smiled as she was set free and the little boy tried to rescue the rest of his kite from a nearby bush.

The man told them – or rather Addie, because she was the only one he seemed to have eyes for right now – 'I told him to wait until we're in a bigger space, but...'

'No worries. I have a son of my own and telling him to wait is like asking for the impossible.'

The man smiled and seemed to remember his manners. He held out a hand first to Addie, then to Susanna. 'I'm Samuel, by the way, and this is my son, Billy.'

'Addie,' her sister replied.

'I'm Susanna. Good to meet you.' He looked in his late thirties, maybe early forties, and she noted he wasn't wearing a wedding band.

'Dad... come on!' Billy cried, his kite gathered up now.

'I'd better go. But good to meet you both. I'll see you around.'

'Sure,' said Addie.

Only when he was out of sight and they began to walk again did Addie notice Susanna's grin. 'What?' she asked.

'You tell me.'

'I don't know what you're talking about.'

'Addie, whoever that guy is, I'd say he's *very* interested in you.'

'Oh, come on, we met for a split second.' She hooked her arm back through her sister's.

'That's all it takes.'

'Yes, well, the only man I need in my life right now is Isaac.'

'If you say so.' And she only let it go because Addie had steered her past the mouth of Evergreen Close. 'Where are you taking me? I thought we'd finished our walk.'

Addie stopped when they were almost at the Sweet Life Café.

'I don't want us going inside for the first time on the day of the living funeral in six days. We need to do it now.'

Her heart thudded. 'Wait a minute. I thought I was the decisive one,' she said to her sister.

'I'm all grown up now, and maybe sometimes I have to be the one to make decisions.'

She couldn't argue with that.

A reel played over and over in her mind of the times she'd come here as a teenager, and then the time she'd come here the day she got back to the island earlier than expected. She'd wanted to surprise her little sister, but Addie wasn't at the cottage and so she'd come to the café. She'd thought Addie would be inside at one of the booth tables doing schoolwork or having something to eat, desperately waiting to see her sister, but when Susanna went inside and up to the counter she'd seen through to the kitchen. There, next to Aunt Gayle, had been Addie with an apron on and the biggest smile on her face. Laughter ricocheted off the walls from Gayle and Addie over and over again, torturing Susanna that their world might well be different from hers and she'd felt like she was losing Addie bit by bit. She'd slunk back out and gone down to the harbour again, where she'd hung around for a couple of hours until she walked back up to the cottage. And when she'd asked Addie what she'd been up to that day, Addie had told her she'd been busy with school and homework and hadn't uttered a word about Gayle or baking puddings with their aunt.

They were about to go inside when Susanna stopped. 'Isn't that Louisa?' They watched the young woman putting something into the rear of the bright pink van used for deliveries, with the café's logo emblazoned on the side panels. 'So she's on holiday but has a job working here?'

'I've no idea,' said Susanna. They were right outside the front door and her feet suddenly wouldn't move.

'Come on,' Addie urged.

'I don't know if I can.'

Addie shook her head. 'You can, and you will.'

19

ADDIE

'You've definitely taken on the role as the bossiest,' said Susanna, as Addie slipped her arm into her sister's to lead her inside the Sweet Life Café. With her other arm, she opened the door.

The familiarity hit the second they stepped onto the classic black and white tiles that she remembered so well. The same turquoise upholstery and chrome fixtures and fittings spiralled her back in time, as did the booths she'd sat in more times than she could remember, the menu board behind the counter with that day's specials, and the sweet aroma.

'Well I never, if it isn't the Rafferty girls,' came a voice.

Addie turned and felt an overwhelming emotion when she saw Nancy. She hadn't thought about the woman in years, but right now it felt like her past was reaching out with both hands.

Nancy hugged them both. 'It's good to see you back on the island.'

Addie heard Susanna say, 'It's good to be here.' The comment earned her a sideways glance.

Nancy hadn't changed much at all, apart from shorter hair in a bob level with her chin, grey rather than black. She was still confident and just as bubbly as she'd always been.

Nancy lowered her voice. 'I know Gayle got you here on false pretences, but she really was quite desperate.'

'We're working things through,' said Addie diplomatically. It was the best explanation she could give to the woman who was likely the closest thing to family Gayle had had for years.

Nancy reached out and squeezed her arm. 'I'm glad, for all of you.'

'Is she here?' Susanna asked.

'No, she nipped home for a break.'

'We must have just missed her,' said Addie.

'She'll be glad you came in. And you'll stay for the party?'

'You mean living funeral,' Susanna corrected.

Nancy smiled. 'That is what she's planned, but I like the word party instead. Whatever it's called, I'm glad you're here for it.' Nancy pushed her pencil into the wire loops of her small notepad.

'I see you've still got the cute notepads for taking our orders,' said Addie with a grin.

'You should've heard your aunt Gayle when a customer suggested we start using those QR things and let people order at the table.'

Susanna began to laugh. 'I bet she was horrified.'

'That's an understatement!' She waved the little notepad. 'Personally, I love the old-fashioned method.'

'Me too.' Addie told her. 'So, the living funeral…'

'Time and place all on the invite,' said Nancy, 'but we could always use some extra help setting up on the day, if you're amenable to that.'

'We can come early to help,' Addie agreed, earning a slight nod from Susanna.

'I assume you're closing the café for customers,' said Susanna.

'We will, but to be honest a lot of the customers are guests. We'll shift all the moveable tables to the middle of the room in a long line, and move chairs to the edges for those who want to sit down. Then the tables will hold the puddings. And there are a lot of them. Gayle wants everyone's tastes catered for. She wants to see everyone tuck into the food and mingle, chat and have a really good time.' Her eyes danced as she added, 'Now, what's it to be?'

'Excuse me?' Addie asked.

'Puddings, of course!'

'We'd better look at a menu,' said Susanna, reaching for one.

Addie looked at her menu, and the third item down caught her eye, the past coming at her in a rush. She couldn't believe after all these years the baked cheesecake with fresh raspberries was still listed for customers to enjoy.

After Susanna left for the mainland and it had just been Aunt Gayle and Addie, they'd often talk recipes back at the cottage or when Addie was here in the café. For a while, Addie had been desperate to make a baked cheesecake. She wasn't sure why, it was just that baked cheesecake didn't feature on the menu and she had a real hankering to try a recipe out. And so, one day, dressed in her little apron and in the kitchen at the café, Addie had given it a go. She'd made a perfectly buttery crumbly biscuit base, she'd topped it with her cheesecake mixture and baked it in one of the professional ovens. As she sat on a stool beside the oven, making sure nothing went wrong, she'd daydreamed that this place was where she worked, with Aunt Gayle, that she would walk to work every morning and when inspiration struck, she'd make something new altogether. She'd topped the baked cheesecake with fresh raspberries and nervous as anything, had taken it out to one of the booths and told Nancy and Gayle to sample it. But all the while she'd been serving customers, she'd had one eye on her aunt and her friend, watching their reactions, giddy when they both put their thumbs up and Gayle called over, 'It's on the menu!'

'The special today is the butterscotch brownie,' Nancy informed them both now, pointing up to the board.

Addie closed the menu, her emotions running high. 'I'll take one of those,' she said.

Susanna smiled. 'And I'll have the same.'

They took a seat in the familiar booth they'd sat in as girls, Addie keeping her memory to herself, and when she noticed Susanna frowning, she followed her sister's gaze.

'There's Louisa again,' said Susanna.

'Aunt Gayle's Airbnb-er?' She looked outside to see the young woman with the crazy blonde curls climbing into the driver's seat of the café's pink delivery van.

'It's a little odd, don't you think? Visiting an island on your own, staying at an Airbnb and grabbing a job while you're at it.'

Addie shrugged. 'I wonder how many of Gayle's former guests have done the same. I suppose it's still relatively busy here, even though summer is behind us.'

Their desserts arrived in no time and didn't disappoint. They were heavenly.

Addie scooped up another piece of the butterscotch brownie, still warm, with the vanilla ice-cream on the side starting to melt enough that it was even creamier with the pudding.

'I can't disagree with you there.' Susanna was close to finishing hers.

'Are you going for seconds?'

'What? No way. This is good, but it's enough. Any more and I'll risk being hyper with too much sugar.'

'Isaac would love this. He has a sweet tooth like me.'

'I know. He chose treacle sponge at the supermarket when I took you both there the last time you visited.'

'Well, you did tell him to choose whatever he liked.' Addie grinned.

Susanna sat up a little straighter as she put her spoon down and nodded towards the doorway. 'Aunt Gayle's back.'

Addie paused, and when Gayle's gaze met hers, waved over at their aunt, who looked as shocked as expected to see her nieces inside her café after all these years. She pointed to the kitchen, which presumably meant she was going to take off her cardigan and put her bag away. Or more than likely to catch a breath at the enormity of the moment.

'Do you think she's slowing down?' Addie asked after Susanna picked up her spoon and ate the last mouthful of her pudding.

'Because she went home for a break?' Susanna put down the spoon into the empty bowl. 'Maybe.'

Their aunt was in her seventies, so perhaps she was starting to taper off with work. Addie had always thought she'd be well and truly retired come her sixties never mind seventies, although maybe she wouldn't have much choice in the matter as a single parent who didn't own her own home yet.

'What do you think will really happen at the living funeral?' Susanna asked. 'Do you think it'll be exactly as Nancy said, just a gathering, a party, with food and laughter and chatter?'

'I'm not sure. Hey, I wonder if there will be a speech, or speeches, I mean, in lieu of any eulogy?'

Susanna pulled a face. 'Hadn't thought of that. Maybe.'

'I guess we'll find out soon enough.'

Gayle eventually emerged back into the dining area, and as she came their way she tied on a half apron around her waist. 'I'm glad you came in. It's good to see you both.' She sounded formal, most likely rehearsing the best greeting for them both. They were used to each other in the cottage, although far from relaxed, but in here it felt totally different.

'Nancy said you'd gone home,' said Addie. 'We must've just missed you.'

'I just took a little break, did a few bits at the cottage.' But she didn't meet either of their gazes. 'Nancy tells me you had the butterscotch brownies. What's the verdict?'

Addie gushed, 'Amazing!'

'Really good,' said Susanna.

'It's Nancy's recipe,' Gayle added cheerfully. 'She's my right-hand man. Or woman, rather.' She lifted up their empty bowls. 'I'll take these to the kitchen.'

They let the significant moment settle and talked between themselves, and when Gayle came back into the main area once more the girls went up to the counter. 'We're heading back to carry on with sorting through Dad's boxes,' Susanna told her.

'Are there still quite a few to go through?' Gayle asked.

'There are,' said Susanna. 'Did you really not go through any of it in all these years? I'm not complaining, just wondering.'

'I didn't feel it was my place.' Gayle pushed fresh napkins into an aluminium dispenser. 'I'm glad you're here to do it. It's what Harry would've wanted.'

'We've run out of room in the bin and the recycling bin,' said Addie with a grimace. 'That's why we've slowed down. Well, partly because of that, partly because it's hard work.'

Gayle smiled. 'Just pile what won't go in the bin at the far end of the utility room. I'll get rid of it gradually if needs be.'

'Are you sure?' Susanna asked. 'You don't want us to try to get it collected or anything?'

'No need. I don't mind.' Gayle locked eyes with Susanna in a way they hadn't really done before. Was it a look that suggested peace, forgiveness?

Or was Addie, as usual, trying to read too much into it?

Susanna glanced outside to where the pink van was parked, although there was no sign of Louisa. 'Is your holidaymaker working here?' she asked Gayle.

Gayle faltered but not for long. 'It worked out well. We needed the help and she was happy to earn some extra cash on her holidays.' She set the napkin dispenser back in its place at the end of the counter before offering them a quick smile. 'I'd better start pulling my weight for the afternoon.' And she disappeared into the kitchen again. Escaping.

Susanna's smile was replaced with a frown as she and Addie left the café. 'I think she's hiding something.'

'Like what? She's already tricked us once, not sure what else she could possibly be keeping from us.'

'I've just got a feeling, that's all. I really don't want any more surprises.'

'I'm pretty sure no surprise from now on could be as big as finding out she's not actually dead.' When they reached the end of the path that led to the street, she glanced back at the Sweet Life Café and the beautiful balcony. The venue really had stood the test of time – it was just as she remembered, and she'd never forgotten the joy of baking with their aunt until it seemed that Gayle had her own life and it was time for Addie to get on with hers.

When her phone rang, she took it from her pocket and smiled to see it was Maurie, although the first thing she asked was, 'Is everything okay?' when she saw Maurie's face.

'Of course.' And she was soon pushed off screen by a beaming Isaac.

'Hi, Mummy!' His infectious smile had always had the power to transform her in an instant if she needed a pick-me-up.

When Susanna leaned so that she was on camera, Isaac's smile widened. 'Auntie Susie!' He was the only one ever allowed to call her Susie. He'd called her that from when he was tiny and the habit stuck.

'Hello, you. How's my favourite nephew?'

He rolled his eyes. 'I'm your *only* nephew.'

'Wait a minute,' said Addie, registering the fact he wasn't at school, 'What's going on? You're not at school. Are you sick?'

'My tooth was hurting,' he said, putting a hand to his mouth.

'Your tooth?'

Maurie leaned into the picture. 'He was complaining of toothache this morning so I took him to the dentist. I did send you a text.' She disappeared briefly but was soon back on screen holding her device. 'Ah, it didn't send. Honestly, I am useless. I was rushing, I should've checked.'

'Don't apologise, Maurie, please.' She went above and beyond for her grandson, and Addie had zero complaints.

'I let the school know,' said Maurie.

'Is he okay?'

'Totally fine. One of his adult teeth is starting to push through and it's hurting a bit, that's all. It was a little inflamed, so I thought better to get it checked in case it was infected, and now he's had a couple of painkillers he seems settled. Oh, and I bought some Bonjela—'

'It's yummy!' Isaac piped up. 'It tastes nice. Can we get some?'

'It's not for eating,' Susanna told him, 'although from memory it does taste pretty good.'

'Not helping,' Addie whispered to her sister. Then to Maurie she said, 'The dentist saw you quickly.' Maurie and Jarrett had all of Isaac's particulars because they looked after him so often, but they'd never had to take him to a dentist or a doctor until now.

'I took him to our dentist instead.'

Oh no – that meant it was a private appointment. 'You didn't have to do that.'

'To be honest, it was easier.'

'How much do I owe you?' She dreaded to think of how much it cost.

'He's our grandson, so we're happy to cover it. I could've called your regular one, but it was my choice not to because it made things easier. You forget about the money, love.'

Jarrett's voice from the background called out, 'Listen to her, she's always right.'

'Well, thank you.'

Isaac was soon hogging the whole screen again and Susanna joined the conversation.

'Are you at the beach?' Isaac wanted to know.

'Not right now,' said Susanna. 'But we've just had pudding.'

His eyes widened. 'At the Sweet Life Café?'

'Yes, at the Sweet Life Café,' said Addie.

Susanna told him all about the butterscotch brownie, how the menu had so many choices they could probably have something different every day for a fortnight at least.

'Mummy, I *have* to come to the island. *Pleeeeease...*'

Addie wished she could agree just like that. 'We'll see.'

'Jaimie at school says *we'll see* is what parents say when they have no intention of doing something.'

She almost laughed. Since when did Isaac – or his little friend, Jaimie, for that matter – use the word *intention*?

'Well, you can tell Jaimie that this mummy *does* mean it. You can visit one day.' She exchanged a look with Susanna, who actually didn't seem as against the idea as she might once have been.

'And I can try a pudding?' he rambled on. 'And go to the beach, and run all the way around the island?'

'Hold on, squirt, one thing at a time.'

Isaac started talking about the Lego boat he'd built with his grandad and how he'd been allowed to use it in the bath and it hadn't fallen apart, and when she hung up Addie felt a yearning so vast for her son that she thought she might cry.

'He's fine,' Susanna assured her. 'He's having a great time. Talking of a great time…'

'What, you're going to tell me that's what you're having?'

'Not exactly. But look, we're almost done with the sorting, and we still have six days to go until the event itself. I have some work but not much. I'm walking a lot and so are you, but why don't we do something else?'

'Such as?'

'Why don't we try to have a bit of time for ourselves? I haven't had a holiday in ages, I know you haven't, and we don't get much time together, just the two of us.'

'I miss it.'

'Me too. So what do you think?'

Addie beamed. 'Actually, I think it's the best idea I've heard in ages.'

And when they let themselves into the cottage it was the first time that Addie had really felt like most of the weight they'd been burdened down with for years had been lifted.

20

GAYLE

When Gayle stepped through the front door to her cottage she was devastated to see a suitcase in the hallway.

They were going? They really didn't want to stay, even after they'd come into the café?

Perhaps that had been their goodbye.

It was only when Addie came out of the kitchen and put her arms around her that she realised she'd stumbled. Had she been about to faint?

'Come and sit down,' Addie urged. 'Susanna! Susanna!'

Footsteps descended the stairs, and her eldest niece came into the kitchen, her face etched with concern. In that moment Gayle realised she meant something to her eldest niece and she felt her heart soar. Except then her spirits depleted. Even if she meant something to Susanna and to Addie, they were still leaving.

'I'm fine,' said Gayle. 'Stop fussing.'

'Drink this.' Susanna handed her a glass of water. 'And I'll put the kettle on, make you a sweet tea.'

'I don't want tea. I just want to go to bed.' She couldn't hear about them leaving, she couldn't watch it happen. Not again.

The day Susanna had packed her things and they'd all gone to the harbour to see her off for a new life with university on the mainland had felt like it was underlining her failure. She'd lost one of them. And then the day Addie left after all those months of happiness before Gayle remembered her promise and never let Addie follow her baking dreams, at least not alongside her, had almost broken her. Nancy had had to look after the café for an entire week. Gayle had spent most of it with flu-like symptoms, Nancy had called a doctor, and he'd concluded it was most likely stress.

'We're having salmon for dinner, I was about to start making it,' said Addie. 'Why don't you rest for a bit then you'll be able to eat some.'

Gayle didn't say a word. She barely glanced at the suitcase in the hallway as she made her way past, climbed into bed and pulled the duvet so high she was buried beneath it.

She hadn't fallen asleep – she'd barely dozed – when a knock came at her door.

'Dinner's ready.' Addie poked her head around the frame.

'Give me a couple of minutes.'

'Are you feeling better?'

'I am, thank you.'

She got out of bed after Addie left the room. It was time to face it. The girls were leaving. They'd never really wanted to be here in the first place.

'Susanna and I have news,' said Addie the moment Gayle went into the kitchen.

She sat at the table, a plate of salmon, vegetables and scalloped potatoes in front of her. She wasn't sure how she was going to stomach any of it.

She braced herself.

'We're going to Guernsey tomorrow, then on to Sark,' said Susanna, sprinkling a little bit of salt across her own dinner. 'Addie and I decided that as we're almost done with Dad's boxes and the weather is still so nice, and we don't get much time together these days, that we would make it into a bit of a holiday.'

If someone had waved a feather at her head, Gayle was sure it would've knocked her down.

'Is that all right, Aunt Gayle?' Addie asked. 'I mean, we'll be back the day before your event.'

'Yes, it's fine.' Still in shock, she barely knew what to say. But she appreciated Addie's use of the word 'event'. The term living funeral, or rather the second word of the phrase, had begun to haunt her, never more so than when she'd felt faint at the sight of the suitcase.

Gayle managed a few mouthfuls of food. The girls had gone to a lot of effort to make her a meal, and she could summon some appetite now she knew they weren't running away.

'We thought we might do some shopping on Guernsey,' Addie went on. 'Although that's more Susanna than me.'

'We're doing other things too,' Susanna put in. 'Addie wants to spend more time near the water, so I've promised we can try out paddleboarding or snorkelling or whatever she likes. Within reason.'

'I've got some savings,' said Addie. 'They're put away for a house deposit eventually but I'm nowhere close to buying anywhere, so...' She shrugged, just about turned both palms upwards, knife in one, fork in the other. 'I'm making the most of the time, put it that way.'

'Good for you.' It was almost as if they were all on the same wavelength, making the most of their lives, doing things before it was too late.

They chatted more over dinner about what the girls planned to do. It was the most animated conversation that had happened under her roof in a long time.

Gayle managed to eat most of her dinner too, which was a first. But she found fish light and whoever dished up must have been sensitive to the fact she didn't eat much and had given her a smaller portion.

'I'm afraid I didn't bring back a pudding this evening,' said Gayle and once again, just like every other night, the girls insisted they wash up.

'I can whip up something,' said Addie. 'As long as you don't mind me raiding your pantry.'

Gayle wanted nothing more. 'Go ahead.' Susanna looked just as happy about it, which meant more than her eldest niece would ever know.

Over the next hour, Gayle and Susanna watched Addie bake a type of mille-feuille. Gayle longed to leap up and help but she was afraid she might feel dizzy or light-headed and really, watching her niece was a joy in itself. She had skill, that was for sure – she made puff pastry from scratch and took it out of the oven when it was lovely and golden, all ready to make the French-style dessert with layers of pastry and cream. She used the electric beaters to get the cream as thick as it needed to be before she added the custard, she prepared the strawberries, blueberries and raspberries to decorate the dessert. She did all of it without so much as a glance at a recipe and it made Gayle both happy and devastated at the same time. Her niece had held the same passion as her, but she'd followed a different path when she could've stuck to what she loved.

After they finished their dessert and went off to bed, Gayle felt the happiest she had in a long time. It felt like her family was back together and she only hoped that what she still had to tell the girls wouldn't ruin what they had only just managed to find.

* * *

While the girls were away for four days Gayle had split her time between the café and the cottage, where she rested. She wanted to embrace the girls' return and then her living funeral. It was as if both things were a last hurrah, but right now, she didn't care. She was excited.

This morning Louisa had picked fresh blue asters for the vase in Susanna's room and pink asters for the vase in Addie's. She'd been up early, ready to go to the café and put in way more hours than they'd agreed on account of Gayle's increased absence, but she didn't seem to mind. And Gayle would be there later on, just as soon as she'd caught up with her nieces.

Gayle put the vases in their rightful places upstairs and then went to sit down in the kitchen to wait. She only got up when she heard the letterbox go and was over the moon to see a postcard from Guernsey from the girls. To get it here that quickly they must have written it as soon as they arrived, and she clasped it against her chest, briefly relieved that they had been thinking of her as well as taking some time by themselves.

That night in the kitchen over the mille-feuille – which incidentally had been one of the best she'd ever tasted – the girls had asked whether she wanted to join them on their holiday, and if it hadn't been for her persistent headaches and the nosebleed she'd had shortly before the pudding was ready, all of which sent her into a tailspin about her health, she might have said yes. She'd cited how busy the café was – an excuse – and she'd despised herself for it because it was the biggest peace offering yet. But she hadn't been able to bear the thought of having to hide her symptoms, which would be near to impossible if they were all together on a holiday.

Plus, she suspected the girls needed the time away, that actually it might be better if they did it without her. They could enjoy themselves, be young, reflect and come back to her cottage to spend more quality time together.

The hour left to wait for them to get back home ticked by so slowly she'd thought she'd go mad until she heard the sound of a key in the lock, the chatter of female voices, and there they were, her nieces.

The three of them had never quite had the relationship where they hugged a lot, although as soon as they came in both of them hugged her tightly and couldn't wait to recount their adventures.

'Guernsey was wonderful,' said Addie. 'Susanna shopped a lot – boring work clothes.'

'Hey!' But even as she said it, Susanna looked more carefree than Gayle had ever seen her.

'Did you get our postcard?' Addie asked.

She pointed to the fridge where she'd popped it beneath one of the cookie magnets which had faded over time. It used to be where she put reminders for the girls – *don't forget P.E. kit, I'll be home later this evening, let me know what pudding you'd like after dinner*, that sort of thing.

'Guess what we did right after sending that?' said Addie. The postcard had detailed a bit of shopping, the views and the delightful little restaurant they'd found where they'd eaten fresh lobster.

'What did you do?'

'We had a kayaking lesson,' said Addie, her face filled with excitement.

And as Gayle listened to them describe the best parts, the

challenges and the fun, she knew she couldn't ask for anything more. She'd got them here to the island, but they'd done the rest – they'd slowly allowed themselves to settle and feel comfortable, and there was no feeling quite like it.

21

SUSANNA

It was only one more day until the living funeral and Susanna was glad they were going. After their break in Guernsey and in Sark, she'd managed to put all of her troubles out of her head – no stressing about Alex, no feeling guilty about the pull she felt towards Mateo, no worrying about how she'd been as a teenager to her aunt. She'd felt a freedom like never before, but today, now they were back on Anchor Island and had a good catch up with Gayle before she disappeared off to the café, it was time to sort through the last of their dad's things.

Addie opened up the flaps of another box and pulled out a black and white print. 'Look, this one is Mum and Dad.'

Kneeling next to her sister, Susanna leaned closer. 'They look really happy in that picture, don't they?'

'Mum had great legs.' Addie giggled. 'Wish I'd inherited those.'

'Oh, come on, you did. Your legs in shorts every summer were the envy of all the girls and the delight of every boy on this island.' Susanna took the framed photograph into her hands.

Their parents looked blissfully happy, like nothing could ever come between them, as they beamed into the camera, their hands together on the handle of a knife about to cut through one of the tiers of their wedding cake. Their mother was wearing a beautiful veil held in place with a ring dotted with dainty flowers. Her dress, knee-length and flared from the waist, as well as the white heels she wore, showed off her long and slender legs.

Addie's phone pinged and she looked at it.

'What's wrong?' Judging by Addie's face there was something.

'It's a text from Maurie. Jonty's in town and he wants to see Isaac tomorrow.'

Jonty, Isaac's absent father, had barely seen the kid since he was born. In fact, Susanna could count on the fingers of one hand how many times he'd visited Isaac. He'd even come to London and not bothered to get in touch. Addie put on a brave face, but Susanna knew her heart broke for her son when it seemed his own dad didn't care all that much about him.

Susanna asked, 'Do you think he'll actually turn up this time?' The guy had done that too, arranged to see his son and then bailed at the last minute.

'Maurie has said she's not telling Isaac until tomorrow in case he doesn't.'

'Try not to worry, eh?' Although she knew her sister would. 'Come on, let's get on – it'll take your mind off it.' She pushed the box in front of Addie closer to her to encourage her to continue. It was better than thinking about useless Jonty.

During their holiday, Addie had had a really good time. Susanna knew she missed Isaac, but when she'd phoned him to say she'd been on a kayak he'd been so excited to hear about it, especially about his Auntie Susie's attempt to get on when she stepped too close to the edge and fell in the water. Susanna wondered whether perhaps Isaac was so happy because his mum was smiling into the camera in a way she hadn't done in a long time.

They pulled even more photographs of their parents from the box. Mostly they were black and white shots, and Susanna couldn't help wondering why they'd left them here for so long. They were beautiful pictures, after all. Perhaps it had been fate's way of giving them a pat on the back for coming back to the island at long last.

Susanna soon got bored of the box she had started to go through – it contained a load of old paperwork for the Cuppas and Treats Café. Why their dad had kept it, she had no idea. Nostalgia? Tax purposes? It would all need to go, it simply wasn't needed any more.

Instead, she looked at the photographs Addie was going through. 'That's the café in Oxford.' The photograph was of Harry and Gayle Rafferty standing out front.

'They're both so young,' said Addie. 'Look at Aunt Gayle's hair, it's gorgeous with all those curls.'

'You have those same curls.'

'So did you when you were younger.'

'I did, until perimenopause started. Now any body or waves in my hair seem to have disappeared.' Susanna harrumphed.

'I've heard women at the office talking about what perimenopause is like,' said Addie. 'I'm dreading it.'

'Some women sail through it. I don't think I'm doing too badly, most days,' she added with a cheeky smile.

Addie's own smile faded. 'Mum didn't even get to the right age to have to face it.'

Cynthia Rafferty had died aged thirty-nine, just a year older than Addie was now. Susanna assumed Cynthia hadn't gone through menopause, nor had she known what it was like to have her hair go grey. She hadn't got to grow old or see her daughters turn into women. Harry Rafferty hadn't really got to see much more, and some days Susanna wasn't sure what she accepted easier – the car accident that snatched their mother away from them or the terminal illness that took their father. The outcomes were the same.

Susanna looked again at the picture. 'I wonder who runs it now. I wonder if it's even a café any more.'

'It is.'

She started. 'You've been?'

'You know I visit Oxford sometimes.'

'I do know. But I thought you went to the city.' And she'd never pressed for details.

'I usually do, but the café is only a short walk from the main drag. Isaac even has a favourite order there – lemon and blueberry muffin with a glass of milk.'

'You never told me, Addie.'

Addie took a deep breath, and when she eventually spoke it saddened Susanna to hear what she had to say. 'I didn't want to talk about the café because that would lead to talking about Dad, and we know what happens between us when we do.'

She felt terrible that her own sister hadn't felt able to tell her about visiting the café, but then again it was her own fault. She hadn't divulged the truth, she'd kept it to herself, so how could Addie ever understand why she felt the way she did?

She wondered what else Addie didn't want to go on about because seeing Addie here on the island made Susanna admit to herself that her sister had felt a lot more attached to the place than she ever had. She'd tried to deny the glaring fact for so long, bury it and start over back on the mainland. She hadn't been fair in doing that though, had she?

She moved away from the direct subject of their father. 'You know, I can't imagine Dad and Aunt Gayle working together.'

'I can't imagine Aunt Gayle taken orders from anyone,' said Addie.

'Nor Dad,' they said at the same time, making them both laugh.

Addie wasn't unpacking anything else; she was looking at Susanna in a way that suggested she had more to say.

'I've been looking up living funerals on the internet,' Addie blurted.

'And what did you find?'

'Not much. It seems people do them the way they see fit, a bit like a funeral, I suppose. But... there are eulogies, or I guess they'd be called speeches if she isn't actually dead. I was thinking...'

Susanna knew where this was going. 'You're thinking of giving one, aren't you?'

'Well, we might have all lost touch, but she *is* our family. And we've all had some really good days lately.'

'We have. But... Addie, I can't do it. Gayle and I have had so much between us for so long, it would feel false. I know everything is good at the moment, but we've not talked about what happened. And I just don't feel I can stand up in front of a crowd and go on about the aunt I'm not sure I ever really knew properly.' She took out another framed photograph.

'I understand. But would you mind if I said something?'

And there it was. The very different relationship her sister had had with their aunt, and if Addie gave a speech everyone would know it more than they probably already did.

'I'll say it's from both of us,' Addie leapt in. 'So it'll sound like we wrote it together. And it won't be gushing, it won't be saying we had the best childhood ever... I just think a few words would be nice and the right thing to do.'

Susanna thought for a moment. 'Would you read me the speech before?'

'Of course. Then you'll know what's coming.' She gave her sister a hug. 'And it won't be long. I hate long speeches, so I'll keep it brief.'

'You're a good person, Addie.'

'As are you. Now, what's that picture?' She nodded at Susanna's hands.

Susanna smiled when she turned the framed picture over and saw that it was a photograph of her in her mother's arms.

'How old are you in that one?'

'I must've been about three, I think.' She was dressed in a ballet tunic, her little dark bunches protruding from either side of her head.

'You're so cute.'

'I don't remember the ballet lessons.' What she did remember was their mum's hugs and the Dior perfume she wore, the way it would comfort her and linger on her clothes, even after the cuddle had long finished and they were separated again. Those sorts of memories were incredible, evocative, and it pained her that Addie would never have as many as she needed.

'When you came along, she was so careful not to exclude me,' Susanna went on.

'Did you ever feel left out?'

'Never. I was six years old when Mum was expecting you, and I still felt loved and seen. And... I would go to bed every night and wish for a brother.'

'You never told me that!'

'I never told anyone. I felt terrible!'

'How did you feel when I arrived, clearly a girl and not the brother you'd dreamed about?'

'I was besotted by you. From the moment I met you in the hospital, I was in love. I couldn't imagine it any other way.' She added to the memories for Addie. 'When you were really tiny, Mum would feed you and then hold you in her arms, and I would run my finger along your forehead. I was so scared you might break. Mum let me push the pram sometimes, once you were a little older. She'd meet me from school, and we'd walk back together and go into the Cuppas and Treats Café where Gran and Grandad would boast to the customers about both of their granddaughters. I loved it when they did that.

'You cried a lot, but Mum and Dad were both hands-on parents, passing you between them. Mum would keep you calm by singing to you, or she'd put you in your bouncer and take you wherever she was. If she was folding laundry, you'd be at the side of the room; if she was cooking, there you would be; if she was in the garden, she'd put you in a shady spot beneath the tree. It got harder when you began to move because you were so inquisitive, into everything. Your favourite thing to do was to go into the pantry and hide behind the boxes of cereal.'

'How was that even possible?'

'Their pantry was huge.'

'I remember it having those funny silver-fish things.' Addie turned her nose up.

'Yeah, well, if they were there when you were tiny, you didn't care. You must've got choosier the older you got.'

After a beat, Addie said, 'Thank you, Susanna. For telling me... again.'

'I like telling you things.' She paused. 'I wish they could've met Alex.'

'They would've loved him, you know.'

Susanna felt sure they would've approved of him – more so than Mateo, who had always had a bit of a wild streak, and maybe still did. But she'd never know what either of them thought of her life choices, and because she'd lost them so young she'd never got to know them as a grown up when things might have been very different.

She'd texted Alex when her and Addie were away, she'd sent him photographs. He'd replied, it had all been fine, but it wasn't right either. They didn't chat – it was as if it was easier to hide behind the texts for both of them rather than have an actual conversation.

Was it a sign of things to come?

'You're still worried about Alex,' said Addie.

A slow smile spread across her face, 'You don't miss much. Yes... I am,' Susanna admitted. On their holiday she'd confided how worried she was. The ability to share things with her sister was far easier when they were away from the noise of everyday life.

'He wouldn't cheat on you, I just don't see it.'

'Well, whether you see it or not, he's different, secretive, and I don't know what else it could be.' She added, 'His new dental nurse is very attractive. Ten years younger than me, no grey hair or hormonal swings.'

'Bit cliché, isn't it? Dentist and his dental nurse.'

'Well, yes, but...'

'Why don't you ask him outright?' Addie opened up another box but didn't pull anything out yet. 'Give him a call.'

'He probably won't answer.'

'Then you call over and over again until he does. Then come right out with it. Say you feel there's something he's not telling you.'

'How did you get so good at relationship advice?'

'I've no idea.' She pulled out a bulging document folder from the box. 'It's not like I have men beating down my door.'

'You're beautiful, Addie. You know that, don't you? And what about that guy with the kite we bumped into the other day?'

Addie laughed. 'A stranger who I'll likely never see again.'

'You don't know that.'

Addie sighed. 'Unfortunately, men run a mile when they learn about Isaac. I've had that happen on a couple of occasions, although to be honest, in a way I was relieved every time. The effort of dating on top of motherhood and a full-time job would be a lot.'

'Well, no man is worth it if they're put off by your gorgeous boy.'

They went through the next box, which was full of more bills, more handwritten documents their dad had kept from the café, and which were no longer needed – training materials from his move into the travel sector.

'He's kept a lot of crap,' said Addie.

'Hmmm... He was a bit of a hoarder, really.' For once their discussion didn't feel like the usual clash they had when it came to talking about their dad.

Addie stood up. 'Shove all that back inside, I'll take it down and dump it in the utility room ready for rubbish.'

Susanna heaped the papers into the box again and once Addie left her to it, she dealt with the next box. Inside this one she found a few pieces of artwork from both her and Addie, which made her laugh. This made her glad their dad was a bit of a hoarder, and she set them aside to show Addie when she came back upstairs. There was also a bumbag of old watches, of all things – very odd – plus a scented candle that smelt of nothing but dust and a couple of padlocks with the keys still attached.

She took out a black folder, the sort that was like a little box with bands at the edges to keep papers together.

A call came up the stairs from Addie. 'Do you want a lemonade?'

'Please!' she hollered back as she undid the elastic at each corner of the folder.

She went through the few things inside, but when she saw the next piece of paper a sense of doom descended upon her because it catapulted her back thirty-three years, right back to the moment when she'd hidden behind her bedroom door as she listened to her parents argue.

She sat back on her heels and closed her eyes. She remembered it all as if it was only yesterday.

That day her mum had been sobbing – a horrible, raw sound Susanna would never forget.

'How could you do this to me?' Cynthia's voice had come out strangled and barely recognisable.

'I'm sorry,' Harry had said more than once.

Susanna had stayed hidden, her heart beating wildly inside her chest. She didn't want either of them to know she was there.

'Do you love her?' Cynthia's voice had juddered with the question.

'No. I love *you*, Cynthia,' her dad had said. 'It's over with Lily. I promise.'

'How many times?' Cynthia had demanded.

How many times? Were they talking about sex? She'd learned about sex at school – some of the girls talked about it, what the words meant, about their parents and the thought of them doing something like that. Did this mean her dad had done the sex thing with someone else?

She dared not move an inch from behind her bedroom door. Her parents thought she was out with a friend, but she'd come back to get her favourite pyjamas, and although she'd called out to them, neither of them had heard because they'd been too busy fighting, again. She'd snuck up the stairs, slipped into her room quickly, but her parents had emerged from their bedroom at the end of the corridor, and it was impossible to get out of the house without them knowing she'd heard them. She didn't want that. Sometimes she did. Sometimes she wanted to scream at them and tell them to stop arguing; sometimes she wanted to tell them that if they didn't stop then she would run away.

From her position behind the bedroom door, she could hear the name Lily batted back and forth.

Who was Lily?

Her mother's cries continued, her dad's claim that he still loved her rang out, and as Susanna peaked through the crack between the door and its hinges, she saw her dad reach for her mum's hand, but her mum snatched it away. She snatched it away and ran down the stairs, and then next thing Susanna heard was the slam of the front door followed by the roar of a car's engine.

That day was the last time she'd got to hear their beautiful mother's voice. She'd managed to sneak past her dad and go back to her friend's house, but less than four hours later her dad had come to collect her and delivered the devastating news that there had been an accident. Cynthia Rafferty had crashed her car into a tree, and she was gone. Just like that.

Susanna remembered being glad that Adeleine hadn't overheard the argument, that she hadn't had to stay in her bedroom, quiet as a mouse, until it was safe to sneak out. She was glad her little sister didn't know any of the events that led up to their mother being snatched away from them. And from that day on, Susanna vowed to keep the truth from her little sister, to protect Adeleine the best she could. She didn't ever want her to know that their dad had been unfaithful and that their mother had crashed her car after one almighty last row. Nobody suggested she crashed the car on purpose. Susanna hoped that she hadn't, but even if she did? Well, then it would be Harry's fault, because she'd driven away angry and upset, and that was how accidents happened, wasn't it? When you weren't concentrating. When you had other things on your mind.

Susanna had never forgotten what she knew, though, and she'd never quite looked at her dad the same way.

Susanna became aware of Addie moving about downstairs, fixing them drinks of lemonade. She clasped the letter she'd pulled from the black folder against her chest after reading it for a second time. What she knew now couldn't be kept a secret any more. Because she'd found so much more than she'd realised there ever was.

She looked at the date on the letter. She calculated that date to be just over three weeks before their father passed away. He must have received the letter right before he got sick and slipped it into the hidden part of his folder, crammed with work papers, until he knew what to do with it. The letter, signed, from a Lily Miller, informed Harry that although their past affair had been brief, the lasting effects were not. In the letter, she apologised for not telling him sooner. She'd considered it but knowing that he was married, she'd decided not to let him know that she was pregnant. She hadn't wanted to destroy a family. She was telling him now because she thought it her duty to not conceal the truth. She said she didn't want anything from him financially and if he chose not to get in touch she wouldn't bother him again.

Lily went on to say that she'd had a little girl, Louisa, and in case Harry wanted to contact her she'd included her address and phone number. Judging by the date of the letter, Harry had likely not got a chance to do anything much at all with the new information.

Susanna had never wanted to add to Addie's hurt. She'd always wanted to protect her little sister, except now she had no choice because part of their father's secret was right here on Anchor Island.

Louisa – Miller, she assumed – wasn't a random Airbnb-er on a seemingly weird working holiday.

Louisa was their half-sister. Harry was Louisa's father as well as theirs.

22

LOUISA

Louisa was helping out in the Sweet Life Café getting everything ready for the living funeral which would kick off in a couple of hours at 4 p.m.

She wasn't supposed to be on an island somewhere between the coasts of England and France; she was supposed to be on holiday with a group of friends in Devon on their annual girls' getaway. And while she was missing out on some fun, there was no place she'd rather be right now.

Louisa had taken a while to get up the confidence to talk to Gayle Rafferty the first time she came to the island six weeks ago. She'd found out that Gayle owned and ran the Sweet Life Café on Bay Street, so it had seemed simple at first: arrive on the island, go to the café, enter and announce herself. The reality, however, had been far different. She'd stood outside for ages, looking at staff on the balcony and wondering whether any of them were Gayle. Eventually, she'd gone inside and ordered the apple crumble, not knowing whether it was even on the menu. She'd practically run to the booth at the farthest end, which had just been vacated, waited for her pudding and ate it slowly, all the while trying to pluck up the courage to approach Gayle.

It had taken her almost an hour, a second order of crumble and three soft drinks to finally speak up when Gayle herself came over to the booth to take away another empty dish. Her heart had been in her mouth as she blurted out, 'My name is Louisa Miller and Harry Rafferty was my father.'

Gayle had just looked at her, expressionless for a moment, and then slowly she'd sat down in the seat opposite, the table separating them, and looked across at her. Louisa knew then that this woman knew nothing of her existence.

'I'm sorry,' Louisa had said, 'there was no easy way to tell you so I thought I should just come out with it.'

Gayle took a few more moments to gather herself before she asked, 'May I ask how old you are?'

It was obvious why she wanted to know. Harry's wife had died before him but not long after she was conceived, and depending on Louisa's age, Gayle would know whether Harry had an affair or only embarked on a new relationship once he was a widower.

'I'm thirty-two,' she told Gayle.

Further realisation dawned for this poor woman.

'My mum, Lily, met Harry outside a café in Oxford.' She watched Gayle's face take on emotion, but she couldn't decipher what her pained expression meant. 'I believe it was outside what was once the family business.'

Gayle's shoulders sagged and there was an air of acceptance or relief, Louisa had no idea which, when Gayle said, 'It originally belonged to our parents. Harry took it over.' She paused for a minute. 'I had my own dreams.' She looked around her as if it explained everything.

'Were you close to him?'

'At one point, Harry and I were very close, but I'm afraid he wasn't happy with me when I decided to do my own thing.'

'Mum told me she was at the café for a job interview one day,' she began to explain. 'It hadn't gone well. She took a coffee outside and sat at one end of a bench. A man – Harry – was at the other end, just staring at the café, and they got talking.'

'He took it hard when he lost the business,' said Gayle after a pause. 'I can imagine him sitting there, wishing things had been different.'

'Mum said he was really miserable that day. He'd talked about working in a job that paid the bills but said he had no interest in it. They went their own separate ways after their conversation, but bumped into each other again shortly after, and they went for a drink. Harry confided how distraught he'd been to lose the family business. Mum said he was so sad.' She had rehearsed telling Gayle all of this. She was pretty sure she was making a mess of it, but she had to keep going, get it all out. 'They slept together once, and Mum, Lily, didn't know he was married until afterwards. He was cut up about what he'd done and Mum hated that she'd slept with a married man. She didn't want to split up a family. And that's why, when she found out she was pregnant, she didn't try to get in touch with Harry.'

Gayle shook her head. 'I never thought Harry would ever have an affair, even a brief one.'

'I'm sorry.'

'It's hardly your fault.'

After what felt like an unbearably long amount of time – in reality, probably less than a minute – Gayle began to smile. 'There's no doubt about the genetic link.' She indicated Louisa's cascade of blonde curls reaching down her back between her shoulder blades. 'I had curly hair just like yours when I was your age.'

Louisa smiled. 'Mum always said my curls didn't come from her side of the family.'

'Harry had the same hair type. Your mother wouldn't have known that unless he told her, because he always had his hair cut so short you could never tell – not unless he let it go too long between appointments.'

It felt odd hearing about her dad, talking about his hair and hers when she'd never even met him.

'My niece, Addie, has curly hair still. Her older sister, Susanna, did once, but hers has gone straight now, like Cynthia's was.'

That was another thing. Not only did she have an aunt, she also had two half-sisters who may or may not appreciate her existence.

She explained to Gayle about the letter her mum had sent to Harry. The letter should've arrived before he died but may have coincided with time in hospital. She had no idea. 'Do you think Harry even read the letter?'

'Going by the date he died and the date you say your mother wrote to him, he was still in what we believed to be good health. So I would expect he did read it. Unfortunately, things turned rather quickly. Not long after that date, I saw him at the hospital, and the news was devastating.'

'I'm sorry.'

Gayle nodded. 'He might have received the letter but had no idea what to do. And then...' She chose her words carefully. 'Harry was the sort of man who would have faced up to his responsibilities, but I imagine your mother's letter would've been such a shock that he would've needed to take a bit of time to think about what the next step might be. He loved Susanna and Addie, and I believe that his first thought would've been his girls and what it would mean for them.' She shook her head. 'He just got sick so fast, went downhill so rapidly, he never would've got the chance to do the right thing, even if he wanted to.'

Louisa was heartbroken all over again that she and Harry never got the chance to meet.

Gayle suddenly gasped. 'I remember something.'

'Something important?'

She put her head in her hands. 'It makes sense now.'

'What does?'

'Before he died, he said your name.' She placed her hands firmly on the table. 'Of that I am certain.'

'Are you really sure?' Louisa felt her pulse quicken, a small modicum of hope daring to enter her heart that the father she never knew had thought about her.

'Absolutely.' She recalled, 'One day he asked me to find Louisa. I thought it was one of the nurses so off I went, but there was only a Louise or a Loulou when I asked the staff. I was going to ask him if he meant one of those names, but he was asleep by the time I reached his bedside again. I didn't wake him and then I forgot all about it.'

Gayle leaned back against the booth seat. 'That was thirty years ago. I'm not sure why it just popped into my head, but it did. I'm positive he said your name, which means...'

'He read the letter.' Louisa didn't realise she was crying until Gayle passed across a tissue.

'I really think he would've found a way to include you in his life,' said Gayle. 'I only wish you'd had the chance to meet him.'

'What was he like?'

That day, Gayle had told her all about the man who was her father, starting with stories from their childhood, continuing into their days working at the family café and on to when Harry got married, and the arrival of Susanna and then Addie into the world. He might have had an affair, but it didn't dampen Louisa's view on the man, the connection that existed, even though he'd never got the chance to be her father.

Over the last six weeks, Louisa had continued to get close to Gayle, even after she returned home to England. They'd talked on the phone a lot, and Gayle had told her more and more about Harry and his two other daughters. And when Gayle first mentioned the idea of a living funeral and that it would hopefully get the girls to the island, she'd also told Louisa that it might be the right time for the truth to come out and for her to meet them both. Louisa had been terrified at the thought. What if the girls hated her given what she represented – an affair! What if they were suspicious of her motives?

Before she could change her mind and chicken out, she'd cancelled her plans and come over to the island. She wanted to meet the girls properly, even though she was scared. She'd initially booked into the inn, but Gayle was having none of it and offered up her accommodation out the back of the cottage. She'd said she would've let her have one of the spare rooms, were she not hoping that Susanna and Addie would come. And one afternoon when Gayle and Nancy were rushed off their feet at the Sweet Life Café, the opportunity to help out and earn some extra cash had come up. She could waitress, work the till, wash up and clear up, and Gayle even trusted her to do some of the deliveries around the island, which was fun. Gayle had opened her arms and her heart from the first day they met, and Louisa couldn't be happier with how she was. She loved Gayle's company. Gayle reminded her a lot of her late grandmother, the way she was strong yet kind. What she'd come to realise too was that despite her successful business, and her apparently together demeanour, Gayle was lonely. Her nieces were rarely in touch, apart from on dutiful occasions, her brother had gone, and while she had plenty of friends, Louisa suspected by the things Gayle said about her days bringing up Harry's girls that she had a lot of regrets from that time. She'd urged Gayle to try to repair things with the girls and not leave it the way it was and had encouraged the idea of the living funeral. She'd even helped Gayle get the invites for the event sent out – she'd written all the envelopes, but she hadn't seen the invite itself until Gayle handed her one to make it official. And by that time Nancy had already raised the alarm that Gayle had made a mistake.

'Should I put that in the holding cabinet?' Louisa asked Nancy who had just finished making another jam roly-poly.

They were following Gayle's plans to the letter for today. Before guests arrived, they intended to pre-make as many puddings as possible, and as choices laid out on the tables dwindled, Nancy would be out here again if needs be. Gayle was off duty, her only task to talk to her guests, and because she was feeling a bit off-colour this morning Nancy had made a big vat of her signature vanilla custard under her instruction.

'Is there much room left?' Nancy deftly sliced the roly-poly and the pieces of fresh sponge fell gently onto each other, showing off their swirls of jam in the centre.

'This one is only half full,' Louisa confirmed as she checked the second holding cabinet which would keep food at the required temperature until it was ready to be served.

Nancy was already clearing down her workspace in preparation for the next thing. 'On to the spotted dick and the sticky toffee pudding. But keep an eye on the space in the holding cabinet so I don't get carried away, otherwise we'll have to eat a load so it doesn't go to waste.' She grinned at Louisa. 'Perk of the job.'

'It certainly is.' The smell of the sponge had already induced yet another rumble from her tummy. The guests were going to be very happy with all these yummy choices.

Her mum had given her blessing for Louisa to be here. They'd never had secrets. Lily had told Louisa about Harry when she was very little, and when Louisa was old enough to understand she'd told her about the letter he'd never responded to and that he'd had a family of his own when they had their brief affair.

For years, Louisa had resisted any urge to find Harry. She didn't want to acknowledge a man who'd ignored her mother's contact, a man who ignored the fact he had another daughter, and she'd held on to that feeling for years. She'd never wanted to do anything about finding him. It had been just her mother and her for such a long time that bringing anyone else into the equation would've felt weird, but both of them had started to talk about Harry more and more as the years went on. Her mum had told her that Harry already had two daughters, and they discussed what might happen when the girls found out about Louisa.

'They probably don't even know I exist,' Louisa had said. 'And when they find out, I bet they'll be upset.'

'Well, there is that,' her mum had conceded.

'I don't want to destroy someone else's world.'

Lily smiled. 'You're my daughter, all right. That's why I didn't tell Harry for a long time.'

'And when you did, you heard nothing back from him. He's clearly not interested. And that's fine.'

But it wasn't fine. It never really had been. It had just taken her a while to admit to herself and to her mum that it stung.

Over the last nine months, ever since a friend of hers had made contact with her birth parents and talked about it with such positivity, Louisa had started to think about things a little differently. Her mother had sent a letter, but what if the letter had been lost in the post? Or what if Harry's wife had opened it first and destroyed it? Or it could've been thrown away with the junk mail. She knew that happened because she'd accidentally binned a birthday card from one of her best friends last year and had to go fish it out of the recycling bin.

They'd had a long talk about it, her and her mum, and together they decided that Louisa would try to find Harry Rafferty. Discovering that he'd died had upset her more than she ever thought it would. She'd never known him after all, but in that moment she'd known that she never would. She'd shed tears for a man who had never been her dad, not really, and her mother had comforted her.

They'd started talking more about Harry's sister, who they knew from their search for Harry was still alive. They knew where she lived and the business she owned.

'Harry was devastated that his sister didn't want to run the café with him,' her mum had said. 'He told me they'd always got on so well, but that had driven a wedge between them. He said that his sister's business took off, but the café had ended up losing money and he wasn't able to keep it going. At the same time, the Sweet Life Café was going from strength to strength, and it made him feel like more of a failure. He'd not visited his sister for a long time as a result of his jealousy. It's very sad.'

'You really talked to him, didn't you?' Louisa had said.

'In the short time we knew each other, yes. I think that's why he had an affair. His life was messy, he felt like a failure in so many ways, and never wanted his wife to think he was. What started off as the two of us talking and confiding went further than it should have.'

That day, Louisa had decided she was going to find Gayle Rafferty and she was glad she had.

The only thing she was worried about now it was almost 4 p.m. was meeting two of Gayle's guests in particular. Because after today's event, she and Gayle were going to sit down with Susanna and Addie and tell them the truth.

People began to arrive. Gayle was here at last and greeting everyone at the door as they came inside.

When Susanna and Addie Rafferty came into the café, plenty of people were happy to see them. They had hugs from so many different people, and as Louisa turned from the counter where she'd placed a fresh tray of glasses ready to serve drinks, she caught Susanna's eye.

And in a few seconds, she felt her insides plummet. Because judging by the way Susanna was looking at her, she got the distinct impression that Susanna didn't need to be told who she was.

Somehow, she had already found out.

23

GAYLE

All these people were here for her. Gathered in the Sweet Life Café, friends from all around the island had turned up wearing bright clothes – pinks, mauves, turquoise, bright yellow – as per the part of the invite she'd actually got right. And it wasn't until this moment she realised how emotional she was going to feel, especially seeing Susanna and Addie come inside.

Last night, Addie had wanted to know all about the puddings that would be served today. In fact, after Susanna went to bed, they'd talked at length even though Gayle was fast running out of energy and had had to fight her tiredness and nausea, if only to treasure the time with her niece. They'd talked recipes, the trials and errors making various puddings, and Gayle had embraced wholeheartedly the feeling that Addie had never lost the joy of baking. She hadn't totally ruined that for her niece, and as they'd chatted she'd brought to mind the memories of Addie coming into the café, excitedly pulling on one of their aprons and waltzing about like she was always meant to be there.

She smiled across at Addie. Then she caught sight of Mateo

as he came into the café wearing the gaudiest Hawaiian shirt she'd ever seen. He winked at her the way he'd done in his younger years once they got past their clash over Susanna. She didn't see him for a long time after he and Susanna ended their relationship – she was pretty sure he avoided her on purpose, even when he returned to the island – but then one day a few years after their conversation at the marina, he came into the café. She'd expected him to confront her, mention what had happened, but instead he'd simply placed an order for an apple and blueberry crumble that he intended to take to his mother's place that evening. He'd come in regularly after that and she'd come to like chatting to the man who was refreshingly uncomplicated and polite.

She looked around again. It seemed as though everyone was here.

Should she open the door? It was already rather hot in here.

'Let me,' said Nancy, reading her mind. Or perhaps she'd noticed Gayle flapping the frilly collar of her cerise blouse.

Once the door was open, Gayle knew it was time for her to say a few words. She moved along the counter so she was more in the centre and facing the doorway and the crowds. She was nervous and had almost talked herself out of doing this, but she was honestly so grateful for all these people in her life that it wouldn't feel right not to say something to that effect.

She tapped the side of her plate with her spoon, having barely touched the piece of summer pudding that lay on top.

She set the plate down once the room quietened and reached for a glass of water. Her mouth was so dry, probably from the nerves she was feeling, even more so now the gathering was underway. 'Thank you, everyone, for coming along today,' she began.

'She's alive!' came a cry from someone in one of the booths, local doctor, Chas, calling through both of his hands.

It might have been funny had she not pulled the wool over her nieces' eyes to get them here. Gayle nodded in Chas's direction and only looked at Susanna and then Addie as she said, 'My sincerest apologies for scaring everyone with my enormous faux pas on the invites. I'm not sure I'll ever live it down, but I thank every single person who has come here today.' She hesitated. 'It means a great deal to me.'

This was harder than she thought. But she didn't want to get upset, she didn't want this to be a miserable affair where she thought about her regrets, and everyone felt bad for her. The whole point of the living funeral was to celebrate, to feel joy, to smile, with everyone she cared about, and by God she was going to do that if it really was the last thing she did.

Louisa was smiling over at her, which was nice. She only hoped that Addie and Susanna would give her a chance when they knew everything. She was digging herself a rather big hole by keeping it quiet for so long.

'I've lived on Anchor Island for almost fifty years,' she continued. 'When I first came here, I never expected it to become the community and the world that I've found myself in. Launching this business was scary, a leap into the unknown. I had no idea whether it would work or not, and I sometimes questioned whether I'd made the right choice. But, having been here, having established the Sweet Life Café as a part of the island, as much as the harbour and the fish and chip shop, the book shop, the bakery and the lovely inn, I am so pleased I didn't give up, even when things got tough.

'The Sweet Life Café, like any other business, has endured its tough times especially in the early days and then again when the world changed in 2020.' She'd read this speech so many times she didn't really need the notes in her hand, a hand that was shaking somewhat with all eyes on her. 'It's thanks to all of you, the local community, that I was able to keep on going. Instead of gathering here, there was home ordering and the reason I bought that lovely pink van outside.' There were a few chuckles amongst her guests. 'None of you could stop by for a chat like we're doing now, but I had many a good conversation with a passerby on the street as I stood on the balcony upstairs, just trying to be a part of the world when I was on my own.'

She couldn't look at her nieces now. She didn't want to make them feel guilty – she was doing enough of that for the three of them. What she'd meant by her words was that during the pandemic she didn't have all the customer interaction she was used to, and she'd felt it so badly on some days she'd wanted to curl up in a ball and cry or scream.

She hadn't realised she'd stumbled until she felt Nancy's hand on her shoulder and the chair suddenly behind her.

'You okay?' Nancy whispered in her ear.

'All this standing up,' said Gayle with a laugh for her guests' benefit. 'And at my age...' Best to make a joke out of it – that would stop anyone thinking the worst, even if the worst might well be closer than she would like.

She took another sip of water before she smiled and said, 'I have so many of you to thank, and I hope by letting you gorge yourselves with all the pudding you can eat – for free! – you realise how much you all mean to me.'

There were cries of approval and agreement and the clattering of spoons against bowls or glass vessels like a chant or round of applause.

She scanned the crowds for one of her favourite people. 'I'd like to say a few special thank yous. Now, where is Moses?'

'Here,' came a low baritone of a voice, and she saw a hand go up from the chairs adjacent to the door. Moses was a slight man and dwarfed by some of the teenagers who could almost eat her out of pudding on some days.

'Moses. A big thank you to you. You are one of my most dedicated supporters. How you stay so trim is beyond me.'

'It's the sea air,' he called over from behind a cupped hand.

'Well, I say a big thank you from the bottom of my heart. For anyone who doesn't already know, Moses has been coming here since the day I opened, the day I had fewer than a dozen customers across six hours and wondered what on earth I'd done. Moses spread the word—'

'True that!' he hollered.

'Moses let everyone know about the Sweet Life Café and I think he's been here every single Sunday, mostly to feed me information from across the Channel, letting me know what his niece in France has in the way of gossip on sweet treats – she works in one of the finest patisseries.'

She looked at Nancy, who was hovering nearby. She reached her hand out until her employee and good friend took it.

'Nancy here came to me for a job when she'd raised her family and wanted to get back into the workplace. She told me straight that she would do anything to help – scrub floors, wash up, run errands, man the till. We're similar in age and I had a feeling then that we were going to get on, but I had one test she needed to pass. I gave her a pudding and the fact she cleared her bowl meant she passed with flying colours.'

'Luckily it didn't contain walnuts,' Nancy interrupted. 'Can't stand them. Mind you, I probably would've eaten them anyway just to get the job.'

Gayle kept looking at her employee, her friend. 'Ever since that day you have been reliable. You've grown your talents, you've been fun to be around and you've been a constant companion.'

The room spun a little even though she was in a chair, and she took another sip of water.

Nancy wrapped her arms around Gayle and for a moment Gayle thought she might cry. But she had one more thank you to give.

She looked at Susanna and Addie this time, standing next to each other, together in the way they'd always been. 'I want to thank my two beautiful nieces, Susanna and Addie.' They both seemed so nervous, or maybe it was her who felt that way, and Susanna had been quiet ever since last night. 'Thank you for coming back to the island, thank you for staying.' She took a deep breath. 'Life can be a real shit sometimes.' She paused to let the giggles from the younger mob pass, the younger mob who never expected her vocabulary to contain anything but polite words. 'Things don't always go to plan. There are unimaginable losses but seeing you here now and the fine women you have become is a real blessing.'

She cleared her throat, emotions doing their best to trip her up. 'It feels a little smug to say that this gathering is a celebration of me, of my life, but that's what it is. I wanted to get everyone together, everyone I love and admire and cherish, at the Sweet Life Café. I decided at my age I'd rather do that now while I could be a part of it. And to have you both here, Addie and Susanna... well, it means everything.'

She was about to announce that everyone could continue with their pudding, choose another and another, until they were full to bursting, except Addie stepped forwards.

'I'd like to say a few words,' she said to Gayle. 'If that's all right.'

Gayle felt Nancy's hand on her arm as she nodded, totally taken by surprise.

Addie stood to address the crowd, and although she was so

suited to baking and a place like this, Gayle could well imagine her in an office. Even if she didn't like her job and it wasn't what she'd dreamed of doing, she wouldn't mind betting Addie still did well and tried her very best.

'I thought I'd say a few words on behalf of me and my sister, Susanna.' She briefly looked across to Susanna who smiled back although she still wouldn't look at Gayle. Maybe she was choked with emotion and too afraid she'd let herself go in front of all these people. After all, they'd had a wonderful catch up yesterday as the girls told her all about the holiday. The night before the girls left, they'd all had dinner together and it had been so... normal.

'Susanna and I came here as young girls,' said Addie. 'Gayle opened up her home to us when life had been rather unfair. Neither of us ever forgot our time here and we never forgot the puddings or this place, which we were delighted to see hasn't changed much.' There were murmurs of agreement from the crowd and as Gayle adjusted to hearing her niece say such kind words it felt as though this was the moment she'd been waiting for, when her past met her present and there was a calming of the storm that had once tried to obliterate her family ties.

'We've both been gone for a while,' Addie continued, 'but since we've been back on the island, we've come to learn how much a part of the community Aunt Gayle really is. We remember some of you from years ago. We have fond memories of cycling around the island, which, after living in a city, was something entirely new for us. Being back here has been quite a journey but thank you to everyone for making us feel welcome. And we're thankful from the bottom of our hearts that there are so many people who care for our aunt in the way she deserves.'

Addie finished her speech with a smile and came to give Aunt Gayle a hug, as Gayle insisted everyone continue to enjoy themselves and eat as much pudding as they liked. She could barely hold back her tears after Addie's speech. The three of them had come a long way in such a short time. They still had a way to go, but maybe they could really make it and be the family they should've been all along.

24

ADDIE

Aunt Gayle had seen the last of the stragglers to the door and as the sun began to set, it was time to get underway with the big clean-up.

It was Susanna who had suggested they help out now. At first, Addie had thought it was because she felt guilty about not helping with the setting up, as they'd initially said they would. Instead, Susanna had had them boxing their father's belongings that they wanted sent back to the mainland, and she'd even gone all the way and arranged for their shipment. What had changed Addie's mind, however, was when right after Susanna's suggestion they help now, she'd added that the sooner they cleared up, the sooner they could get out of here.

Susanna had been unusually tetchy since last night, a different person to the woman who'd been in the kayak laughing her head off, the sister who had relaxed as they ate and drank and shopped and enjoyed one another's company. And Addie hadn't had the chance to ask what was wrong because Susanna seemed to be on autopilot, getting things done as fast as she could.

Maybe Alex was the problem. The sisters had talked about him on their holiday, but not much. In fact, Susanna had been having fun and seemed to have put him out of her mind, but maybe now she was getting closer to going back to Cambridge, she was worrying all the more about what might be happening in her marriage.

Addie thought of how her sister had looked at Mateo during the gathering, and the body language which suggested there could easily be something between them again. She hoped Susanna wasn't going to do anything silly. She and Alex belonged together – surely they could work it out. She'd been sorely tempted to call her brother-in-law and have a word with him, but she didn't want to interfere. Susanna wouldn't ever thank her for that.

Addie took her phone out when it buzzed with a message from Maurie. She felt her insides settle when she saw a picture of Isaac with Jonty. For once, Isaac's dad had actually shown up, and despite the unease she felt that Jonty wasn't used to parenting, she knew Maurie would have everything in hand. She'd hit the jackpot with her and Jarrett as her son's grandparents.

As she picked up some debris from the floor and left it on the side of a table to pop in the bin later, she thought about her encounter with Samuel earlier. She'd wondered whether the man who had rescued her from being tangled with his son's kite would be on the guest list today, and although she hadn't spotted him when she first arrived, her eyes had locked with his right after she finished her speech.

She'd finally plucked up the courage to go and say hello after chatting with Nancy, Gayle and some of the other locals who welcomed her back.

She'd caught him midway through a mouthful of pudding.

'Sorry.' She grimaced. 'I didn't time that well, did I?'

His hand covered his mouth for a moment. 'I've had four helpings already. Maybe it's a sign I should stop and talk instead.'

'Don't worry, I could never resist Gayle's baking, either.'

'My son would've loved coming home from school to fresh bakes, but I'm afraid I'm not all that good in the kitchen.'

Susanna had told her that she'd noticed Samuel hadn't been wearing a wedding ring when they'd met for the first time, and she found her gaze drifting to his hand to double check. Susanna was right.

Billy came barrelling over to his dad.

'Lovely to meet you again, Billy. Did you ever get to fly your kite properly?' Addie asked.

'We got it so high!' His hands flailed out to demonstrate. 'I almost got it tangled around a post, though, and then I almost let go of it.'

Samuel put a hand on Billy's shoulder. 'First kite. It's a learning curve.'

Addie had thought how marvellous it would be to let Isaac have a go at flying a kite. She could take him to one of London's many open green spaces, but how lovely would it be to have vast open spaces and the beach at your fingertips the way everyone on Anchor Island did.

'How old are you, Billy?' she asked.

'I'm seven,' he announced with confidence.

She looked into the same big brown eyes that his father had and told him, 'I have a little boy too, and he is seven just like you.'

'What's his name?' Billy asked.

'Isaac.'

But Billy had caught sight of more chocolate puddings arriving on a tray and wriggled out of Samuel's grasp.

'Careful, Billy,' Samuel called after him, wincing as he

narrowly missed knocking into someone on his quest to reach the pudding. 'I'm afraid he's overdosed on sugar today.'

She laughed. 'I think we all have. My son is just as energetic, with or without sugar.'

'Is Isaac here today, with your husband?'

'No, he's staying with his grandparents for a while. And there's no husband, I'm not married.' It all tumbled out when perhaps it sounded a bit desperate.

'Me neither, not any more. Wife, I mean, not husband.' He grimaced at the muddling of his words.

'It's okay, I knew what you meant.' It was endearing and suggested Susanna might be right. Perhaps he *was* interested.

Samuel pulled a face, his attention flitting from Addie to across the room. 'I'm going to have to follow Billy around before he knocks something or someone flying.'

'I should go and help out a bit in the kitchen.'

'We'll talk later?'

She'd smiled. 'That sounds good.'

She hadn't got the chance to catch up with him again after that, but she sincerely hoped she did before she left the island in a couple of days' time.

Susanna was mopping the floor. Addie finished picking up the remaining debris from various surfaces, and as she picked up her cloth to wipe down a couple of sticky tables, she said to her sister, 'Mateo seemed chatty today.' She could bring up his name when it was just the two of them, with Gayle and Louisa in the kitchen dealing with the clean-up in there. 'Susanna,' she repeated when it appeared that her sister was in her own little world.

'Sorry, what?'

'I was just saying that Mateo seemed chatty today.'

'Yes, it was good to catch up.' She dunked the mop back into the bucket, squeezed out the excess water, and then carried on mopping.

'Is he married?' Addie asked.

Susanna didn't stop. 'What does that have to do with anything?'

'Just a question. I wondered if he'd settled down, that was all.'

Maybe she wouldn't ask anything else. She just hoped her sister knew what she was doing if she was getting close to him again when she had problems with Alex.

She wiped the back of one of the chairs that had a smear of something or other on it. The breeze from the open window – which would help to dry the floor quicker – sent goose-pimples all the way up her bare legs. The weather had cooled but given the request for colour on the invite her navy linen knee-length spaghetti-strapped dress, coupled with a lightweight lime-green cardigan with dainty white flowers on the top had been the best choice for the occasion. When she'd packed, she hadn't really thought it through and brought many options, and she felt good in the dress too.

She turned to see a couple more stray bowls on the lowest windowsill near the door. 'I'll just take these to the kitchen.' There was, it seemed, a never-ending supply of crockery in this place.

She made her way behind the counter where she noticed one more bowl on the very edge that she skilfully picked up as she passed through the short corridor to the kitchen. She was almost at the open doorway but stopped when she heard the name *Harry*. She hadn't talked much to Aunt Gayle about her dad since they'd come back to the island – she was usually wary of going on about him in front of Susanna – so now she wanted to pause and hear what her aunt had to say, especially because she'd also mentioned the Cuppas and Treats Café. Addie loved hearing the Oxford memories, a lot of which she couldn't recall given how young she had been.

'Harry always wanted the café to stay in the family,' Addie heard Gayle say to Louisa. 'I hate that I couldn't help him with that.'

Addie never realised their aunt had felt guilty about not being able to help Harry. The story she had pieced together, mostly from what she remembered her dad saying and what Susanna had told her, was that their aunt had left and never looked back. Her focus had become the Sweet Life Café.

'You had a dream, and you followed it,' came Louisa's voice. 'You shouldn't feel guilty.'

'He'd like seeing this.' Addie could hear a smile in her aunt's voice and expected Gayle to expand about the event or the fact that Addie and Susanna were here, but she went on to say, 'You and I working alongside each other.'

Addie was confused. Why on earth would he like the fact that Louisa was here when she was a random stranger?

She didn't have to wonder for long. The next words almost caused her to drop everything she was carrying when she heard Louisa say, 'I've enjoyed getting to know my father through you.'

'He would've been proud that you came here to find family,' said Gayle.

Addie took a step backwards, then another and another until she was back behind the counter. She turned and dumped everything she was holding with a clatter.

Her gaze went to the outside where Susanna was emptying dirty water from the mop bucket.

She couldn't move.

Susanna came inside, one arm wiping her brow, and looked over. 'Everything all right?'

Addie said nothing.

And now her sister knew something was up.

Susanna abandoned the empty bucket and the wet mop beside the front door and came to her sister's side. She guided her from the counter to the nearest chair. 'Addie... What's wrong? You look like you've seen a ghost.'

How could she possibly find the words to tell her what she'd just overheard?

'Addie, you're scaring me.' With Addie seated, Susanna sat opposite. 'Tell me what's wrong. Is Isaac all right?'

She felt her shoulders sag a little because her son, her most precious thing in the world, was safe with his grandparents. 'It's not Isaac.'

'Then what?'

'It's Dad...'

'Dad?'

'Louisa.'

Susanna's brow furrowed. 'What about Louisa?'

'I think her dad... is our dad.' Her voice caught. She shook her head. 'He wouldn't do that. He wouldn't do that to Mum or to us. She must be lying. She must be here to take advantage—'

'Do you think Gayle could be fooled so easily?' Susanna said softly.

It sounded crazy, even to her own ears. But what other explanation was there?

Susanna's hand came out across the table and held on to Addie's firmly. But what was missing was rage that their dad could do such a thing, any protest her sister was usually so good at when it came to Harry Rafferty.

And that was when she realised.

Slowly Addie pulled her hand away. 'You knew?'

'I didn't know who Louisa was, no.' She reached for Addie's

hand again, her grip firm enough to plead for her to stay there. 'Yesterday, I found something in the attic. It was a letter. From Lily, Louisa's mother. I was going to talk to you about it after this gathering today, I promise you.' She grasped for the right words. 'Addie, I wanted to protect you just a moment longer. I didn't want you taking that burden to the living funeral, not when there's a sense of peace with Aunt Gayle, for the both of us.'

'But she kept it from us. She's known all this time. Why aren't you furious?'

'I was, last night. I've calmed down a bit since then, and given Aunt Gayle and I have clashed so spectacularly in the past I felt I needed to wait before confronting her. Today, this event, it wasn't the time to do it. But we will.'

This sounded nothing like her sister, the sister who could never ignore something so huge. Her usual reaction would've been to demand the truth, immediately. She had never been one to sit back and wait patiently, for anything!

Addie snatched her hand away. 'I don't believe you,' she said without breaking eye contact. 'I don't believe you only found out yesterday.' The pieces in her mind were beginning to find their way to each other. 'It all makes sense now, why you rarely want to talk about Dad, and when we do you don't have many good things to say about him. You knew about Louisa all along.'

'I promise you, I didn't.' Susanna gulped and looked away, a sure sign she was gearing up to say more. 'But…' She held out her hand and Addie took it after a pause, like they were those two young Rafferty girls who first came to the island.

Susanna led her outside and they walked to the end of the path, turned left and went past the trees so they wouldn't be seen from the café should Aunt Gayle look outside to see where they'd got to.

Susanna's voice shook as she said, 'You're right, in a way, I did know something before yesterday. I knew about Dad's affair. But I didn't know it resulted in Louisa.'

Addie felt the ground fall away from beneath her. Her wonderful dad. He wouldn't do that to their mum, no way in the world. 'Why didn't you tell me?'

'I didn't want to hurt you, Addie.'

'But I deserved to know!'

Susanna nodded. 'You're right. And now I'll tell you everything.'

'There's more?' Addie asked. 'How could there possibly be anything else?'

'The day Mum died was the day she and dad had the big argument, and I heard about the affair.' She waited. 'That day, Mum was angry, upset, and she walked out of the house, got into the car, and never came back.'

'That was the day of the accident.' Addie tried to take it all in.

'For years I blamed Dad,' said Susanna. 'I told myself that if he hadn't had the affair, if they hadn't argued, Mum would still be alive.'

Addie didn't know how to process it all. It was too much. Her dad, an affair, her parents' argument, her mother's death, Louisa.

Voice wobbly, tears flowing, she said, 'But Mum and Dad never argued.'

Susanna looked down at the ground, at her polished black boots against the patchy grass near one of the tree's visible roots. 'They argued a lot in the year leading up to the day Mum died. You were so young. I always tried to protect you from it, hide it from you however I could. Sometimes I'd go into your bedroom, close the door and make up a loud game or put music on, or other times I'd make sure we were in the garden so we wouldn't overhear what they were saying to each other.'

Addie felt her whole body stiffen. 'What did they argue

about? Tell me, I'm not a kid any more. You don't need to hide things from me. You shouldn't!' She couldn't imagine her parents arguing. But she'd been so little before they lost their mum. Had her rose-coloured little-girl glasses stopped her from seeing what really went on? 'Susanna, please... I need to know.'

'Mostly it was about money, the demands of the café. The only different argument I remember was the one that day, about the affair with a woman called Lily.'

'Was Dad in love with this woman?'

'No, he said it was over. He told Mum he loved *her*.'

Addie slumped against the tree trunk. 'You never told me the truth, in all these years.'

'Believe me, I thought about it, but I knew what it would do to you. You idolised Dad, you missed him so much. You missed Mum too and you couldn't even remember much about her. I gave you as many memories as I could, but that one?' She shook her head. 'Why would I torture my sister with thoughts that take up too much room in my head, thoughts that have haunted me for far too long?'

Addie realised something else. 'That's what you fought about.'

'Who?'

'You and Dad. When we were going through his boxes, you found Mum's bracelet with the tiny blue flowers and you said that you and Dad had argued.'

'Yes. I thought he'd given it to her... to Lily.'

'I *knew* there was more to it. You denied it!'

'Addie—'

'No! No more.' Addie began to cry, and she felt her sister's arms around her, but she pushed her away. She turned. She ducked beneath the low-hanging branches of the tree. And she ran.

She ran down the street. When she reached the point where she'd got tangled in the kite's strings, she headed for the pathway beyond that would take her all the way round the island. And she kept on running.

She didn't stop at the first bench, nor the second; she only stopped when she had no more energy left.

She stood, got her breath back, looked out at the vastness of the ocean.

It wasn't long before she began to feel the cold. She needed comfort. She had to hear her son's voice.

She took her phone from her cardigan pocket and, hands shaking, she made the call.

'Hello, love,' said Jarrett when he answered, only briefly getting a word in before Maurie was on the line.

'Addie, what's happened? Are you okay?' Maurie asked.

'I'm fine, I promise. I just wanted to say hello to Isaac, ask him if he had a good time with his dad today.' She got up, moved around, jumped a little on the spot to keep herself warm.

Maurie hesitated. 'I knew you'd be worried, but he's safe and sound. He's fallen asleep on the sofa. They played a lot of football. I can wake him up?'

'No, no, don't do that.' She wanted to hear his voice, but knowing he'd had a good time with his dad was suddenly enough. 'How long is Jonty staying with you?'

A pause.

'Maurie. Are you still there?'

'I'm still here.' But her voice juddered.

'Maurie, are you upset?'

After a pause Maurie sniffed. 'He's never going to change. I thought... We thought... After the good day they'd had that Jonty might realise what a fine young boy he has. We thought he'd finally realise he still has time to be a proper father to Isaac.'

Addie could've told them they were dreaming, but she suspected if Jonty was her son she would be hoping for the best outcome too. 'Has Jonty left already?' she asked delicately, putting her own troubles aside for the minute.

'As soon as they finished at the park.'

Addie's heart sank. He'd not even managed to spend time with his parents after the visit. What was wrong with that man? 'I'm sorry, Maurie.'

'It is what it is.'

'But Isaac was all right when Jonty left?'

'You know, I was more sad than Isaac was. He took it in his stride, as if it was perfectly normal. He might not always feel that way if and when his daddy dips in and out of his life, but whatever you've done for that boy, Addie, you've made him resilient, and he doesn't doubt everyone else's love for him even though his dad is useless.'

'I'm so sorry, Maurie. It must be hard for you.'

'It is, but we're tough. We're fine.'

'Jonty has always done his own thing.' It was the politest way to describe him. Talking about him with Maurie and Jarrett was always a balancing act between getting her point across and not totally alienating them by criticising their son.

'We worry.'

'About Jonty?' Addie asked.

There was a longer pause before Maurie told her, 'We worry that without Jonty making an appearance, you and Isaac will move on, we'll lose touch.'

'Oh, Maurie, that will *never* happen. I can promise you that.'

'Really?'

'Really. You two are our family. Isaac and I love you to bits.' She let Maurie have a few tears down the line. 'Isaac and I would be stuck without the pair of you. You always step in, no question, and you've well and truly earned your grandparent stripes. I would never take Isaac out of your lives, and he would never want me to either.'

As she paced to stay warm, she looked out at the sea, at the moonlight casting a glow across the surface of the water, a sense of calm descending even when she shivered again. She was glad she'd called, not just for her own benefit, but for Maurie's. She hated that Isaac's grandparents had been having these doubts about their place in her and Isaac's lives.

'Isaac has been asking to see Anchor Island, you know,' Maurie told her. 'What's it like?'

'A lot more beautiful than I remembered. And it's half term soon so I was thinking he could see it then.'

'Right,' said Maurie who frequently had him during the school holidays. 'Well, that will be nice.'

'Maurie, there's something I need from you and Jarrett.'

'Anything, love. Just say the word.'

'I want you and Jarrett to come to the island too.'

Maurie's voice wobbled. 'Really?'

'Yes. I'm sure Isaac would be thrilled if you two came, and so would I. You could see the place for yourselves, have a bit of a break – even head over to Guernsey or Sark like me and Susanna did. And I'd love for you to meet my Aunt Gayle.'

'Oh, Addie, I would love nothing more.'

Addie wrapped up the phone call as she made her way back along the track in the direction of Bay Street and the Sweet Life Café. It was time to face the truth and get some answers from Aunt Gayle about Louisa, the younger sister she'd never known about, but who was right here.

Harry Rafferty had done a terrible thing, but unlike Jonty, he'd been there for his daughters. She couldn't hate him for the one thing he did wrong and already she knew she couldn't blame Louisa.

Neither she, nor Susanna, nor Louisa, had had any control over Harry Rafferty's behaviour. But it was time for Susanna to stop trying to protect her. She was a grown up, and her sister had to remember that she could deal with things and had her own life to lead.

25

SUSANNA

Susanna stood outside the café. Addie had run off; she needed to process what she'd discovered, especially the part about Susanna keeping some of the details about their parents' marriage and their fight from her, and Susanna was desperate to cling to some sense of normality in all of this.

With Gayle and Louisa still busy in the café kitchen, she called Alex's number. It rang and rang. She tried once, twice, three times. On the fourth attempt, he picked up the call.

Everything that had happened came out in one garbled message.

'It sounds a lot to cope with. Are you okay?'

His question almost floored her, and her voice trembled when she said, 'Yes. I think so.' Although right now she felt as though her whole life were imploding.

'You never told me all that before, you know.'

'I wanted to try to forget. Except it didn't work.'

Now probably wasn't the time – in fact, she knew it wasn't – but hearing his voice, she couldn't wait any longer to say, 'We can't carry on like this, Alex.'

'Like what?'

'We need to talk.'

'We *are* talking.'

'Not about my family woes. About us.' She didn't wait for him to say anything else before she added, 'I have to know. Are we done?'

'What's that supposed to mean?'

She looked up at the sky. It was already dark, September bringing with it shorter days. 'I mean, is our marriage over?'

'Why would you ask that?'

Her breath hitched. 'Because there's something you're not telling me. And I'm done with secrets. I can't take much more. I haven't pushed for answers, I've given you space when you needed it.' She heard their doorbell sound in the background.

'I have to get that,' he said. 'But I'll call you back in a bit.'

'Alex—'

'We'll talk, I promise.'

And then he was gone, just like that.

She was still looking at her phone when she saw Mateo across the street.

She stood up straighter as he noticed her, pulled herself together as she called over, 'I thought you'd be long gone.' She felt a sense of calm she'd been so desperate for finally descend. How did Mateo still have the power to make her feel that way when it should've been hearing Alex's voice that did it?

He hooked a thumb over his shoulder as he walked towards her. 'I own the flat above the newsagent. I rent it out but my tenant just left and it needs a repaint. I thought I'd do a bit more of it while I'm this way, before I head back to my place.'

She noticed his hands when he was in front of her. 'You've got most of the paint on you.'

'It certainly seems that way.' His laughter rumbled out and

took her back decades to all those lazy evenings at the marina, down on the sands, on the decks of boats whenever they could, hiding from the world together. 'I'm not sure doing it with only artificial light was the best thing, but what could go wrong painting a ceiling white?'

It was her turn to laugh. 'Go check it out in the morning, see the damage.' She swatted at a sharp sting on her arm. 'Ouch.'

'Did you get bitten?' He took her hand, looked at the place she'd swatted. 'Mosquitoes are out in force right now. You got repellent on?'

She was still trying to adjust to the feeling of skin on skin, still looking at his hand on hers. 'I hate the stuff.'

'Then the mosquitoes will love you.' But then he jumped. 'I think one of the buggers just got me.'

She giggled. 'They're persistent, I'll give them that.'

'Hey, do you remember that time a fly went up your nose?'

'How could I forget?' She'd been sitting on one of the benches with Mateo looking out over the water, having just come up the steps from the beach and a serious making out session they'd hit pause on when they realised they were about to be discovered by some beachcombers. A fly had buzzed around for a while. She'd swished it away, and as she laughed at something Mateo said it returned and its timing was perfect. Or not so perfect – she'd inhaled and up it had gone right into her nose.

'You were panicking,' he said.

'Wouldn't you be? I could feel it!' She put her finger against her sinuses on one side of her face. 'The blessed thing only came out when you grabbed some wildflowers, held them under my nose and the pollen made me sneeze.'

This was nice. Mateo was easy company and there was no wondering what he meant or what he was hiding.

She slapped her arm again as another mosquito decided she was a good target.

'The perils of the island.' He was standing so close she felt her heart beat even faster, and before she knew it she was looking into his eyes and was back there as a seventeen-year-old when they'd started dating and he became the first man to teach her what passion was.

'One of them,' she said.

'What are you doing lurking out here, anyway?' he asked.

'Family stuff, you know.' She looked behind her, through the window into the café. Gayle and Louisa must still be ensconced in the kitchen.

'Family stuff was always a thing for you.' He reached out, tenderly hooked her hair behind her ear on one side and then did it with the other. 'You can talk to me, you know.'

She should be talking to her husband. But he was answering the door. To whom, she had no idea.

'I'm just waiting for Addie,' she said, looking down the street, but there was no sign of her yet.

'Well, you know where I am.' He stepped a little closer, or maybe she had, she wasn't sure.

'I do.'

'I meant what I said, you know.'

She could feel the warmth of his voice raking up feelings she'd thought long since buried. 'What did you say?'

'That you haven't changed all that much.' He put a hand against her cheek. 'The way we ended things...'

'I never forgot it.' Her words came out soft against the evening air.

'I hated myself for it.' He closed his eyes briefly before fixing his gaze back on her.

'Don't feel guilty.' Her face, tilted upwards, left her inches apart from being able to kiss him.

'I wish you were happy now,' he said.

Her eyes prickled with tears. 'I'm doing okay.'

'You deserve to be more than okay.' And then his lips touched tenderly to hers, for one brief moment before he pulled back. 'I'm sorry, I shouldn't have done that.'

'It's not your fault.' Because she'd wanted him to, very much. And she leaned in again, almost kissed him properly, but in that split second, she realised what she was doing.

'I have to go.' She turned and scuttled down the path towards the front door to the café.

'Susanna!' Mateo called after her a couple of times, but his voice was blocked when the door shut behind her.

Louisa came out from the kitchen while Susanna was still standing by the front entrance. 'We wondered where you and Addie had got to,' she said, all smiles. 'Just the kitchen floor to be done now.' Louisa, with her beautiful blonde curls and the hint of youth that Susanna felt she'd long since left behind, picked up the mop and bucket to take to the kitchen.

'Just going to the bathroom,' Susanna said before Louisa could respond. She needed a minute before she could deal with anything else.

If Alex was having an affair, she'd be devastated. But if she did the same? It wouldn't make it any better, would it?

In the bathroom, she stood with her back against the closed door and took a few deep breaths. Addie had run off, she'd almost cheated on her husband by kissing Mateo, and she still had to face Louisa and Gayle.

When her phone rang it made her jump. It was Alex calling, and she wished he'd forgotten to call her back.

She let it ring out. But he rang again.

'Where are you?' he asked when she answered. 'It sounds echoey.'

'In the bathroom at the café.'

'Should I call you in a few minutes?' he asked.

'I almost kissed Mateo,' she blurted out, the words leaving her lips before she could change her mind. She couldn't keep it to herself. She just couldn't.

'What?'

'Mateo, he still lives here, and he was here today, at the café…' Her words were tumbling out as if she was worried she wouldn't get the chance to say them if she didn't do it right this minute.

A knock at the bathroom door was followed by Aunt Gayle asking, 'Susanna, what's going on? Are you okay? Where's Addie?'

'Alex, I'll have to call you later.' Gayle's timing couldn't have been worse.

'No, we nee—'

But she cut off the call because Aunt Gayle was still knocking, anxious to know what was happening.

She emerged from the bathroom, but she didn't say a word until she was in the café where she turned to her aunt and said, 'Addie ran off.'

'What do you mean, she ran off?'

'She knows.'

'Knows what?'

Louisa appeared at that moment, picked up on the atmosphere, and remarked, 'Sorry to interrupt. I'll leave you both to it.'

Susanna's voice stopped her before she could head back to the kitchen. 'She knows about you, Louisa. We both do.'

She wasn't sure who looked more shocked, Louisa or Gayle.

Gayle let out a big breath. 'I think I need to sit down.'

Louisa rushed over, held her arm and guided Gayle over to a chair. Louisa didn't really meet Susanna's eye when she said, 'I'll go and make us all a cup of tea.' She rushed out to the kitchen.

Susanna sat down opposite her aunt.

'I was going to talk to you after today,' said Gayle, voice soft, a hand to her chest. 'I wanted to do it right.'

'Doing it right would probably have been before today,' said Susanna defeatedly. 'I found out yesterday when we were looking through Dad's things.'

'Oh, I've messed this up good and proper. I should've done it differently.'

'I'm not sure anything would've lessened the shock.'

'I should've done it *all* differently.'

Susanna's eyes filled with tears. The remorse in Gayle's voice stopped her anger rising and when she thought about Addie, how much she'd tried to protect her over the years, how her choices had become Addie's, this all felt like too much. 'It wasn't all your fault, you know.'

Surprised, Gayle looked across at her niece.

'I bet you never thought you'd hear me say that.' And right now, no matter the revelations, it felt like a good time to admit that things hadn't been so clear-cut back then.

Gayle's expression softened. 'I knew deep down you had a good heart. You were just angry at the world, and I got in the way.'

'I should've given you more of a chance, I should've let Addie be more independent.' She looked around the Sweet Life Café. 'I remember how often we'd come here and wait for you to finish up your working day. I think the smell of pudding was in the walls, it was always so comforting.'

'I thought you always hated it here.'

'I never hated it. I resisted it. There's a difference.' She remembered fond things about living here. She'd tried to block them all out, but lately they were creeping back in. 'Do you remember joking that the Raffertys would always do pudding before dinner?'

Gayle's distress was replaced with a smile of her own. 'I do remember that. I thought it was a little bit of fun.'

'Even that I tried to resist, thought I knew best, that you were being irresponsible to teach us such a thing.'

'You were forced to grow up too quickly when you lost your parents.'

Louisa emerged with a tray holding three mugs, a teapot, a little jug of milk, a small bowl of sugar cubes, and spoons. She looked nervous, unsure of herself.

Susanna picked up the teapot. 'Let me.' As she poured them each a cup, nobody said a word.

At last, with her cup of comforting tea in front of her, Susanna explained, 'I've known about Dad's affair since I was eleven years old.'

'Oh, Susanna.' Gayle shivered.

Susanna prompted Gayle to drink the tea. She looked pale. Perhaps it was the shock, the panic that Susanna was going to get mad with her at this latest revelation. Maybe she remembered how mad she'd got over Mateo, how she'd yelled at her aunt, told her she couldn't wait to leave this shitty island.

'I'll go get your cardigan from the kitchen,' said Louisa and went off to fetch it.

'Did Addie always know too?' Gayle asked desperately, when it was just the two of them.

She shook her head. 'Addie has always had Dad on a

pedestal. I never wanted to ruin that for her. What would've been the point? I kept it to myself.'

'You always protected your sister. You always looked out for her.'

'I probably did it too much. And now she's upset, especially with me for withholding the truth. That's why she ran off tonight.'

'She'll forgive you, of that, I'm sure. But she just learned her dad wasn't infallible.' A look of concern passed across her face. 'This explains a little why Addie always talked about Harry with such devotion and you always... Well, you held back a bit.'

'It's not that I hated him for it. I was angry, but I still loved him.'

'Of course you did,' said Gayle as Louisa returned with the cardigan and wrapped it around her shoulders.

Louisa sat down again and finally she spoke. 'I'm sorry, Susanna. About all of this.'

'You don't need to be sorry.'

'But I am. It must've been horrid to find out about me before Gayle and I had the chance to explain it all. We've been getting to know each other and wanted to do it right. I hate that it backfired.'

Gayle frowned. 'Come to think of it, how *did* you find out?' she asked Susanna. 'You said you were going through things in the attic. What was there?'

'I found a letter,' said Susanna and judging by Louisa's face she knew exactly what letter she was referring to. 'You knew about it?' she asked her.

Louisa nodded, in shock. 'I can't believe it still exists after all this time.'

'It was tucked away in a folder of Dad's. I assume your mother is Lily.'

'Yes. Lily Miller.'

'And she told you about Harry?'

'Only when I was older and better able to understand. She told me the affair was brief, that my biological father chose his family, and then she told me about the letter she'd sent that Harry never responded to. I saw it as a rejection. I decided at that point that I never wanted to track down a man who wasn't interested in me.'

'What changed your mind?' Susanna asked. 'Presumably you're only in touch with Gayle because you tried to find Harry.'

Louisa hadn't touched her tea. 'I started to wonder, what if? What if someone else had found the letter first and got rid of it? What if it never actually arrived? Mum supported me and we tried to find Harry. I decided that if he told me he wasn't interested, I'd be hurt, but I'd know once and for all. I discovered he'd passed away not long after Mum sent the letter. I also found out he had a sibling.' She smiled across at Gayle who smiled right back. 'I wanted to at least find out a bit about him. It's hard not knowing where you really came from, always wondering. At least now I know a bit. And I see where I got my curly hair from.'

The remark relaxed all three women and Susanna told Louisa, 'Addie still has the riotous curls – I lost mine as I got older, but it's certainly a Rafferty trait.' She looked at Gayle, remembered how crazily curly her hair had been when they first came to live with her on the island, how young their aunt was. She hadn't ever really acknowledged what a grenade the arrival of her nieces must have set off in her aunt's life. It had been all about her and Addie, their new life, their survival.

Susanna winced at the lukewarm tea and set her cup down.

'I'll get us some more,' said Gayle.

'No, let me.' But Susanna wasn't quick enough.

'I'm capable of making some tea,' Gayle insisted, standing up.

She briefly rested her hands on the back of her chair. 'I'll bring back those last few mini-Eton mess puddings, shall I?'

'Good idea,' said Susanna, watching as Gayle walked slowly around the back of the counter and towards the kitchen.

'I've had about five different desserts today, not sure how I'll go with fitting anything else in,' said Louisa, in an attempt to lighten the conversation.

'You'll manage. The Eton mess, from what I remember, is very light and very good.'

Conversation lapsed without Gayle until Louisa eventually said, 'Gayle told me you lost your mum when you were very young. I'm really sorry.'

'Thank you. I remember quite a bit about her, Addie not so much, which always makes me sad. She remembers more about Dad.'

Her comment lulled them both into silence again.

'Is your mum okay with you being here?' Susanna asked for want of anything better to say, because no matter whether an affair took place, it wasn't Louisa's fault. And by the sounds of it, it was incredibly brief, a mistake. One anyone could make. After all, she'd almost done it with Mateo this evening. If she hadn't stopped that kiss...

'Mum supports me being here.' Louisa smiled. 'We're very close.'

'Did she ever meet anyone else?'

She shook her head. 'No, which always made me a little sad.'

'Are you with anyone?'

'Currently single.' Louisa smiled. 'Gayle tells me you're married.'

'Yes, to Alex. We live in Cambridge.' And she desperately hoped that wouldn't change.

'And you're a solicitor?'

'I am. And what do you do? You probably know lots about us, but we know nothing about you.'

'I did a degree in drama. I was a bit stuck as to what I wanted to do, and that seemed like fun. It never led to steady work, though. I've had some different jobs. I worked at a ticket office for a while, then helped out with a theatre group, but lately I've been picking up work here and there at garden centres. I love gardening. I hadn't realised quite how much until I started doing it at my mum's when I was stuck at home so long during lockdown.'

'Finding something you love is half the battle.' And it reminded her how much Addie had loved to bake and how her life might have turned out very differently if she hadn't been so encouraged to leave the island and pursue an academic path.

Louisa looked down into her lap. 'I'm sorry this has all been so secretive.'

'It's not your fault. We can get to know each other now.'

She lifted her gaze. 'Do you mean that?'

Amusedly, Susanna said, 'Don't tell me – Aunt Gayle said I'd be the hardest one to convince.'

'She didn't say that exactly...'

'It's all right. I know I'm headstrong but being here... Well, let's just say I'm slowly beginning to realise that it wasn't always Gayle who was the problem.' And it was a sobering thing to come to terms with. She'd known for a while, but coming here and confronting it head-on was quite different.

'Louisa, I have to ask – was it really a mistake, putting the word *funeral* on the invites rather than pre-funeral or living funeral?'

'It really was a genuine mistake. Gayle was so annoyed at herself, but you know, I think it might have been fate playing a hand. She didn't think you'd come for anything other than something so final.' She paused. 'It might not be my place to ask, but was she right?'

'Honestly? Yes, probably – at least in my case. Addie might have come, but with me being the *difficult one*...'

They shared a smile.

'Wherever Addie and I landed after losing Mum and then Dad, whoever we were with, we would've pushed against it,' Susanna confided. 'Our whole world had changed. Everything was daunting, hard, different.'

'Maybe you should tell Gayle that.' But Louisa's expression immediately changed. 'Oh God, now I really am speaking out of turn.'

She looked across at the entrance to the kitchen to make sure Gayle wasn't about to emerge. 'Please, go on, I want to hear what you think.'

'Gayle blames herself for you and for Addie, for the fact she couldn't make either of you happy enough to stay here on the island. She says she failed you both, and I don't think she ever made peace with the fact.'

Guilt washed up on her like the tide coming in on the shingle beach nearest the marina. 'Maybe we should have come back before now.' She shook her head, almost talking to herself. 'I fought so hard to get away from this beautiful island. Spending time here again, I can't work out why.'

'It sounds like you had a lot of grief back then, and you were only young.'

She smiled at her half-sister. 'I appreciate the sympathy. I feel like you understand me, even though you don't know me.'

'I hope that can change.'

And when she said, 'So do I,' she really meant it.

Louisa gathered up the cups and put them all onto the tray

she'd carried them in on. 'I'll go and see where those puddings are, shall I?'

Susanna stayed in her seat as Louisa left. But seconds later she leapt up at a scream coming from the direction of the kitchen.

She tore out the back.

Gayle was lying on the floor, with Louisa kneeling beside her.

Susanna took her phone from her back pocket and called the emergency services.

26

ADDIE

Addie was almost back at the Sweet Life Café where her sister, her aunt and her half-sister, Louisa, would be waiting for her.

Louisa. With her blonde hair and her curls. Louisa who had never known her dad. Harry Rafferty's other daughter, taking Addie's place as the youngest of his children. It was a weird feeling, like she was being dislodged in a way.

She stopped when she reached the tree where Susanna had told her everything. She looked up at the sky, the stars prickling against the darkness. 'Oh, Dad,' she murmured. She'd started talking to the sky as if he could hear her after she and Isaac once had a candid conversation about death – seven-year-olds had an endless list of questions on the topic, it seemed. Isaac was adamant that when someone died, they 'went to the stars'. It turned out that Isaac had heard someone in his class say that his granny had gone to the stars, and he'd latched on to it and lodged it as a fact in his head. And Addie had never wanted to contradict him, because it was a nice way to think of those who were no longer with them.

She closed her eyes. She thought about her wonderful dad, all those summers he'd carried her on his shoulders, the times he'd read her bedtime stories, the cuddles, the laughter. She'd thought of him as perfect and today, she'd found out his faults. She wasn't silly, she knew he'd have them; what she hadn't thought was that they would be quite so significant.

The sound of footsteps coming towards her made her snap out of her daydream.

'Addie!' It was Louisa, calling for her.

'What's wrong?' she asked, quickening her pace, approaching the café.

'It's Gayle. Come quickly.'

As they began to run a man climbed out of the car that had pulled up kerbside. He followed them inside, carrying a small bag. He went straight to Gayle, and Addie realised he was a doctor. He carried out his checks, talking to Gayle in a soothing voice, while Addie stood back. Susanna was at Gayle's side as he said that a call had already been put in to initiate the marine ambulance. There was a medical facility on the island, but it wasn't for emergencies. Aunt Gayle would need to be transported to the hospital in Guernsey.

Addie went to her aunt's other side opposite her sister and took her hand. Gayle had a blanket over her and a rolled-up towel under her neck to make her comfortable until help came.

'I'm so sorry I ran off,' Addie said softly.

Gayle groaned.

'I'll go outside and wait for the paramedics to arrive,' said Louisa.

Susanna reached across Gayle to give Addie's hand a squeeze. With her other hand she took Gayle's, and for a moment all three of them were joined in a circle, the little family that had fractured apart. If only they would get more time with Gayle to make sure they got everything out in the open, truths told, admissions made, and the past addressed rather than ignored or run away from. It's what Addie had always tried to do with regards to Isaac and his dad. She'd always been truthful about Jonty and the way he was. No secrets, no lies, then there was less hurt. But then again, would she really have wanted to know her dad had cheated on her mum? Would she want to know that that was the reason she'd gone out in the car that day and that the state of her emotions could have had something to do with the car accident?

No. She knew she'd got the better end of the deal, and she realised now the hurt Susanna must have felt keeping all of that to herself.

It felt like they waited for an age, voices soothing, encouraging Gayle, telling her that she was going to be fine. And then they were joined by two paramedics and the girls stood back with Louisa.

'What do you think is wrong with her?' Susanna's voice wobbled.

'Maybe she's exhausted,' said Addie. 'Today would've been a lot.' But then she looked at Louisa. 'Do you know something?'

'I... I...' They watched on as the paramedics attended to Gayle.

'Come on,' said Susanna. 'Out with it. The Raffertys have too many secrets as it is, we don't need any more.'

'I've been trying to get her to go to the doctor since I arrived on the island,' Louisa blurted out. 'She's had nausea, been really tired... She told me she's had blurred vision on and off, but put it down to perhaps needing glasses. She kept saying she'd get around to sorting herself out. But... Well, I think she might have been scared of what she'd find out.'

Addie looked at their aunt. Aunt Gayle who'd done so much

for them both. Aunt Gayle who they'd pushed away because she wasn't their parent, because they were so desperate to escape island life and go back to the mainland, where they thought they belonged.

The thought of losing her was terrible. Since coming to the island, Addie had wound back those years, seen herself and Aunt Gayle in the way she'd pushed out of her memory bank, held it at arm's length. All that baking together, the way they'd laughed and talked in the kitchen and then at the cottage. How had she ignored that for so long?

The paramedics remained tight-lipped about possible outcomes. They wanted to get Gayle to the marine ambulance and over to the hospital on Guernsey.

'One of us should go with her,' Susanna declared.

'No room I'm afraid,' said one of the paramedics.

Addie was beside herself. 'Then we need to get a ferry.'

Before they had a chance to wonder when the last ferry went, a voice came from the doorway. Mateo. He was holding the door open for the paramedics to take Gayle outside to the ambulance that would head down to the harbour.

'How can I help?' he asked them all.

Susanna didn't seem surprised to see him back here and she told him everything. Mateo pulled her into a hug to calm her down, and Addie pushed aside the fact that Mateo was there for Susanna when it should have been Alex.

'What time is the last ferry to Guernsey?' Susanna asked Mateo as Addie began turning off the lights and making sure everything was off in the kitchen.

'The last ferry just left,' he said.

'What the hell are we going to do?' Susanna had her hands to her forehead.

'Stay calm,' said Mateo. 'Remember, I know a man with a boat.'

Susanna gasped. 'You could take us to Guernsey? Now?'

'I'll take you. Go home and get a bag with a few clothes. You can find accommodation once you're on the island.'

Addie locked up the main door once they were outside. The girls tore home. Mateo drove his van around to the cottage and picked them up in less than ten minutes. They were on board the boat in another ten.

Addie put on the life jacket Mateo passed to her.

When Susanna's phone rang, she answered. One finger in her ear, she said her husband's name and gave a garbled explanation that she couldn't talk right now.

'Life jacket,' Mateo prompted from beside Susanna. 'Put it on. I'm not leaving the marina until you do.'

'Alex, I have to go. What? No, I—'

And then she had the phone back in her pocket and wrestled the life jacket on.

'Alex?' Addie asked as Mateo powered up the boat ready to leave.

'He hung up the call. He heard a male voice. And now he knows I'm with Mateo.'

'He must know you're not *with* him.'

Susanna looked at her. 'That's the thing, he doesn't. Mateo and I almost kissed and earlier on the phone, I told Alex.'

'Oh, Susanna.'

'It's okay. I'll explain everything to him when I'm home.'

It was a distraction of sorts as the boat raced over to Guernsey. Susanna told Addie what had happened with Mateo, how she'd stopped it before it went too far.

'It's all such a mess,' Susanna said when Addie put an arm around her sister.

'You'll work it out, you and Alex, I just know you will.'

And when they arrived on Guernsey, it was time to refocus.

Aunt Gayle was family, and right now they had no idea whether she was going to be okay or whether they were about to lose her for good.

27

LOUISA

'Louisa, is that you?' Her mother's voice on the other end of the phone made the tears flow even more. Louisa was outside the hospital on Guernsey, leaning against a wall. The skies were dark, and the world carried on around her in this place of emergency.

'It's me,' she whimpered.

'What's happened? Are you all right?'

'Yes, I'm fine. Sorry, I didn't mean to panic you.'

An exhale of relief was followed by, 'Take your time. Tell me what's going on.'

Louisa had been an anxious child. She wasn't sure why. Sometimes she'd wondered whether it was because it was just her and her mum, no dad to rely on, no siblings in her corner, and maybe she hadn't learnt how to deal with things quite the way she should have. She'd shared her theory with a friend once who thought the opposite, who said she would surely be stronger if she was used to only having her mum to rely on and nobody else.

Louisa had no idea which of them was right. All she knew

was that she hadn't felt this anxious since her teenage years. She'd forgotten the feeling of having the walls of the world closing in and what it felt like to have to remind herself to take a proper breath in and let it go each time.

'Gayle is in the hospital,' she said, as she moved further along the wall so she was well out of the way of the ambulance bay.

'What happened?'

She recapped what she knew, told her mum that Susanna and Addie were here in Guernsey too. 'Mum, they know.'

'They know?' A pause. 'Oh, they *know*.'

The way her mum said it so conspiratorially had the power to calm her.

'So, you and Gayle told them both?' her mother asked.

'Not exactly.' The whole story poured out: Addie hearing them, Addie running off, talking with Susanna and Gayle, then Gayle collapsing and the boat trip over here because the medical facility on the island wasn't equipped for emergencies like this.

'And how is Gayle doing?'

'We don't know yet. Susanna and Addie are in the waiting room, but I needed to come outside for some air and to call you.'

'What are they like?' her mother asked after a beat.

She smiled. 'Susanna is so obviously the older sister. She's strong, she's very much in charge. Addie is softer. She has a kindness about her – not that Susanna doesn't. And Addie has curly blonde hair, not as blonde as mine, but the curls are the same. Harry had curly hair.' She was babbling, perhaps a mix of excitement and adrenalin, she didn't know why. 'He would have it cut really short so the curls didn't show. The only time they did, according to Gayle, was if you caught him between haircuts.'

'I didn't know him very well at all, did I? It's moments like this that remind me. The girls must have been so upset.'

'Addie more so.' Addie hadn't found the letter, she hadn't

overheard her dad like Susanna had and been somewhat eased into the secret of the affair. The information had hit Addie right in the face when she overheard the conversation in the kitchen.

'Well, they know now,' said her mum.

'I should get back inside, find out what's happening.'

'Keep me up to date, won't you? And Louisa... I hope you and the girls can work through this.'

'Me too.' She turned and followed a paramedic into the hospital.

Her mum saying she hoped they could work through this meant she hoped the girls weren't too angry, weren't too mean to her. It had been Lily's biggest concern with the search for Harry, not only that he might reject her but that the rest of his family might make things unpleasant for her daughter. Of course, Harry was no longer around which represented another hurdle, but her mum's relief when Louisa had told her that Gayle Rafferty was really kind and hadn't told her to get lost, was palpable.

She found Susanna and Addie in the waiting room. Mateo was on the phone at the far end. 'Any news?' she asked when Addie looked up as she approached.

'None yet,' said Addie.

Mateo came over. 'I've found you a couple of rooms in a guesthouse. Two of you will need to share, but it's a place to stay.' He passed on the address. 'I have to go back to Anchor Island soon, I need to be at the marina in the morning.'

'Thanks again, Mateo,' said Addie, with the others echoing the sentiment.

Addie turned to Louisa. 'Susanna and I will share – you can have your own room.'

Louisa suddenly felt like an intruder. Maybe it was better to return to the island. 'Why don't I go with Mateo, if that's okay?' She looked in his direction, and he agreed it would be fine. 'This is your family. I haven't known Gayle all that long and I don't want to be in the way.'

Susanna put a stop to her protest. 'You probably know more about Gayle than we do. And she likes you. Plus, you *are* family.'

'Are you sure? I—'

Susanna reached out for her hand. 'We are sure.' She looked at Addie.

Addie smiled at Louisa. 'Gayle will want to see us all when she wakes up.'

These two women had no idea how much it meant to her to feel such acceptance, even in the wake of their shock.

Susanna spotted a vending machine with bottled water. 'Anyone else parched?'

Both Louisa and Addie nodded, and while Susanna and Mateo went to get the waters Louisa quietly observed them. 'They're close,' she said to Addie.

Addie smiled. 'They used to be together. They dated for a long time before Susanna went back to the mainland and started university.'

'Do you think they still have feelings for each other?'

'She's married.'

Louisa caught herself. 'I wasn't suggesting she'd cheat. Sorry, I shouldn't have asked the question.'

'It's fine.'

'I don't think it's okay to cheat either, neither does Mum. She knows it was a mistake. With your dad.'

'*Our* Dad. And mistakes happen. Nobody is perfect.' She added, 'I know about the letter now, Susanna told me she found it.'

'My mum sent that to Harry to let him off the hook, if that was what he wanted. I always thought he'd ignored it, but between us Gayle and I worked out that he must have received the letter right before he got sick.'

Addie paused, taking in the new information. And then she turned in her seat to face Louisa. 'The fact that he kept the letter says a lot, in my opinion. I was only eight when he died but I remember enough about him to know that he was a kind man, a loving man and a good father. Keeping the letter tells me he was probably working out how best to handle everything. He had us two girls to think of and if he hadn't got sick so quickly, I really do think he would've got in touch with your mum and wanted to get to know you.'

'Really?' She was making this moment about her, but she wanted to grasp at whatever she could, while she could.

'I really do,' said Addie.

Addie was being so kind, but when she glanced over at Mateo – who would be leaving any second now – she didn't want to miss her chance. 'I really think it's best if I go, let you and Susanna digest everything.'

'No,' said Addie firmly. 'Please stay. I've seen how kind you are to Gayle, how much she likes you. And the Raffertys, in case you hadn't noticed, are a bit thin on the ground these days. We need you for the numbers.'

They were interrupted by a nurse intercepting Susanna returning with Mateo and the bottles of water. The nurse must have met the Rafferty girls this evening already because she didn't ask who they were here for.

'Just two visitors at a time,' said the nurse once she'd shared the information that Gayle was doing well and resting.

Addie linked an arm through Susanna's. Of course, they would go through first. But then Addie announced, 'We're sisters, we're all Gayle Rafferty's nieces. Can we be the exception tonight, please? We came all the way from Anchor Island.'

The nurse, obviously deciding whether it was more than her job was worth, relented. 'Very well – but not for too long.'

'Come on,' said Addie. 'Let's go see how she's doing.'

Half-sisters, by her side, something she'd never had. And it was something she was so grateful for. They could've refused to have anything to do with her, they could've excluded her this evening, but instead they were embracing her into their family.

28

ADDIE

Aunt Gayle looked vulnerable and small in the hospital bed. She'd never been like that in the whole time Addie had known her. Right from when they'd arrived on the island as two girls in crisis, Gayle had always been strong with the energy and drive to match her curls.

The doctor who met them as they approached Gayle's bedside pulled another chair in so that all three Rafferty girls could sit down.

After he'd introduced himself, he quietly informed them, 'She's doing well. Gayle shared some concerns when she arrived at the hospital this evening, worries about her family history. We've already done a few tests and there will be more tomorrow. Don't worry, we will be thorough. For now, spend some time with her. Visiting hours are over but you can stay a while as long as you're quiet.'

When the doctor left them to it, Addie had wanted to run after him and demand to know more, but she supposed no news was good news, wasn't it? And once the test results came through, they'd know what they were dealing with.

'This is my fault,' said Louisa as they sat at their aunt's bedside and waited for her to open her eyes, say something, anything, to put their minds at rest.

'How do you work that out?' asked Addie.

'I should have made her go to the doctor. I knew she kept having these symptoms.'

'Don't even think that, Louisa,' said Susanna firmly.

'She's right,' Addie added. 'This is nobody's fault, least of all yours. We all noticed little things about her.'

'I saw her taking an antacid a couple of days after we got here,' said Susanna. 'She said she felt a bit sick and her tummy hurt. She explained it away by saying she'd drunk milk past its use-by date. I didn't argue the toss.'

'She's had a sore back,' said Louisa. 'She said she was getting old and it was expected.'

'She's been so tired,' Addie put in. 'And she's had frequent headaches. Her appetite has been off too, but I put that down to her being busy with the business and organising the living funeral. She was never one to sit still for five minutes. Although that's what's different this time, she's not been on the go. I put *that* down to her being in her seventies.'

'And it might still be that she's getting older,' Susanna interjected. 'Let's not panic until we know more.'

Sitting there, thinking about all the dramas of this evening, Addie realised something. 'Susanna, you were all right on the boat crossing. You didn't feel sick. That's the first time in a long while.'

Susanna smiled. 'I think the emergency was such a distraction, my body knew it couldn't misbehave.'

'I'm so glad we managed to get here,' said Addie, looking across at Gayle whose eyes were closed. They all had so much to work through, she only hoped they got the chance. If she had pancreatic cancer like Harry, they might lose her quickly, and she wasn't sure she could bear it if that happened before they all made their peace properly. To a certain extent, she and Susanna had already repaired some of their relationship with their aunt by being here, by staying at the cottage and by not leaving as soon as they knew about the mix-up with the living funeral. But there was so much more to talk about for all of them, especially with Louisa now in the picture.

They stayed at Gayle's bedside a while longer before they said goodnight to her and headed for the guesthouse a short taxi ride away. They checked in, and whatever Mateo had told the owner, the man at the front desk was kind enough to ask whether the girls wanted anything to eat. They settled on a pot of tea and some toast with jam to be eaten in their rooms.

'Can we have all of it brought to room nine?' Addie requested and to Louisa said, 'Come on, we all need to talk for a bit. You can't go to sleep straight away after all that's happened.'

They filed up the stairs, along the corridor, first to room eight where Louisa left her bag and then on to room nine where Addie slumped on the bed. Susanna and Louisa flopped onto the paisley sofa near the window. The toast and jam arrived not long after.

They ate quickly, all of them finally hungry again after all the earlier puddings.

'That was the best toast I've ever had,' Addie declared, using her finger to pick up the last of the crumbs.

Louisa piled the plates on top of each other and set them on the edge of the dresser.

'Do you really think Aunt Gayle might have pancreatic cancer, like Dad?' Addie asked, figuring she might as well come right out and ask the question. 'Or she could have heart problems like her sister.'

Susanna pulled a few crumbs from her top and dropped them into the bin. 'Let's keep everything crossed that it's neither.'

'Gayle will be one of the lucky ones,' said Addie. 'She has to be.'

The room quietened.

Addie broke the silence. 'You know, for so many years I thought our dad was so bloody perfect.'

'Nobody is,' said Susanna.

'Well, to me, Dad was. I guess by eight years old I hadn't quite worked out that people weren't necessarily all good or all bad. I blame those movies with princesses and villains, the evil and the good, no in between.'

Louisa moved from the sofa over to the bed when Susanna pointed out there was only one blanket and it was getting chilly.

'I always fantasised about who my dad might be,' said Louisa once she was settled. 'I'm embarrassed to say that for a while I lied. I told the boys in my class that he was off fighting for his country. I said he didn't get to come home often but we missed him and wrote to him all the time. I'm not sure if they knew I was lying but it made me feel better.'

'How?' Addie asked.

'Because otherwise I was Louisa Miller, mother Lily Miller, father absent. I hated the thought of people asking me about him, so I made stuff up. When I went to high school, I changed the story to something far more exciting. I said that my dad was a hotshot film director in Los Angeles. That one came back to bite me, though, because it turned out the teacher had a sister in the LA film industry.'

Susanna began to laugh. 'What were the chances?'

'I know!' Louisa was laughing now too. 'She took me aside one day. She said that she had met my mother at parents' evening and knew that my dad wasn't on the scene. I burst into tears, not just because nobody else would think he was a hotshot film director but because I had to remind myself that he wasn't and that he wasn't a part of my life.'

'It must've been really hard for you,' said Addie. 'I had Dad for eight years at least.'

'I had him for fourteen,' said Susanna.

Addie rolled onto her back, extricating herself from beneath the blanket. She was warm enough now. 'Susanna... did you idolise Dad even a little bit, before... well, you know...'

'Before the day I overhead him admit to the affair? Of course I did, he was Dad. He was strong, funny, capable.' And then a sadness came over her face. 'I couldn't look at him the same way when I knew that he'd cheated on Mum. I had a lot of resentment stored up inside of me for a while and held him at arm's length. The only thing that made me feel compassion for him was knowing that he had been trying to do the right thing by telling Mum the truth. I loved him, but... well, I never let go of some of that anger. And then he got really sick. I hated myself then, Addie.' Her eyes filled with tears. 'By the time we were sent to Anchor Island, I loathed myself and thought I'd made his life so miserable at the end.'

Addie turned onto her back again. 'You didn't make Dad's life miserable, Susanna. He was always saying how proud of you he was, when you won those go-karting medals and beat all the boys in the local area, you should've heard him.'

Susanna swiped at the tears on her cheek. 'I was a legend.' She smiled.

'And so modest,' Addie teased. 'He knew you loved him. And you told him you loved him at the hospital too.'

'I thought I did, but I didn't know whether he heard me.'

'They always hear you,' said Louisa. 'Mum said that when my gran was in hospital and it was nearing the end, she recalled snippets of conversations with Mum, even when Mum had thought she was asleep. I bet your dad was the same.'

'Hey,' said Susanna. 'He was your dad too.'

'I'm not sure I'll ever be able to talk about him in that way.'

'Maybe if you got to know more about him,' Addie suggested.

'Gayle has told me quite a bit,' said Louisa.

'Well, we're here to tell you so much more.'

And so for the next hour they talked until all three of them were struggling to keep their eyes open. They talked about Harry Rafferty – husband, father, man, café owner and then travel agent. They talked about fun times, frustrations, the things he'd said and his laugh; they'd talked about his curls and the Rafferty family as a whole.

Most of all, Addie realised as they talked, all three of them were struggling with the revelations, but what they could do was start processing their feelings together.

Perhaps if Susanna, Addie and Gayle had done that years ago, things might have been very different.

29

GAYLE

Gayle opened her eyes when she felt a hand on her arm. 'Addie…' She turned her head and saw Susanna and Louisa. All three Rafferty girls here at her bedside, and despite the circumstances in many ways it made her feel like the luckiest woman alive.

'How are you feeling?' Addie asked.

'So-so,' she said. She was tired. She'd been poked and prodded around, needles for this, that and the other, and she'd had a scan as well as an ultrasound. 'What day is it?'

'Thursday,' Louisa informed her.

'Did I sleep a whole day away?'

Susanna smiled. 'Kind of. You had more tests yesterday. We all popped in a couple of times, but you needed your rest.'

She leaned forward a little while Susanna put another pillow behind her head to prop her up some more. She was still tired and she was still worried. Her mum had always said to her, *never go into hospital or you won't ever come out again*. What if that time was now?

'Did you sleep well?' Addie asked her.

She shook her head and said quietly, 'There's either someone yelling, or alarms by the beds going off, beeping, lights flickering. I'll be better once I get back to my cottage.' If she was going to die, she wanted to die at home, not in a sterile environment like this. She wanted to keep eating the most delicious puddings and for the sweet smell of them to drift up the stairs as her big send off.

'Did you all come by ferry?' Gayle asked the girls.

'Mateo brought us over the night you collapsed,' said Addie. 'You came here in the marine ambulance while he brought us by boat and got us sorted with accommodation too.'

'He's a good man.' Her gaze flitted briefly to Susanna, who nodded in agreement. It felt like some sort of reprieve after what she'd done decades ago to break them up, when she did what she thought was best.

'What was your breakfast like?' Louisa asked.

'Questionable.' Gayle liked that they all giggled. The three of them together was quite something. Harry would've loved to see it, of that, she was sure.

When Susanna had revealed that she'd known about Harry's affair for years but never told Addie, Gayle's heart had gone out to her for harbouring the secret, and to Addie who had idolised her dad and had to find this out now. Gayle had been terrified that the revelations would be too much for Addie to handle. And yet, here she was. Perhaps collapsing had been the best thing that could've happened. And at least now she was here in the hospital having tests she was no longer avoiding her failing health.

When she saw the doctor approaching, she sat up a little further. It looked like it was time to face facts head-on, and she was glad the girls were with her.

'Should we give you some privacy?' Susanna asked.

'Most definitely not,' said Gayle decisively, before she addressed the doctor. 'Give it to me straight. How long do I have?'

Never one to beat about the bush, she added, 'My brother died of pancreatic cancer and my sister had heart problems at a very young age. So what is it for me?'

The doctor's neutral expression morphed into a kind smile. 'Gayle, we've run quite a few tests, and we are confident that whatever made you pass out and is responsible for your other symptoms, isn't cancer. And you don't appear to have any problems with your heart, either.'

'Are you sure?'

'As sure as we can be. But there are some concerns.'

Here it was, the truth. She was ready. She had the girls at her side and she could take whatever he threw at her now.

'We believe that the reason you passed out was because your blood pressure was very high. That can cause damage to the body and the internal organs, but we've given you some medication and it has come down significantly. It may take up to a few weeks to fully stabilise.'

'Well, that's good,' said Susanna.

The doctor continued. 'Our tests have also revealed that you are in the pre-diabetic range, Gayle, which isn't so good. But on the positive side, we know now and we can act.'

'Would that have caused her other symptoms?' Addie asked.

'We can't be sure. Sometimes there are no obvious symptoms with pre-diabetes. What we do know is that there is plenty we can do at this early stage.' The doctor looked at Gayle. 'How is your diet? Do you eat regular meals? Healthy snacks?'

Addie leapt in with, 'She runs on empty a lot of the time, snacking here and there in the kitchen while she's cooking. She makes puddings. *Great* puddings.'

'Then it would be wise to make some changes,' he said. 'Lifestyle plays a pivotal role in a lot of diseases, type 2 diabetes included.'

'I'll do my best,' Gayle replied, albeit a bit begrudgingly.

The doctor smiled. 'Don't get me wrong – puddings are great, but you need to prioritise nutritious meals. I'll get the nurse to bring over some leaflets with more information. Lifestyle changes don't need to be complicated.'

Everything he was saying was true, but one thing remained – she had a business to run, while she was still able to do it. She had to make him understand. 'Young man...' He barely looked old enough to shave, let alone to have been to medical school. 'I'll have you know, I own the Sweet Life Café on Anchor Island. Puddings are kind of my thing.'

His face lit up. 'Well, I never. I love the Sweet Life Café!'

'You know it?'

'Know it? I *love* it. I've been going there on and off since I was a young boy.' He still was a young boy in her eyes, but her life was kind of in his hands so she wasn't about to voice that thought. 'Whenever I eat there, it reminds me of my grandmother's home cooking. It didn't matter how big the dinner, there was always room for pudding.'

Gayle laughed. 'I like the sound of your grandmother. Wise words. And I can't give up puddings – I have to taste test, sample a lot of different puddings with a vast array of ingredients. I have to eat what I make, or how can I expect anyone else to?'

He smiled. 'I wouldn't dream of suggesting you never eat a pudding again, just prioritise your nutrition first with some decent meals and then perhaps work with a process of elimination to see whether anything in particular makes your indigestion or tummy pains worse. You might find that by eating properly as well as the necessary taste testing, you'll feel far better anyway. Make sure you get plenty of fresh fruit and vegetables, lean protein. Do you do any exercise?'

'I walk – not as far as I used to, but enough – and I'm on my feet a lot at the café.'

'Well, living on an island with all its fresh air is probably at the top of my prescription.' He nodded, smiled, and bid them farewell. Gayle had to hand it to him – he had a lovely bedside manner. It was only when he left that Gayle realised how relieved she was that they hadn't found anything too sinister.

'I'm really glad it's nothing too serious,' said Susanna. Gayle saw her hand move as if she was going to reach out to her, but she stopped short of doing so.

'Me too,' said Addie. 'Although you want to avoid developing diabetes, so you really do need to make some changes.'

'And I will. I promise.' Because now she had even more incentive to hang around for many years to come. She had these three wonderful girls, her family, or at least she hoped she did from now on.

Addie suddenly asked, 'Wait, is this why you wanted to have the living funeral? Did you really think you were dying?'

She grimaced. 'I was convinced my fate was sealed. I had so much to say to you both and I thought if I called it a living funeral the word *funeral* might make you realise we didn't have forever.'

'The word *funeral* certainly did that,' said Susanna. 'We should've come sooner.'

'We all should have dealt with things sooner,' said Gayle. 'All three of us struggled in different ways with how things were. I know I did plenty I'm ashamed of.'

'Gayle, you kept us safe,' said Addie. 'You brought up two girls who were strangers, really.'

'Yes, well, I didn't do a very good job of it.'

Addie smiled. 'I think you did a better job than you give yourself credit for.'

'I agree,' said Susanna with a smile so kind it made Gayle want to weep for all the years they'd missed.

Louisa stepped closer to the bed. 'Gayle, you're a wonderful person. I'm glad there's nothing sinister wrong with you because I quite like being a part of this complicated, messy family.' Her comment made them all laugh. 'I mean it! I've never had it before.'

Gayle leaned back against her pillows. 'Imagine if I hadn't missed that wording off the invites.'

'We might never have come,' said Addie. 'But I'm glad we did.'

'Me too,' Susanna agreed. 'But that will do for drama for a while.'

Oh, sod it, Gayle thought. If Susanna wouldn't make the move, she would. She reached out and put her hand over Susanna's much warmer one. 'That will definitely do for drama.'

Susanna's eyes were filled with tears when she looked up.

Gayle needed to talk to Addie as well, but right now it was Susanna's turn. Without taking her eyes from her eldest niece, she said to Addie and Louisa, 'Would you two please give us a moment?'

'We'll go for a wander and give you some time,' she heard Addie say.

Once Addie and Louisa had gone, Gayle patted the bed. Susanna moved from the chair to the mattress.

'Didn't think this was allowed,' said Susanna.

'Leap off if the nurses come,' Gayle suggested. Susanna had popped her bottom down this same way when she first arrived and was promptly told by a porter that she shouldn't be sitting on the bed. But right now, Gayle wanted her as close as possible.

'I wasn't ever very nice to you,' said Susanna without hesitation. She said it as though she'd known what to say since she was fourteen, but had only just given herself permission to come out with it.

'Susanna, I never thought that. You were a teenage girl. You were hard work, but teenagers generally are, even I know that with my limited experience of parenting.'

'I wish I'd been able to see how hard you were working for us rather than the fact that you were gone out of the house so often. You know, it was Mateo who helped me see that. He told me that being there was one way to care for a family, but so was earning a living.'

Gayle felt awkward when she delivered an apology she should've given Susanna a long time ago. 'I'm sorry I split the pair of you up. That wasn't my intention. I wanted you to get a bit of distance from each other, enough so that you could pass your exams and get into university, but I never asked him to end it completely. I just wanted him to think very carefully about your needs and your life. It totally backfired when he got a job elsewhere and left. I was so annoyed at myself that I hadn't been able to convey to him my concerns without making him feel like he had to walk away for good.'

'I hated you a little bit for it.'

'A little bit?'

'All right, quite a lot.'

'I was worried that you'd rebel and not bother trying at school, just to spite me.'

'I thought about it briefly,' Susanna admitted. 'But then I knuckled down with my schoolwork because I knew that was the only way I'd get to go to university. Without Mateo, I wanted to stay on the island even less.'

'University and a return to the mainland had been your goal for so long. I didn't want to see you miss your chance. I just wish I hadn't got in between you and Mateo.'

'We can't rewrite the past.'

'I wish we could sometimes.'

Susanna smiled. 'Me too.'

'You know, before you girls came to the island I used to go to the café much earlier every day.'

'Really?'

'Oh, yes, but after I had you both living with me Nancy took over the really early shift, and I adjusted. I'd take paperwork home rather than work on it in the café, and I often did some of the baking or preparation at the cottage. I wanted to be there to see you girls when you got up, I wanted to hang around for breakfast and at least wish you a good day at school.'

'You worked hard,' said Susanna, 'and I took it for granted.'

'I expect I was the same at your age.'

'I never let myself get close to you.'

'I know you didn't.'

'I almost did once.' She paused. 'Do you remember the time I found you making pudding in the middle of the night?'

'When I'm stressed, I bake. I must have been fretting about something.'

'We sat and had ginger steamed pudding.'

'I remember.' Gayle smiled. 'It was something I was trying for the café. Inspiration had struck when I couldn't sleep.'

'It was pretty good.' Susanna smiled. 'That night, I wanted to talk to you so much, but the words wouldn't come. I wanted to tell you that I was hurting, how scared I was.'

'I knew. I wish you'd been able to confide in me.'

'I guess I'd learned to be tough and to be Addie's protector. I had an armour around me, and I kept it, shielded myself from getting too close.'

'You never let me hug you. I found that really difficult,' Gayle admitted. 'From the moment you came to live with me, any form of touch was forbidden.'

'Mum and I used to cuddle on the sofa a lot. When she died, I really missed it, but I had Addie, and she always wanted to be hugged.'

'You took it upon yourself to be a mum to Addie. Sometimes I think I pushed that on you, asking you to take care of her after school, when I was working.'

'I didn't mind. Well, sometimes I did.' Susanna took a breath before she said, 'I'm pretty sure Addie would've stayed closer to you if it wasn't for me.' Her face fell. 'I'm sorry I did that. I'm sorry I made her honour a pact we'd made as young girls, a pact we didn't really think through. But all I could see at the time was that I'd lost Mum, then Dad. I couldn't lose Addie too.'

'I would never have taken her away from you.'

'No, I don't believe you would have.' Susanna's chin wobbled; she was doing her utmost to keep herself in check.

'Your sister loved to bake at the café. She showed a real interest once you were at university and I encouraged her, at first. But then I realised it might well come between you if Addie and I got closer. Am I right?'

'At the time, probably, and I'm ashamed to admit that.'

'At one point I thought about what she might say if I invited her to work with me full-time.' When Susanna stayed quiet she added, 'But I couldn't do that, because I made a promise.'

'A promise?'

'To your dad. When he died, he told me he was sorry. We put our differences aside. We both realised what we'd lost by not having each other. He never wanted that to be you and Addie, so I assured him I would never let it happen. The only way to keep my promise was to push Addie away, not encourage her, make sure she left the island as you'd both always said you would.'

Susanna looked upwards to stem her tears. 'I took that from her, and I shouldn't have.'

'We all made mistakes. You thought you were looking after your sister and yourself.'

Susanna paused. 'You saying that makes me see the intention behind you talking to Mateo about our relationship. You were trying to look after me just like I was doing for Addie by getting her to go through with our plan.'

'That's one way of looking at it.'

'You know, Addie was furious I never told her what I knew about Dad until now.'

'Why would you? It wouldn't have benefited her. But maybe with Addie grown up now, it's time to stop mothering.'

Susanna nodded. 'You know, I saw the two of you together at the café once. I could see her settling in, enjoying herself, and I panicked. I thought perhaps she wouldn't come to the mainland at all, and I'd lose her. I couldn't wait to get us both off the island.'

Gayle chuckled. 'I wouldn't have been surprised if you'd had a calendar, crossing off the days like you were in prison.'

Susanna's smile soon gave way to a seriousness again. 'I was happy here sometimes, you know.'

'When you were with Mateo?'

'Not just then. I loved it when Addie and I explored the island, went out on our bikes, all that fresh air and freedom here compared to what we'd had in Oxford.'

'You always seemed quite happy when you came into the café. Even on the days you protested because you wanted to be with friends rather than babysitting, you'd slowly ease into it, and you looked content enough. I'd watch you so many times. I never let you catch me doing it, though, you'd have scowled over at me.'

Susanna grinned. 'You know, I think you're right.'

'So, how is this new world of yours on the mainland? Married, with a posh job and, I expect, a lovely lifestyle?'

Susanna briefly got up when a nurse came to check on the patient opposite, but as soon as she disappeared Susanna perched her bottom on Gayle's bed once more. 'To be honest it's not all a bed of roses.'

Susanna spent the next twenty minutes telling her all about Alex, the good and the bad, the worry, the concern about her marriage.

'Do you still love him?' Gayle asked when she'd finished.

'I do. I really do. But I've never felt more lonely in my life.'

She reached for Susanna's hand. 'I hope you and Alex work it out.'

'So do I. But he wasn't happy when he heard Mateo's voice in the background on the boat when we came here. And I haven't heard from him since.'

Gayle gripped her hand for reassurance, in a way she'd never been allowed to before, and only hoped that it would go some way to comfort her. 'Talk to Alex.'

'I'll try.'

She waited a beat before she asked, 'How do you feel about Louisa?'

'Strangely okay.'

'You are?'

'I've surprised even myself. Addie is slowly getting her head around it, and it's not Louisa's fault that her mum had an affair with our dad, or our dad had an affair with her mum, whichever way you want to put it. I can see that, you know, with my forty-four years of wisdom.'

'Rather than your fourteen-year-old self?'

'Not sure how I'd have felt back then if I'd discovered Dad had fathered another child.'

She had so much to catch up on with Susanna and she wanted to know, 'What did it really feel like coming back to Anchor Island after all this time?'

'Honestly? Weird, terrifying, confronting, eye-opening... especially when my dead aunt suddenly came alive.'

Gayle stopped a giggle in its tracks. 'Maybe we'll laugh about my faux pas on the invites someday.'

'What a story, eh?'

'So, the island... Do you like it, or is it a case of you can't leave soon enough?'

'I've pushed it away for so long, the same way I pushed you away. But it's beautiful. I love all the open spaces, the water from different vantage points, the quaint streets, the absence of traffic. I wish I'd appreciated it more and not been so selfish to see that Addie liked it here.'

'You are not selfish. You have turned into a wonderful woman, despite all the crap thrown at you along the way.'

'We did have a lot of crap. All of us.'

'Maybe it's time we faced the crap together,' said Gayle.

Susanna's voice shook as she laughed, 'Stop saying crap or I won't be able to take you seriously.'

Susanna was different to the girl who had left the island, angry, desperate to escape. Maybe Anchor Island had finally worked its magic on her.

30

SUSANNA

Susanna was at the cottage, getting everything ready for Gayle's homecoming. Gayle was finally being released from hospital and she wanted everything to be perfect. She'd dusted Gayle's bedroom, vacuumed and cleaned the bathroom. A fresh arrangement of pink gladioli, sunflowers and cerise roses had been placed in a vase on the kitchen table and a smaller vase – this one containing white spray chrysanthemums – was on Gayle's bedside table.

She looked out of the kitchen window. It was early October already and autumn was on its way. Soon the tree at the front of the cottage garden and the trees dotted along Bay Street would shed their leaves, leaving a crunch underfoot, and the island would take on a whole new personality.

She turned her attentions to preparing the vegetables to go with the almost-cooked chicken casserole. Once the timer beeped she'd give it another forty minutes or so to rest and let the flavours really develop.

Now all that was missing was Gayle, and when she heard a noise at the front door she almost skipped to open up and welcome their aunt over the threshold. It wasn't lost on her how many years she could've been like this and hadn't. But it was no use constantly regretting the past.

She pulled open the door and froze in shock. 'Alex?'

He didn't step closer, he didn't beam a smile – he looked so uncertain, but Susanna wasn't.

She stepped towards him and enveloped him in a tight hug. Since the day she'd told him about the near kiss with Mateo, and after he'd overheard Mateo with her on the boat, she hadn't been able to get hold of her husband. She'd been texting, calling, but every attempt went unanswered.

She inhaled the familiar scent of the Paco Rabanne aftershave she'd bought him last Christmas, the warmth of his skin, the feel of his firm body beneath his clothes. 'I'm so pleased to see you.'

'Susanna...'

'There's nothing between me and Mateo, I promise.' She was still holding on to him. She never wanted to let go.

His chest rose on a breath, a sign he was contemplating the right words to use. 'You almost kissed him,' he said as he pulled away. 'And then when I called... you were with him.'

She stared at her husband. He looked so crushed.

'Alex, the near kiss was a mistake, a horrible, silly mistake. And there's a reason I was with him when you called me back. I'll tell you all about it, but first I need some answers from you.' She stood back and waited for him to step inside. When she closed the door behind him, she said, 'You've been distant for a while. Something is going on, and you refuse to tell me.'

When he said nothing, she folded her arms across her body, ready to feel the brute force of a confession when she asked, 'Are you having an affair?'

'Am I what?'

'Are you having an affair?' she repeated. Maybe he was stalling, grasping for the words he could utter that might get himself out of this.

'Whatever gave you that idea?'

'Well, are you?'

'No, I'm not.'

'I found a receipt. I wasn't snooping – I was in your study trying to find the number for the window cleaner and I saw it. It was from that little Italian restaurant where we celebrated our anniversary.'

He let out a deep sigh. 'You're right, I went there.'

'Who with?'

He shook his head. 'It's not what you think.'

When the oven timer pinged she went into the kitchen and turned the oven off. The meal could stay in there until it was time to eat.

He'd followed her and sat down at a chair at the table.

She sat opposite. 'Wait, did you only turn up here because you thought I was cheating on you?' she asked, piecing it together. 'Because I'm not. I promise.'

'Hearing about the almost kiss and knowing you were with Mateo did instigate my visit.' He looked at her now. 'But not because I'm angry and wanted to have it out with you. It made me realise how long overdue our talk is, that I should've confided in you before now.'

Oh God. He *was* having an affair.

'I promise you I'm not cheating,' he said.

And then something else dawned. Something far worse. 'Are you sick?' Gayle's upcoming return had probably triggered the thought. Had she totally missed the mark with her suspicions?

'No, I'm not sick.'

'Then what is it?'

Instead of answering, he looked around. 'Where is everyone?'

She explained the dash to the hospital, the emergency and the stay in Guernsey. 'I tried to call you back a couple of times to tell you everything. Gayle was taken by marine ambulance. They couldn't accommodate any extra passengers so Mateo stepped in and took us.'

'So that's why I heard Mateo in the background.' He looked so relieved she could've wept.

'We wouldn't have been able to get to the hospital without him.'

He held out a hand and waited for her to take it. 'When I thought you were with Mateo, I panicked. I thought I was going to lose you.' He took a deep breath. 'I've not been myself for a while, I know that, and I've pushed you away every time you tried to get to the bottom of it.'

So he *had* noticed.

'I haven't been entirely honest with you,' he said. 'It's the practice.'

'What's happened?'

He looked her right in the eye when he confessed, 'It isn't doing well at all. It's in trouble financially.' His expression negated any need to ask whether it was really that bad. 'That's what the fancy dinner was about. I took a potential investor out and tried to woo them. With no success, unfortunately.'

'Why did you never mention it? Not just the dinner, but any of it.'

'I didn't know how to. We were both doing so well and then all of a sudden, I wasn't. I kept it hidden out of pride, because I thought I could fix it. I knew your dad had lost his café, and whenever you talk about that time in your life I can tell how sad it makes you. I didn't want my practice to go the same way. You always wanted to help and fix Addie. I didn't want you to feel you had to do it with me too.'

'I never felt I had to with you. You're my equal, in every way.'

'I just wanted to be the one who made life easier for you, never the other way round.'

He rested his arms on his legs, palms clasped together at his knees. 'The practice has seen a reduction in the volume of patients coming through its doors – the cost of living probably has a lot to do with it. Patients who liked a check-up and clean every six months are pushing it to twelve or more, and there's much less uptake on non-essential procedures. At the same time our costs have increased – utility bills are high, equipment prices have been hiked up, and maintenance is costing more than it ever did. Our inventory system wasn't as efficient as I assumed either – there's been wastage, pushing up our expenses.'

He shifted his gaze from her face to his hands. 'I've let you down.'

'No, you haven't.' *She'd* let *him* down by not trusting him and by almost seeking comfort with someone else.

'I think I'm going to have to sell the practice,' he said. He looked so despondent.

'Is it that bad?'

'It is. And that's another reason why I didn't want to tell you. I wanted to find a way out of the mess, but nothing I've tried has worked.'

'Alex, I'm in property law, not family law, but I'm pretty sure we're supposed to be a team. I wish you'd shared this before now.'

'I wish I had too.' He shook his head. 'I'm sorry. It's all such a big mess.'

She moved to sit in his lap and wrapped her arms around him. She'd missed this closeness more than she realised.

'It's my work,' he said. 'It's my job to sort it out. I wanted to give you a good life, and here I am messing it up. We talked about converting the loft, but we don't have the money. We discussed holidaying next year, but we can't afford that either, and we definitely don't have the funds for the driveway that needs repaving.'

'None of that is the end of the world.'

'I thought you'd be disappointed. You love our house.'

'I do, but I love you more.' She rested her forehead against his. 'Let's just say I feel like I've got a whole new perspective on priorities since I came here. I don't need new things in the house, I don't need a big expensive holiday. Addie and I had a few inexpensive days away and it was one of the best breaks I've had.'

He put a hand to her cheek. 'What happened to you?'

'This island,' she said. It had happened to her when she was fourteen and it was happening to her again, except this time it brought with it the ability to see the important things and finally find a sense of peace in letting go of the past.

As they chatted and Alex held her on his lap, refusing to let her even get up and make a coffee, she told him more about the island.

'You never told me whether those bands worked on the crossing over here,' he said.

'The travel bands you gave me? Well, I wasn't sick so yes, I think they did. Thank you.' She hugged him. It felt so good to have him by her side, so close, after all this time.

'I can't believe you never brought me here,' he said, looking out of the window as if it gave him a view of the whole island. 'I've not seen much of it, but the walk from the harbour was spectacular. The views are incredible.'

'I can't wait to show you more. How long are you staying?'

'I'm afraid it'll be a quick turnaround. I'm going back in the morning.'

'So soon?'

'I need to. I have a meeting with a financial advisor to see if there's anything else I can do. Then I'll take it from there.'

She understood. If the practice was in trouble, he had to be at the helm. 'But you'll stay tonight?'

Before he had a chance to answer they heard the front door open and Addie's voice call out, 'We're home!'

Susanna leapt from Alex's lap and raced to greet them, hugging her aunt as she crossed the threshold.

Addie squealed when she saw Alex appear in the hallway.

Gayle, still beside Susanna, whispered, 'That's your Alex?'

'It is,' she said quietly, before introducing him to her aunt and Louisa, who she named as the third Rafferty girl. Quite rightly he looked confused, but he took it in his stride. She'd have to explain that part of the drama to him later.

'And?' Gayle whispered to Susanna when Addie had dragged Alex and Louisa into the kitchen with a yell that she was making teas and coffees.

'Gayle, I really think you should be sitting down. You've just come out of hospital.'

'Not until you tell me how it's going with Alex.'

Susanna hugged her aunt and said softly into her ear, 'Alex and I are going to be okay.'

'Then that's all I need to know.' And she smiled right back at her niece.

'Is it all right if he stays the night before he has to head off?'

'Of course.' She strode towards the kitchen calling over her shoulder, 'I have a set of earplugs.'

Susanna felt herself colour. She couldn't wait to be in Alex's arms tonight, to feel safe, to take on whatever life threw at them next. Together.

She'd never felt quite as much warmth in this cottage as she did right now.

31

GAYLE

A couple of days later and Gayle was getting used to being waited on and fussed over. She'd thought she might hate it, but quite the opposite – she basked in it.

'What have we here?' She looked at the bowl on the table.

'Porridge,' said Susanna, who was at the sink washing blueberries in a sieve. 'Sit.'

'Bossy.' She loved it.

Susanna came over and sprinkled the berries on top of Gayle's breakfast.

Since her homecoming, Susanna, Addie and Louisa had been on top of her nutrition plan. They ensured she had three meals a day, and it didn't matter whether those meals were large or small, as long as they were packed full of goodness.

As Gayle scooped up some porridge from the edge of her bowl, ensuring there was a berry included, she asked, 'How's Alex? Have you spoken to him today?'

'Yes, first thing.'

'You two lovebirds.'

'We're doing well.'

'I enjoyed getting to know him when he was here. Shame it was such a short visit.'

The pair had got on like a house on fire. Gayle and Alex had talked about the island. One of her passions – apart from puddings – was to talk about the place she lived and loved to newcomers who were yet to experience the joys of living here. They discussed puddings in great detail, dentistry, Cambridge, the day he saved Susanna's life, and before Susanna had gone up to bed with him, Gayle had stopped her and pulled her in for a hug. 'I'm glad you found such a good man,' she'd told her. She didn't say anything about Mateo; she didn't have to. In many ways, Mateo had been good for her back then, but Alex was perfect for her now.

'I could get used to being looked after like this,' Gayle said now, her appetite much improved and already halfway through her porridge.

'Well, remember you need to keep going with the good eating plan when you're on your own again. This will get you into a pattern. We'll be checking up on you, you know.'

'I don't doubt it.'

Addie came through next, having already been out for a morning walk around the island with Louisa, who had stopped at the café to help Nancy. Gayle was to take a whole fortnight off work, during which she'd have a couple of check-ups with the doctor. She'd thought she would hate the time off from her beloved café, but instead she knew she needed to get herself back to tiptop health if she wanted to enjoy many more years at the helm of the Sweet Life Café.

'What's on the menu tonight?' Gayle asked, as she popped a stray blueberry on top of her last spoonful of porridge.

Susanna filled her in on tonight's dinner of fish, potatoes and vegetables. 'That will be followed by whatever Addie is making for pudding,' she said. 'Now, I'm just going to run to the bathroom.'

After Susanna left the room, Gayle asked Addie, 'What will you make?'

'I was thinking bread and butter pudding.'

Gayle's spoon paused before it could reach her mouth. 'That was the first thing you and I ever made together. Do you remember?'

'Of course I do.'

She felt happy, honoured, relieved to hear it. 'Do you follow the same recipe?'

'To the letter.' Addie smiled. 'And when Isaac was old enough to help me bake, it was the first thing we made together.'

Gayle felt her emotions rise again. For so long she'd thought of only ever having a negative impact on these girls' lives, but slowly she was coming to realise she'd been way too hard on herself, and actually, they'd all done better than she thought.

Addie's phone went and she excitedly answered a FaceTime call from Isaac via Maurie's phone.

'Hey, my little man. How are you?' She propped her phone up against the big jug of fruit juice in the centre of the table so Gayle was in view. Addie, like the other two, had extended her stay, and Gayle knew how much she was missing her little boy.

'I miss you.' It took seconds for the small frown creased in Isaac's forehead to deepen as he asked, 'Who are you?'

By now Susanna had come back into the room and she nudged Gayle gently. 'I'm pretty sure he's asking you.'

Addie hadn't told Isaac that her aunt had died and that was what was behind the trip to the island, which made it far easier to explain her existence now. 'I'm your mum's aunt. I'm Aunt Gayle.' Oh, this sweet boy, he was just gorgeous, and if she didn't think it would confuse him, she might well burst into tears with emotion.

'You know who this is, Isaac,' said Addie, 'I showed you photographs, remember, of the island, the Sweet Life Café.'

He drew in a breath and his eyes widened. 'You're the pudding lady!'

Gayle roared with laughter. 'Well now, I don't mind you calling me that at all.'

He looked perplexed. 'But if you are mum's aunt like Aunt Susanna is my aunt, what am I supposed to call you?'

'Why don't you call me Aunt Gayle? These girls can call me Gayle now they're older.'

'Mummy is thirty-eight. Is thirty-eight too old to have an aunt?'

'Not at all.'

She talked to Isaac about all sorts – the island, the café, where he lived, her cottage. 'And how's school?' she asked him.

Isaac let out a long sigh. 'I don't want to talk about it.' This made Gayle laugh even harder. 'I want to talk more about puddings,' he enthused. 'Me and Mummy make things sometimes.'

'I wish we could do it more,' said Addie, looking at her watch. 'But right now, you need to get ready for school, young man.'

'I'm ready,' he said. Presumably all he had to do was pick up a bag. Life was easy when you were seven. 'Mummy, are you coming home soon?'

'You know I am. Only two more sleeps and I'll see you again.'

The three girls had worked out a bit of a timetable now that Gayle had been discharged from the hospital. She was fine on her own, not likely to collapse again, but they wanted to get her into new habits before they all got back to their regular lives. And of course, Nancy had been supportive and looking after the bulk of things at the Sweet Life Café.

Isaac still hadn't got the hint that it would soon be time for him to go to school. He said, 'Mummy… Granny Maurie said you'd been on a boat.'

'That's right.'

'Did it go fast?'

Gayle could've listened to him all day, and she was sad when they had to say goodbye.

Having the girls back on the island had turned all of their lives around, and she'd never be sorry for the events that had unfolded because they had all led them to now. It was a new version of the Rafferty family, and she couldn't wait to see where they went from here.

32

ADDIE

A few weeks after they left Anchor Island, Addie was on her way back during the October half term, and this time her trip to the island was about so much more than a visit or a holiday.

She stood with Isaac, hand in hand on the top deck of the small ferry, as they left Jersey en route to the island that still meant so much to her. Isaac was beside himself with excitement at the adventure, and Addie couldn't wait for Gayle to meet her little boy in person.

Over the short time that Addie had been back at the flat in London, she'd done a lot of soul searching. She wasn't in her dream job, she didn't live in a place she loved, and she desperately wanted Isaac to have more. She wanted to give him a life that had some freedom, a childhood where he could get fresh air, not city smog in his lungs, space to run around and be a kid. But it wasn't just about Isaac. After getting back to London, she'd soon realised that Anchor Island could give them both something different, and although she hadn't handed in her notice yet or given up their flat, she wanted to talk to Gayle this week about the possibility of trying something new. They'd had a good talk the last time Addie was on the island, they were in a good place, and she really hoped her aunt would be on board with what she had in mind.

The day Aunt Gayle had met Isaac over FaceTime, Susanna had gone upstairs to call Alex and Gayle had asked Addie if they could talk. She'd had a talk with Susanna in the hospital, so Addie had known this was coming.

'Isaac is a credit to you, Addie,' Gayle had told her as they sat at the kitchen table with a mug of tea each.

'I know I'm biased, but yes, he really is.'

'I love how he has so many questions.'

Addie laughed. 'And then some.'

'He has so much energy.'

'I struggle to keep up sometimes,' Addie admitted.

'How do his grandparents cope?'

'They're brilliant.' And by the wistful look on Gayle's face, Addie wished she hadn't kept herself or Isaac from her for so long. 'I'm glad they're in his life, because his dad isn't really.'

'May I ask what happened with Isaac's father?'

Addie explained the gist of it. 'I got Isaac from the fling, so I'll never be sorry.' She paused. 'Gayle, did you ever have anyone special in your life? A man, I mean.'

'Once upon a time, yes.' She paused. 'Jeffrey. We married, but it wasn't to be. I struggled to have a baby and, well… it broke us.'

'Gayle, I didn't realise.'

'I never told a soul. It was easier that way. It's why I particularly regret that I didn't make more of you and Susanna being in my life.'

'I think you did your best in the circumstances. I'm sorry it was so hard for you.'

'It was hard, but I had my cottage, you girls, my café, and

despite the struggles, I was grateful. But I also had to honour a promise to Harry.'

'Susanna told me you'd promised Dad that you would never let us fall out.'

'Is that all she told you?'

'Well, yes. What else is there?'

'The promise is also the reason why I never showed too much enthusiasm about your love for baking.'

Addie felt taken aback. She should have put two and two together when her sister told her about the promise. 'So I didn't imagine you pushing me away.'

'Oh, Addie, I'm so sorry. I didn't want to at all, but—'

'I understand.'

'I feel so terrible about it.'

'I'm just glad you told me.' She reached out and held Gayle's hand. 'You wanted me and for so long I thought you didn't.'

'I wanted you very much.'

'Over the years I thought a lot about how my life might have been different,' Addie shared. 'If I'd stayed here, if I'd pursued baking, not a career in web design.'

'Do you understand why I did what I did?'

'I do. You made a promise.' But she wished in a way that her dad hadn't asked that of Gayle; he was, in part, to blame for the way things had turned out, heaping an additional pressure on his sister's shoulders. He couldn't have known it would backfire, that it might have kept his girls together, but it had made her life so very different than it might have been.

'You know, I question myself with Isaac all the time,' said Addie. 'I ask myself should I let him have more freedom, am I being too strict, am I creating good memories not bad ones? Parenting is a tough job, no matter which way you look at it.'

'You're being so kind.' Gayle's eyes prickled with tears. 'May I ask you a question?'

'Go ahead.'

'Why don't you ever let anyone call you Adeleine these days?'

Addie smiled. 'Initially, it was because Dad was the one to call me that. My friends called me Addie – so did Susanna, from time to time. When Dad died, I didn't want anyone else to use that name. Not even you.'

'Oh, I know.'

'It's less of a big deal now than it was then, to be honest. My boss *always* calls me Adeleine, but it does sound a bit more grown up in the office, so I let it slide. I suppose I've been Addie for so long that I've grown to like it. It's no longer because hearing Adeleine is painful, it's more that I'm different.'

'I do wish the three of us had worked this out a long time ago. When you two girls came to live with me, I told myself that this was my chance to be a mother figure, but then I kept messing it up.' She pre-empted Addie's disagreement, 'I did. You girls were young, and it should've been me who managed to get you both to a better place. I'll never forgive myself that I didn't.'

'Well, you should. Susanna and I know we have all contributed to the three of us not having a very good relationship.' She paused. 'Susanna also knows that I pulled back from you because of her. My big sister, who I looked up to, I didn't want to do anything that went against her wishes, and so when you weren't particularly enthusiastic about my love of baking, I accepted it, I stepped back. I should've been stronger and become my own person earlier on. I liked it here, felt at home. I always wondered what it might have been like if I'd followed my dreams. I knew that you had, that you'd found a wonderful place to live on a beautiful island and you'd launched a successful business.' She looked fondly at Gayle. 'Do you know how many times over the years I wanted to call you up and talk to you?'

'But you felt it was betraying Susanna?'

'Not only that, I thought I'd left it so long that you might not want to know. You had friends, a life, the café. I wasn't sure if I could, or should, try to edge back in.'

'Then I'm guilty of not making it so that you knew.' Her eyes met Addie's. 'What a pair we are. What a trio, what a quartet with Louisa too!'

'Gayle, what would you think if I said I wanted to bring Isaac to the island for his half-term holiday?'

Gayle's face lit up, and she put her hands across her mouth for a moment before she took them away to utter, 'I'd say yes, please.'

And now Addie and Isaac were almost at the island. The boat was close enough to the harbour that they could start to focus on the people lined up, waiting to greet the arrivals.

'Can you see her?' Addie asked her little boy, who was standing as tall as he could, on tiptoes.

Luckily, she wasn't crouched next to Isaac because he suddenly jumped up, bouncing on his toes now as he waved madly. 'Auntie Gayle, Auntie Gayle!' Isaac had taken to calling her Auntie Gayle rather than Aunt Gayle over their FaceTimes, which Gayle didn't mind one bit, and his little voice might not have carried over the din of the boat as it came in to dock, but his hands in the air certainly caught Gayle's attention.

Addie spotted Gayle waving to them both. She kept a firm clasp on her son's hand until they were safely off the vessel, and it was safe for him to charge up the ramp and into Gayle's arms. Addie suspected if she had the strength Gayle would've picked him up and swung him around, but they both settled on a big hug and Addie went over to get one for herself.

This time, returning to Anchor Island felt a lot like coming home, except to a home she hadn't admitted the true existence of until recently.

* * *

An hour later they were in the Sweet Life Café and Gayle was in her element. She was back at work, although not today and only in a part-time capacity when she was. She'd been talking to Isaac about her pudding business ever since they met down at the harbour and had answered the million and one questions he had.

'Would you look at the pair of them,' said Nancy, as they watched Isaac emerge from the kitchen first, carrying his own choice of pudding topped with a rather generous dollop of cream. Gayle followed after with a more modest portion. Addie wasn't about to comment either, because according to Nancy, Gayle was staying on track with the healthy eating and puddings were no longer the mainstay of her diet.

When a group of four customers came through the door, Nancy announced, 'No rest for the wicked. We're getting busy. I'll get on.'

Addie spotted a spare apron hanging on the hook outside the kitchen. 'I'll give you a hand.' And when she waved over at Gayle who was in cahoots with Isaac in the same far booth the Rafferty girls had always taken, Gayle nodded her absolute approval.

They stayed until closing time, and while Isaac was busy with a colouring book and a full complement of felt-tips, Addie sat at the adjacent table with Gayle and Nancy and a cup of coffee each.

'This one has been a lot of help today,' said Nancy, gesturing to Addie. 'Our part-time help lasted all of a week.'

'Was she that terrible?' Addie asked.

'He. And yes, I caught him smoking up on the balcony and handing out free pudding to his mates.'

'Oh dear.'

'Good job you found him, not me,' said Gayle. 'Louisa was here last week helping out, but by her own admission her skills are more suited to the garden than the kitchen.'

'She sounds like she's doing well with her new job.' Addie, Susanna and Louisa were slowly getting to know each other. They did FaceTime calls regularly and finally Louisa had found full-time work at a garden centre and already talked about someday having her own business. Maybe it was in the genes.

'When you do what you love, it's a lot easier,' Gayle agreed.

'Part-time help is why I wanted to talk to you both, actually,' Addie told the two women. 'I have an idea. It sounds kind of crazy even to my own ears, so please tell me if it is.'

'Spit it out, love,' said Nancy.

'Well... what if I was to come and work here.' She paused, looked from Gayle to Nancy, Nancy to Gayle.

'That would be great,' said Gayle. 'It's a busy week, with half term.'

'No, I don't mean just for half term. I mean, what if I was to come and work here, permanently?'

Gayle looked over at Isaac. 'How would you do that when you live in London?'

Addie felt a smile form. 'I'd move myself and Isaac over here, rent somewhere, enrol Isaac in school, the whole shebang.'

Gayle couldn't have looked more shocked if Addie had said she was going to run naked down Bay Street carrying a tray of puddings.

'We do need someone reliable,' Nancy urged.

'What about your job?' Gayle asked. 'The wages here would be nowhere near on a par.'

'I have factored that in. Wages would be less, but the cost of living here is cheaper. And it's time for Isaac and I to have a new adventure. I have savings given I've been trying to get a deposit together for a long time. I'd rent for a while and take it from there. There are a couple of two-bed apartments that would be perfect for us. I could do however many hours you needed me to do.'

'This is all... Well, it's wonderful,' said Gayle. 'But I have to ask, are you doing this so you can keep an eye on me?'

'Absolutely not. You'd see right through that plan if I tried. This is something for me and for my son. I don't love my job in London. It's been a means to an end for so long, but being here on the island, being at the Sweet Life Café, reminded me of how different my life might be if I only took a chance. Susanna agrees with me too.'

'She does?'

Addie nodded. 'We've had a long talk.'

Gayle looked at Isaac and then back at Addie. 'It's a yes on one condition.'

'Name it.'

'I'll employ you full time but only if you move into the cottage with me, or at least agree to have the garden room. I'll charge you a peppercorn rent so you can save your money and invest in a property on the island if you like it and want to stay.' Firmly, she added, 'Take it or leave it, that's my offer.'

Addie drew in her breath and extended her hand. 'Deal.' And then she raced to her aunt's side and gave her the biggest hug. Nancy disappeared out back and returned with her handbag.

'Where on earth are you off to?' asked Gayle.

'I'm going to buy a bottle of champagne, and I think this calls for fish and chips all round.'

Gayle laughed. 'I'm not sure my doctor recommends champagne.'

'A small glass won't hurt,' she said. 'Isaac, would you like to help me buy fish and chips and carry them back here?'

'Yes!' Isaac stopped his colouring and clicked the lids back on the felt-tips scattered across the table.

Nancy lowered her voice and said to Addie, 'He won't be scarred if he sees me nip into the off-licence, will he?'

'I'm sure he won't.'

Moments later, Isaac and Nancy left hand in hand with Isaac delivering his usual rapid-fire questioning by asking Nancy whether the fish they were going to eat were caught from the water surrounding the island.

Her little boy was going to love it here, and she already did.

33

NEW YEAR'S EVE

Susanna

Susanna was filled with excitement at thought of returning to Anchor Island this time. She hadn't been back since she'd left in October; not because she didn't want to, but because there was a lot to do in Cambridge.

Alex had found a temporary solution to keep the practice going and it was a case of taking it day by day. But they were in it together now, and they talked, every night, without fail. He'd shut her out before, and she never wanted to feel like such a stranger from her husband again.

The passion had returned to their sex life; it was as if they'd been apart for much longer than they had, although emotionally she supposed they'd been distant for a while.

Alex sat beside her on the ferry from Jersey and took her hand. 'It's decent weather, should be a good crossing.'

She squeezed his hand. 'Let's hope so.'

'Do you have your special bands on?' He pulled back the sleeve of her heavy woollen coat to see for himself.

'I do, but I think having you with me is going to be the most calming thing.' And so far so good.

'New Year's Eve on an island,' said Alex. 'Who would've thought? And we've both got two weeks off. Well, kind of for me, but good enough.' With the financial struggles he would only be taking a break from the practical side of dentistry but would be keeping a close eye on the business side. He began to smile. 'I can't believe I got you on this ferry without your laptop.'

'I feel bereft without it.' She shook her head. 'Actually, it felt really good to tell work that this was a total break, that I wouldn't be doing anything. I'm pretty sure I shocked more than a few of my colleagues.'

This was another thing they'd agreed on, as well as openness and communication. They needed more time together, just the two of them. Work couldn't take over every moment of their lives, and since they'd had the discussion it had been surprisingly easy to start separating office time from home time. Alex, while initially devastated at the prospect of having to sell his practice, had started to see the plus points should it happen. They'd talked about him continuing with dentistry – he could do that anywhere – and he wouldn't have the added stress of management, which was taking its toll. They had their marriage, they had each other, and they'd even begun to talk about retiring early and perhaps doing some sort of repeat of the travels they'd done as twenty-somethings. Susanna had added the caveat that they'd at least increase their budget a bit when it came to accommodation, but other than that she was all for it.

When she heard a noise even over the din of the boat's engine, she looked at Alex. 'Was that your tummy?'

'No.' He quickly added, 'Yes.'

'You're hungry.'

'*Really* hungry,' he said. 'But I don't want to get anything to eat as I know the smell of food might make you nauseous.'

She leaned closer and planted a kiss on the corner of his mouth. 'It's better you wait anyway.'

'Oh? Why is that?' He turned and grazed her lips with his own.

'The winter menu at the Sweet Life Café, from what I remember, is pretty good.'

'I predict eating my bodyweight in puddings over the next two weeks. They might not take me back by ferry, I might exceed the weight limits.'

'Totally worth it for Gayle's puddings.'

'And Addie's.'

'And Addie's,' she echoed.

She and Addie had had a long talk on the ferry on the way back to the mainland following the living funeral, and once they knew Gayle was going to be okay. Susanna had opened up the conversation with an apology.

'I'm sorry I made you come to the mainland,' she'd said.

'Why are you sorry?'

'Because it was my plan.'

'It was *our* plan.'

She'd smiled. 'It was, but we'd both changed. You loved baking with Gayle, and I wish I'd seen past my own needs and wants at the time.'

After a pause Addie had told her, 'In a way, so do I. But then again, I love that we stayed so close to each other. It's good that I became independent and did a job for the money, if only to show me what it was like in comparison to doing what I love. And without London I wouldn't have met Jonty, and I wouldn't have Isaac.'

'Very true.'

'I think things worked out pretty well in the end,' Addie had said to her, looping her arm through Susanna's and leaning her head on her shoulder.

They'd come full circle, back to the island, and now here she was doing it again.

'Do you see them?' she asked Alex as they emerged from below deck and up towards where people were greeting arrivals. It really seemed to be just the people here to meet loved ones; nobody else would be here merely to watch a ferry come in when it was this cold.

'There they are,' said her husband, and took her hand to navigate the crowd.

And as she saw Gayle waving and young Isaac desperately trying to spot them too, she felt a pull she hadn't felt in a long time.

The pull of a family life here on Anchor Island.

34

ADDIE

'Well, that was a hit,' Addie said. She was in the kitchen at the Sweet Life Café, having finished for the day. She was only working the morning shift, and she'd just served the bread-and-butter pudding she still loved as much as when she'd made it with Gayle the first time they baked together. That and her cheesecake were permanent choices on the menu these days.

Addie was full-time on the island and in the café now, having moved here the day after Boxing Day. Leaving her job in London had been easy – her boss hadn't even been that surprised when she handed in her notice – saying goodbye to her colleagues a little sad, but the hardest of all had been saying goodbye to Maurie and Jarrett. She'd spent Christmas Day with them though, and they'd already booked to come to the island in February – not the nicest of seasons, but any season according to Maurie would be perfect with Isaac. Addie had told them that Gayle could have a break when they were here, and Jarrett could help Isaac with his Lego which Gayle clearly didn't enjoy doing at all. At Easter, Addie would take Isaac to the mainland, and he could go to his grandparents' house and spend time with them.

They'd promised to keep his room as it was. Maurie and Jarrett were thrilled and Isaac, well, he was being wrapped in so much affection that hopefully as he got older – and even if it hurt that his dad was disinterested – he would know that he was loved by so many people, that he was part of a big messy family.

Isaac came racing through the front door to the café, all rosy-cheeked.

'She's here, Mummy, Auntie Susie is here!' he called out.

Addie laughed, as did everyone else in the café, because Isaac had delivered his announcement as if he was the town crier.

Gayle, Susanna and Alex appeared moments later, and Addie raced over to hug her sister and her husband. 'I'm so glad you're both here.'

'So am I,' said Alex. 'Now, what's on the menu?'

Gayle was already talking about what was being served today on top of the regular menu: spiced blueberry and cranberry pudding, Christmas pudding – which was a hit during the cold months, even after the big day itself had passed – apple and pear crumble, and a melt-in-the-mouth chocolate volcano pudding.

Alex and Susanna both went for the Christmas pudding knowing Addie had made it, and Addie asked her son what he'd been up to with Nanna Gayle.

During the October half term, Isaac had pointed out that Aunt Gayle was the same age as Maurie and only a year younger than Jarrett. He'd asked how Gayle could possibly be an aunt when Maurie and Jarrett were grandparents. Addie had explained the relationship, how Gayle was really his great-aunt, but he said it still felt odd. He'd said he didn't want to call her Granny either because it would confuse everyone and so Addie had suggested, 'Nanna Gayle' instead. Gayle had been honoured with her new title and thoroughly embraced it.

'We went to the playground near my new school,' said Isaac.

He'd be starting school in a week, and he couldn't wait. 'And then we ran down to the marina, and I was allowed to race around the picnic benches.'

Addie could imagine it, Isaac racing ahead, Gayle calling after him to slow down but with a big smile on her face. Isaac racing anywhere in London had been terrifying but here, she felt so much more laid back and he had so much more freedom.

'Come on, you,' said Addie, taking off her apron, 'Time to get you home.'

'I want to stay with Auntie Susie and Nanna Gayle.' He was using his best whiny voice and she was tempted to cave, but she could see Alex, Susanna and Gayle catching up as her sister and brother-in-law ate their puddings. They needed this time together.

'I know you do, but remember you've had Nanna Gayle to yourself for a while since we got here and it's Auntie Susie's turn now.'

'All right.' An eye roll accompanied his words.

As well as giving her sister some time with their aunt, she really wanted to get Isaac home to the garden room. He needed some down time, so she intended to curl up with him and watch a movie before they ventured out this evening down to the green space, with its incredible view of the harbour and the fireworks. It wasn't the busiest spot, or the best spot which was further around the bay, but it would be relatively uncrowded in comparison and it was closer to home for Gayle who wouldn't want to walk too far, especially after a trip down to the playground and on to the harbour and back already.

'Good to see you again,' came a voice from behind her before she could go and collect her bag from the kitchen.

She turned to see Samuel bundled up in a dark green fisherman's jumper, his deep brown eyes warm and gentle, and the quiver in her tummy reminded her of how she'd felt when she got talking to him at the living funeral. She'd not bumped into him over the October half term, but she had seen him in here a couple of days ago. Unfortunately, he'd picked up a takeaway, and they'd been so busy in the café that she hadn't been able to chat.

'It's good to see you too,' she said, conscious that her curls were all over the place, having avoided washing her hair until after work. 'I've just finished my shift, but what can I get for you?'

'A bit of advice, really,' he said.

She moved behind the counter, some separation to calm her nerves. 'Fire away.'

'I wanted to know whether you would take a seven-year-old to watch fireworks at midnight?'

She smiled. 'I'm planning to take Isaac.'

'You are? So it's approved?'

She laughed. 'I don't know about that... What I do know is that he'll be grouchy tomorrow, but I'm pretty sure it'll be worth it. I'm going to take him back to Gayle's now for a rest.' She lifted both hands and crossed her fingers.

'Right.' He smiled. 'So I guess we'll see you tonight then.'

Her heart raced. 'See you tonight,' she said as he made for the door. But before he could open it, she called out, 'We won't be at the harbour.'

He came back to the counter and said softly, 'Any hints as to where you *will* be?'

She explained the alternative destination.

'I... *We* will see you tonight,' he said, heading for the door again.

'Wait, you don't want any pudding?' she asked.

He turned to face her. 'Turns out I'm not that hungry.'

And when he left, she only tried to hide her smile when she noticed Gayle and the others all looking her way.

Back at the cottage she agreed to Isaac having a hot chocolate in front of the movie. 'Tonight, we will break all the rules, and you can have another one, plus as much pudding as you like.' They planned to take a big box of sweet treats down to the green space this evening to enjoy before the fireworks.

Addie snuggled up with Isaac to watch *Home Alone*, and as the wintry temperatures wrapped around the garden room, unable to penetrate the interior, she thought about her dad. She stroked Isaac's blond hair, cut short just like his grandad's had been so you couldn't see the curls. Addie secretly loved it when Isaac's hair got a bit long and the Rafferty trait shone through. She wondered whether Isaac would grow up to look like Harry, her imperfect dad, a man who had a third daughter he'd never had the chance to meet, the man she loved so much it still hurt that he was no longer around.

More than anything, she hoped he'd be looking down on all of them right now glad that she and Susanna had found their way back to Gayle, that they were a family and that Louisa had become a part of that too.

35

LOUISA

It was wonderful to be back on Anchor Island. She'd checked into the inn already and followed the straightforward route from there up to Evergreen Close, where she was meeting Gayle, Susanna and Addie for a big surprise for Gayle's birthday. Her birthday wasn't until February, but she would be getting her present early when they could all give it to her together.

In November, Louisa had brought her mum to meet Gayle. Her mum hadn't wanted to come initially – she was the other woman, after all – but Louisa had talked her round, and despite the nerves it had gone really well. Gayle had cushioned any awkwardness with servings of pudding on repeat until none of them could fit another thing in. Her mum hadn't wanted to return for New Year's, even though she'd been invited – she'd finally booked the trip to New York that she'd always dreamed of, her best friend accompanying her for the seven days, but she'd agreed to come back to Anchor Island in the summer for another visit with Louisa.

She reached the cottage, but before she could knock on the

front door a voice from the side of the house caught her attention.

'Psst...' it said.

She crept past the front window and found Addie crouched down, looking her way.

'Do you have the ribbons?' Addie asked in a whisper.

She took off her rucksack. 'I certainly do.' They had been in cahoots about this gift for over a month and organised between the three of them how this was going to work.

They crept around the back of the house and in the shed – which Addie had unlocked without Gayle being any the wiser – she took off her gloves and put the final accessories on the gift. Then she went outside and closed the door, ducked down and ran alongside the house so she wouldn't be seen, and loudly knocked on the front door.

Gayle opened up seconds later, thrilled to see her, and ushered her in out of the cold.

Susanna came out of the kitchen beaming. 'You're here.' She opened her arms to give her a welcoming hug.

The Raffertys could very well have wanted nothing to do with the love-child of the woman who Harry had risked his marriage for when he cheated, but all three of these women had hearts bigger than Louisa could ever have hoped for. Her mum hadn't mentioned until long after their visit that she and Gayle had had a lengthy chat one quiet day at the café, while Louisa had been talking to Nancy about her gardening needs. Gayle had engineered it that way, with Nancy in on the plan – of course she had, because that was Gayle, a determined woman who wanted things to be right. She and Lily had talked candidly about the circumstances of her affair with Harry before Gayle had assured Lily that she had every intention of embracing Louisa as part of the Rafferty family, as long as that was all right with Lily.

'The puddings are all ready for collection from the café,' Addie announced.

'We're eating those while watching the fireworks,' Susanna confided with a nudge at Louisa's side. 'And there's custard.'

'And I've got some Prosecco,' whispered Addie.

Isaac was right on it. 'Can I try one of those. Is it a pudding?'

Addie ruffled his hair. 'It's not a pudding, and no you may not. Prosecco is a grown-up drink, but you get as much hot chocolate as you like, remember. I'm taking a very big flask just for you.'

His eyes lit up much in the same way they had over FaceTime on Christmas Day, when he'd thanked Louisa for the Lego kit she'd gifted him.

Addie looked at her sisters. That was another thing – they'd decided it was enough of the *half* reference. Technicalities, Addie had said, Susanna agreeing readily, Louisa touched with emotion.

'Ready?' Addie asked.

Both Louisa and Susanna nodded.

Susanna clapped her hands together. 'Gayle, Gayle, where are you?' She found her in the hallway, fiddling with a piece of Lego wedged in the sole of her boot.

'Put your boots on,' said Susanna, 'we're going outside.' She grabbed Gayle's coat from the peg.

'Whatever for?' Gayle asked, as she succeeded in removing the offending Lego piece.

'Just do it,' said Susanna, passing over her coat.

Addie and Louisa put their own coats on, and Louisa held Isaac's hand as they all filed out of the back door.

'It's not fireworks time yet,' Isaac pointed out.

'No,' said Louisa, 'but we have a surprise for Gayle.'

'A surprise for Nanna? What is it?'

Louisa laughed. 'Well, if we told you then it wouldn't be a surprise, would it?'

They reached the shed and stood in front until Susanna put her hands across Gayle's eyes.

Gayle was understandably confused. 'It's not my birthday, and Christmas has long gone.'

'This is an early birthday gift,' Addie told her. 'You're getting it now so we can all be here to give it to you.'

When Addie nodded, Susanna took her hands from Gayle's eyes.

'Ta-da!' the three girls called out, Isaac following on with his own 'ta-da!', never one to miss out.

Gayle stepped into the shed. 'It's a bicycle.'

'It's not just any bicycle,' said Susanna. 'It's *your* bicycle.'

Gayle put one hand on the handlebar of the aquamarine bike. 'This is for me?' She ran her hand across the wicker basket attached to the front. 'But I'm too old...'

'Never too old,' claimed Louisa.

'I don't think my doctor would approve,' said Gayle.

'Nonsense,' Addie argued. 'I think he would approve very much. Now, look in the basket.'

Gayle peered inside and pulled out a turquoise helmet. She roared with laughter. 'You think I'm going to put this on?'

'We *know* you're going to put it on,' Addie said.

'Put it on, Nanna!' cried Isaac.

Gayle always found it hard to say no to Isaac, and his request did the trick. 'What's the verdict?' she asked.

Addie stepped forwards. 'It needs adjusting. Here, let me.'

Gayle spotted that in addition to her bike there were three more in the shed besides the girls' old rusty bikes they'd long since outgrown. 'Where did those come from?'

'We borrowed them,' said Louisa, 'For us three.' She indicated herself, Susanna and Addie.

Gayle was clearly happy, if not a little emotional. 'You have all gone to such a lot of effort.'

'You deserve it,' Susanna assured her aunt, putting an arm around her shoulders. 'Remember when we first rode bikes on the island? Well, you said *another time* when Addie wanted you to come with us. And it never happened.'

'Until now,' said Addie with a grin.

'Don't worry,' Louisa added, 'we were all very rusty when we rode the bikes up here from the hire place. I think I wobbled the most.'

Gayle smiled. 'That does make me feel a little better, Louisa.'

Gayle had been putting Louisa's mind at ease ever since she came to the island for the first time, and now it was Gayle's turn to be looked after. She had a heart of gold, and Louisa wasn't alone in thinking she deserved any bit of happiness that came her way from now on.

36

GAYLE

The temperatures that New Year's Eve may have plummeted further as they ventured out, but they were graced with a clear sky and very little wind.

They found the spot they'd agreed on and spread blankets on the ground. Alex had carried down a couple of fold-up chairs. Gayle was sure he'd only brought two so she wouldn't feel singled out, and she gladly took one of them and Isaac took the other when nobody else wanted it. Seconds after his bottom touched the seat, he jumped up when he saw his little friend approaching.

Gayle smiled. Samuel was here. He seemed nice, and it was clear from the body language coming from him and Addie that this pair were on the verge of something special. At least, that's what she hoped.

'Time to serve.' Louisa pulled tin bowls from the bag while Susanna took charge of opening up the big bag of boxed-up pudding portions and distributing them. They would all be full and warm in time for the midnight celebrations.

Gayle got up to help them get organised. Puddings had always been her thing, after all.

She called over to Samuel, 'Pudding?'

'I don't want to intrude,' he said drawing closer to the party with Addie at his side.

'You're not.' And with that she turned and thrust the steel bowl she'd just had Louisa fill with steamed jam sponge into his hand. She passed him a spoon from the bag. 'Custard?'

'Guess I'm eating the pudding.' Amused, with eyes only for Addie, he took the spoon in his thickly gloved hand.

'I guess you are.' Addie smiled up at him and Gayle didn't miss that twinkle in her niece's eye.

Louisa hooked her arm through Gayle's to stay warm. 'It's almost time for the fireworks.'

'And I'm grateful to be seeing in another New Year,' she said, 'with all my family together.'

'Same,' Louisa replied.

She took a deep breath, inhaling the night air, the feeling of excitement and promise all around as they waited for the first firework to launch into the sky.

The next morning, with their tummies satisfyingly full – more so after Susanna's legendary cooked breakfast – and bundled up against the cold, the four Rafferty women lined up their bicycles on Bay Street. On New Year's Day, the road was deserted as the island slept off last night's celebrations. Gayle had had a practice pedal up the front path to her cottage and back again, three times, and although a little unsteady had declared herself ready.

'I can't believe we're doing this,' said Gayle with a big smile on her face.

'Neither can I!' Louisa giggled nervously.

Addie tugged the strands of her hair from the bottom of her helmet to make it more comfortable. 'Watch out, Anchor Island!'

Susanna began to laugh. 'It's been years!' And then she counted them down. 'Ready, steady, go!'

They set off, slowly at first, and Gayle was glad to see she wasn't the only one wobbling. It was a good job nobody was around to witness this – at least not in Bay Street – and as they turned the corner and began making their way down towards the harbour where they would ride along near the water, Gayle felt the cold wind whip against her cheeks, against her smile and her laughter.

The Rafferty girls. All four of them. Here on Anchor Island, together. And as they raced along gathering speed – yes, she was going as fast as the others! – she sent a silent thank you to Harry that he'd been the one to bring these wonderful women into her life.

* * *

MORE FROM HELEN ROLFE

ABOUT THE AUTHOR

Helen Rolfe is the author of many bestselling contemporary women's fiction titles, set in different locations from the Cotswolds to New York. She lives in Hertfordshire with her husband and children.

Download your exclusive bonus content from Helen Rolfe here:

Visit Helen's website: www.helenjrolfe.com

Follow Helen on social media here:

instagram.com/helen_j_rolfe
facebook.com/helenrolfeauthor
tiktok.com/@helenrolfebooks

ALSO BY HELEN ROLFE

Heritage Cove Series

Coming Home to Heritage Cove

Christmas at the Little Waffle Shack

Winter at Mistletoe Gate Farm

Summer at the Twist and Turn Bakery

Finding Happiness at Heritage View

Christmas Nights at the Star and Lantern

New York Ever After Series

Snowflakes and Mistletoe at the Inglenook Inn

Christmas at the Little Knitting Box

Wedding Bells on Madison Avenue

Christmas Miracles at the Little Log Cabin

Moonlight and Mistletoe at the Christmas Wedding

Christmas Promises at the Garland Street Markets

Family Secrets at the Inglenook Inn

Little Woodville Cottage Series

Christmas at Snowdrop Cottage

Summer at Forget-Me-Not Cottage

The Skylarks Series

Come Fly With Me

Written in the Stars

Something in the Air

Standalone Novels

The Year That Changed Us

The Best Days of Our Lives

So This is Christmas

The Sweet Life Café

www.ingramcontent.com/pod-product-compliance
Lightning Source LLC
La Vergne TN
LVHW030917080826
845145LV00013B/2939